Chapter One

August 1943

'Nothing exciting ever happens to us in Gosport, Eadie.'

Joy was remembering the postcard she'd spotted pinned to the notice-board in the newsagent's shop earlier this morning when she'd collected the issues of *Picturegoer* the manager set aside for her. She gave a huge sigh and stared at her friend while tucking an escaping blonde curl back inside the safety of her white turban. She wore it, with navy dungarees, for work at Priddy's Hard armaments depot, where she tamped fulminate of mercury into copper shell cases. When the girls arrived for their shifts, it was standard practice to exchange their own clothing and shoes for Priddy's uniforms and to leave all personal items, except wedding rings, in their lockers.

The sensitive light brown powder was highly flammable and toxic. Its acidic droplets and toluene vapour discoloured workers' hair and skin, dyeing it orange – hence their nickname: the Canary Girls. It also poisoned the air in the workshop, making the women sleepy.

The information and telephone number on the postcard flitted in and out of Joy's brain.

Look!

Enjoy a holiday in the invigorating Hampshire country air.
Good remuneration.
Accommodation and travel provided.
Come and pick hops with us for the war effort.

Working outside sounded wonderful.

The laughter caused by *Workers' Playtime*'s comedy duo Gert and Daisy rang out, momentarily eclipsing the machinery noise in the huge workroom. Priddy's was named after one Jane Priddy. In 1750 she had owned the forty acres of land beside Forton creek opposite Portsmouth harbour. Now it was home to one of England's main armaments factories supplying shells, rockets, ammunition and mines. More than two thousand women worked there, filling jobs vacated by men serving in the forces.

51446472 0

Please return this item
by the last date shown.
Items can be renewed online at
inderby.org.uk/libraries

The Field Girls

Also by Rosie Archer

The Girls from the Local
The Ferry Girls
The Narrowboat Girls
You Are My Sunshine

THE MUNITIONS GIRLS SERIES
The Munitions Girls
The Canary Girls
The Factory Girls
The Gunpowder and Glory Girls

THE BLUEBIRD GIRLS SERIES
The Bluebird Girls
We'll Meet Again
The Forces' Sweethearts
Victory for the Bluebird Girls

THE CRITERION GIRLS SERIES
The Picture House Girls
I'll Be Seeing You

THE TIMBER GIRLS SERIES
The Timber Girls
Dream a Little Dream

ROSIE
ARCHER
The
Field Girls

QUERCUS

First published in Great Britain in 2025 by Quercus
Part of John Murray Group

1

Copyright © 2025 Rosie Archer

A CIP catalogue record for this book is available
from the British Library

HB ISBN 978-1-52944-296-0
EBOOK ISBN 978-1-52944-297-7

Typeset in Garamond by CC Book Production

Printed and bound in Great Britain by Clays Ltd, Elcograf S.p.A.

Papers used by Quercus are from well-managed forests and other responsible sources.

Quercus
Carmelite House
50 Victoria Embankment
London EC4Y 0DZ

John Murray Group
Part of Hodder & Stoughton Limited
An Hachette UK company

The authorised representative in the EEA is Hachette Ireland,
8 Castlecourt Centre, Dublin 15, D15 XTP3, Ireland (email: info@hbgi.ie)

To Tiger-dad.

For the times we had.

Eadie sat next to her in the line of women on benches at long tables. Deftly she filled a container and set it carefully alongside another shell on the conveyor-belt before briefly contemplating Joy. She, like her friend, was well aware that one false move in handling the explosives could result in them being blown to kingdom come.

'We're at war, Joy. The Germans keep bombing us. Ain't that exciting enough for you?' Without waiting for an answer, the older woman began compressing more powder into yet another bullet case. Then, with longing in her voice, she added, 'I do miss the sunshine, though. I hate working in this artificial light with all the windows covered. I know it's necessary for the blackout but we come to work before the day's properly begun and leave when night's arriving.' Her shoulders rose and fell as she gave a huge sigh. 'Don't mind me, I'm having a little moan. But it'd be nice to see the sun once in a while. Besides, I could do with a fag.'

Eadie smoked like a chimney. Woodbines were her cigarette of choice but she'd smoke anything. It was against the law to smoke at Priddy's, and obviously very dangerous. A brief smile touched her lips. 'Anyway, changing the subject, what about that airman you met at the Connaught Hall dance? You heard from him yet?'

Joy shook her head and was about to answer when a fit

of coughing caused Eadie to freeze. Angry words poured from her lips: 'Steady on, Maureen, you can't jig about like that with a bloody hazardous process like this going on!'

Maureen, seated at Eadie's other side, grabbed at the pocket of her dungarees for a hanky and mopped her nose and mouth. 'Sorry,' she said, her voice muffled to a low whine. A yawn turned into a cough. 'I think I've got a cold coming.' Maureen always wore a turban at work and at home. Her hair was falling out, due to worry, a boozing husband and a six-month-old baby, who hardly slept.

Eadie rolled her eyes. Joy knew that Eadie might have remonstrated even more forcefully, their work was so fraught with danger, but she was aware of Maureen's hard life. Now Eadie turned back to Maureen, whose eyes were luminous in her thin, sallow face. Joy saw the brief smiles of understanding the two women exchanged and she was relieved. Eadie could sometimes be quite scathing about Maureen's apathy towards her violent husband. She said Maureen should pull her socks up and do something about it. Joy interpreted Maureen's submissiveness towards him as fear.

At least once a week Eadie asked her the same question about the airman and received a similar answer. Automatically Joy picked up a shell canister and began filling it. 'I expect he's forgotten about me now. Last May that was. He said he was going on a special operation and didn't know how it would turn out . . .'

'They all say that, ducky.' Eadie laughed, and the creases in her face plumped out. 'If I had a penny for every bloke who told me a tale or two before I was married I could buy a new winter coat!'

Joy grinned. Eadie, in her thirties, was almost old enough to be her mother but she was a good friend. It had been next-door neighbour Eadie who had put in a good word to Priddy's management when Joy's mum was killed in a shelter blast at the beginning of the war. Joy was fifteen then but determined to stay in the two-up-two-down home in Victoria Street that held so many memories for her. For that, though, she needed a job that paid decent money. Eadie had been her mum's best friend, even though she was younger, and the friendship had transferred to Joy. Joy and her mum had intended she should continue her education after leaving Gosport Grammar School but it wasn't to be.

'Remember, ducky,' Eadie had said, 'the munitions pays women well, not as much as the men but enough to live on, if you're careful, and Priddy's is within walking distance. Anyway, when you gets your wage packet, take out the rent first and put it aside, bills next, then food. Always the rent first.' Joy remembered her nodding sagely, then adding, 'Everything else follows if you can afford a roof above your head.' Then she had grinned. 'But you knock on my door if trouble comes to you.' Joy never forgot what Eadie had said. It meant more to her than Eadie would ever know, especially as Eadie had more than enough worries with her own family.

Joy was nineteen now and her home was her nest, filled with crocheted cushions she and her mum had made and bright curtains sewn from material purchased at Gosport market. Everything held a special memory. Books occupied shelves and were piled in corners. Joy remembered her father's words: 'You're never alone with a book.' In her mind's eye she could see him sitting opposite her at the kitchen table reading one of his beloved cowboy novels by Zane Grey, the arm of his spectacles held together with tape. Two years before her mum was killed, he'd died in hospital, finally succumbing to injuries sustained at the Battle of the Somme.

However much she loved reading, Joy's great passion was the pictures. She adored settling down in the darkness of the Criterion Picture House and watching stories unfold on the screen, the characters played by impossibly handsome male stars and beautiful women, whom she would never see walking the streets of Gosport. A creased photograph of a fair-haired man in an army uniform taken during the Great War stood in a frame in pride of place in the middle of the mantelpiece above the living-room range. To Joy her father had been more good-looking than any film star.

Although she smiled at Eadie's warning that the young airman hadn't meant to follow through on his request to write to her, Joy was saddened that she hadn't heard from him. 'I thought he was different,' she said wistfully. 'And I still do.' She couldn't explain why or how as their meeting had been fleeting, just one dance. It had been the last waltz of the evening.

Joy hadn't noticed him in the crowded, sweaty, smoke-filled Connaught Hall until he'd stepped in front of her. She'd been sitting with Eadie, and Madge, who'd been up and down, like a yo-yo, never refusing a request to dance from anything in trousers, when a tall, curly-haired man in air-force blue shyly asked Joy, 'Will you have the last dance with me?' He held out a hand. Joy had smiled, stood up and slid into his arms.

The electric lights had been turned low. Couples snuggled together and moved slowly about the parquet floor. She'd liked the way he'd held her. He wasn't a grabber, like some men with their roving hands. He'd smelt of lemon cologne and the Brylcreem the air-force boys were known for wearing. Hesitantly he'd asked her name, if she was a local girl. Jim was easy to talk to, she remembered thinking, almost as if they were already friends. He'd told her he was on leave from Scampton in Lincolnshire but due to return to the base in the morning.

She'd had to stretch up on tiptoe and listen carefully when he spoke because Mr Prout's band never varied its piercing intensity, but she liked the toothpaste smell and the warmth of the young man's breath. Jim's teeth were white and even, marred only by a tiny missing fragment at the front, which Joy found endearing.

It was as if a cocoon had spun itself about them.

She wanted to know more when he admitted he was the bomb-aimer in a crew of seven men on a Wellington and, at twenty-three, the youngest, but she didn't ask him. Both were aware that careless talk cost lives. Joy was touched when he explained it had taken him ages to pluck up the courage to walk across and ask her to dance, which, he said, was surprising because he was never usually timid in the company of girls.

'I'm so glad you did,' she said, and meant every word.

'I'd like to write to you.' Jim sounded hesitant. A tiny muscle at the corner of his mouth was flickering. 'Oh dear.

I've got cold feet again, asking you.' He was staring at her, clearly half expecting her to say she wouldn't tell him where she lived.

When she said, 'If you've a piece of paper and a pencil I'll write down my address back at the table,' a huge smile swept the apprehension from his face.

The waltz ended. Couples untangled themselves. The National Anthem was played and the mad rush to leave began as the lights were turned up once more. The dinner-suited musicians began packing away their instruments. Cardigans and coats appeared as people made for the exits.

After they'd walked back to the table she'd scribbled her address on a page from his diary, with a pencil stub he'd eventually discovered in his wallet. Madge and Eadie were already among other people exiting the hall and Eadie, thoughtful as ever, had taken Joy's cardigan and handbag, making sure nothing was left behind.

Eadie glanced back at her and shouted, 'We'll have to walk home if we miss the number three. Come on! Hurry up!' She was limping, Joy saw, so her bunion must have been hurting.

'I'm sorry, I'd better go.' It was an unwritten rule that the three women arrived and left night destinations together.

Joy had caught up with her two friends in the corridor. Tucking her arm through Eadie's, she'd looked back at the throng of chattering people but Jim had been swallowed into the crowd.

Madge had dug her elbow into Joy's side. 'He was a bit of all right, wasn't he?'

Now months had rolled by, and Joy had practically given up hoping for a letter. Perhaps it was, as Eadie said, 'just one of those things'. Nevertheless, Joy preferred to believe there was a reason why Jim hadn't written. After all, didn't hope spring eternal?

Joy carefully laid another shell on the conveyor-belt. Last week she had been working in a different part of the factory putting highly toxic azide pellets into shell fuses because one of the girls who did that job was absent. Her hands had been boxed in thick glass panels that helped contain the vapour but she had still contracted a rash that covered her arms and itched like mad, keeping her awake at nights. She'd been given a special ointment but it hadn't helped, and she was relieved to be back alongside Eadie, working at her regular job.

Her mind went back to the postcard. Joy wasn't sure what picking hops entailed but if it was for the war effort it had to be all right, didn't it? Surely the war couldn't go on much longer.

Joy voiced her concern to her friend. 'Do you believe we'll eventually have Hitler on the run, Eadie?'

'Course we will. Our boys and the Allies are doing a great job. What about the RAF's clever plan to blow up them Ruhr dams? Didn't you hear what Alvar Lidell the newsreader told us a while back? Thousands of acres of farmland in Germany was ruined by the water. Factories, mines, power stations put out of order, destroyed or damaged. Adolf didn't like that.'

'I bet that caused a big dent in German production. How come I didn't know about it?' Joy frowned as she set another filled case on the belt.

'I expect you had your nose in one of them film magazines instead of listening to the wireless . . .' Eadie was mocking her but there was no real malice in her words.

'Called Operation Chastise it was,' called Maureen, her handkerchief tucked into her sleeve in readiness to stave off another fit of coughing. 'Though everybody's now calling them airmen the Dam Busters. I reckon they're real heroes.' Maureen's fingers released a fully tamped shell case onto the moving belt. 'They learned to release bombs that bounced from their planes and hit the dams. Two dams, the Möhne and—'

Joy didn't hear the name of the second dam for a resounding roar and a blast lifted her off her seat and threw her into the air, as if she had no control of her limbs.

And then she was flying, opening her mouth to cry out but no sound emerging, as if all the breath was simultaneously being sucked from her body. Projectiles struck her, small stinging particles slicing into her skin. And then she was falling. Darkness claimed her . . .

When Joy came round, she was aware that she was lying on her side, one of her legs pinned down by a heavy object. Dull sounds grew louder, permeating her brain, groping through the deafening silence. Whistles. Screams. Shouting. She could smell burning, smoke. It seemed to be coming from somewhere behind her. She must find out what . . .

A wave of dizziness took away her thoughts.

After a while her head cleared again. She wriggled her toes, thankful that she could use both feet. Whatever confined her left leg was probably doing no permanent damage. Her skin was itching, as if a million gnats were feasting on her. She opened her eyes, the lids smarting with grit. Her mouth was dry and she tried to swallow the dust inside it.

She wasn't dead. She could hear and see. Relief flooded her. Then she looked down to see what was restricting her movement. It looked like part of a piece of furniture: black-stained wood. Comprehension dawned. It was a large section of the solid oak bench, usually bolted to the floor, that she, Eadie and other workers sat on in the factory workshop. How strange. she thought. And she could smell mud. The gaseous, oily stench of mud mixed with the stink of burning.

Where the hell was she? She realized she was lying on thick, fibrous couch grass interspersed with tall weeds, all of which had probably broken her fall. Joy put out a hand and ran her fingers over a spray of ragwort. A tiny yellow-and-black-striped caterpillar was crawling over one of its flowers. Its colours reminded her of fulminate of mercury . . .

'Oh!' Joy gasped. She was no longer inside the work-room, listening to Maureen talking about planes destroying German dams. Eadie? Maureen? The others? Where were they? What had happened?

Panicking now, but using her elbows on the grass to hoist herself, Joy managed to sit up, relieved that, apart from her trapped leg, she didn't appear to be hurt.

She was facing the creek where the original chain ferry that used to carry passengers and freight between Gosport and Portsmouth was rotting in the mud. To the left she could see the wooden jetty Priddy's used to load the flat-bottomed lighter barges with munitions that were transferred to war-ships in Portsmouth harbour.

To her right the creek meandered inland. It appeared

peaceful, deserted even, so whatever was happening, the voices, the commotion, was coming from behind her.

It was then she spotted her feet were bare and the material of her dungarees was shredded. No shoes? How peculiar. She remembered her own clothes and shoes were safely in the changing room, along with her newly purchased and unread *Picturegoer*s. She'd collect them later.

A wave of immense tiredness overtook her and she fell back into the soothing blackness.

'Wake up! Oh, Joy, open your eyes, ducky!'

Joy obliged and stared into her friend's anxious face. Eadie was bending down towards her. Her face was streaked with dirt and her hair was so covered with dust that it looked grey instead of its usual hennaed red.

'Where's your turban?' Joy's first words brought a look of relief to Eadie's face.

'Same place yours is, along with your shoes, I suppose.' She grinned.

Joy put up a hand. Her fingers tangled in matted hair. 'Well, bugger me!'

Eadie slid her arms around her friend's upper body and hauled her to a sitting position so Joy was now crushed against her slim frame.

'Oh, ducky, thank God you're all right.' Eadie's relief was plain to hear in her voice.

Joy could almost taste the smell of cigarettes on her friend's skin – never had it seemed so welcome.

'I've been looking everywhere for you. I thought you'd copped it.' Then, just as quickly as Eadie had grabbed hold of her, she released her. 'Oh, my God! What am I doing holding you so tight? You might have injuries inside.'

Joy brushed away the tears that had run down her face. 'I'm all right,' she assured Eadie, and noticed for the first time how dirty she was. Also she could now move both legs. 'It's gone!' The piece of wood no longer hampered her.

Eadie straightened, looking smug. 'Yeah! Took me a while to shift that heavy bit of oak. You got bruising but I was expecting to see blood and God knows what else . . .'

Experimentally, Joy lifted her knee and flicked her foot up and down. 'It's fine. Feels strange, though . . . However did you manage? Oh, you're an angel. Thank you, thank you. I'm so happy to see you and to know you're all right . . . You are, aren't you?' She was babbling but she couldn't help it.

'I'm all right.'

'Thank God.' Joy stared at her. Eadie was alive. So was she. But they hadn't been alone in the workshop . . . 'What happened? I don't remember.'

Eadie's face darkened. 'The wall at the back of us blew out. We was lucky, if you can call it luck, that the blast took us with it. Though how you landed over here . . .' Her voice wavered. 'I ended up outside on the gravel in the yard with Maureen on top of me . . .' Evidently anticipating Joy's next question, Eadie added, 'Oh, don't worry, she's all right. I broke her fall.'

Eadie was twisting her wedding ring on the third finger of her left hand. Joy knew she did that when she was disturbed. She waited.

'Some women on the other side of the factory floor was killed. It come from that side, see?' Eadie's lips formed a thin line while she was remembering. Then she blurted out, 'There's been a lot of injuries . . . Bad stuff . . . Ambulances back and forth. Trying to clear up now . . .' Her voice tailed off again.

For a moment the sounds of heavy vehicles and shouting voices took over. Joy knew Eadie was gathering her thoughts, wondering how to describe exactly what had happened before she had begun searching for her. 'It was a dropped shell case. Women were screaming . . . trapped, broken . . .' She narrowed her eyes and shook her head. 'You don't want to know, love, but someone was looking out for us on our side of the workroom.' Eadie pointed a finger heavenwards to signify a being of the highest importance. 'We didn't get off scot-free but . . .' Again, she fell silent.

Joy waited. If there was more Eadie wanted to say she'd explain in her own good time.

'We were bloody lucky we weren't all killed.' Eadie put up her hands to cover her face as her shoulders rose, then drooped, and she sobbed. 'A bloody bloodbath! That's what it was! A bloody bloodbath!' She bent down and once more swept Joy close to her.

Joy put her arms around her. Her own heart felt like lead. She was hoping the warmth from her body would comfort Eadie because there were no words that would ease her friend's agony. Memories would linger, perhaps never leave either of them.

There was a strong chemical smell, like rotten eggs, lingering in the air with the stink of burning. It reminded Joy of the stench in the streets of Gosport when she'd left a shelter after an air raid.

She released Eadie. 'All right?' she asked, and Eadie nodded.

Of course Eadie wasn't all right, but the two friends were together and, for the moment, that was all they needed.

Using her as a support, Joy rose shakily to her feet and turned towards the noise. Then, Eadie's arm steadying her, she took a few steps across the grass. There had been so many bombings of homes and premises in Gosport since her mother's death that Joy felt almost immune to the sight of blitzed and blown-up buildings ruined by the Luftwaffe. But this was different. An accident had caused this inferno.

Eadie sniffed. 'Now we're both upright, where d'you think you're going, madam?' She wiped her nose and face with her free hand.

'To help, of course.'

Joy's first view of the wreckage surrounding the remains of the workplace where she was used to spending the major part of her day was worse than she'd feared, much worse.

'You'll be more of a hindrance than a help when there's trained people doin' a proper job. Besides, you got no shoes.' Eadie looked down at Joy's naked feet, then waved towards firemen aiming hoses at dying flames. 'If your feet don't get burned, they'll be shredded by all the rubbish.'

Joy said, 'Don't worry. I'll get my clothes and stuff from the changing room.'

'You'll have a job.' Eadie sniffed. 'That place got a right soaking by the fire brigade.'

Joy sighed. She'd have to walk home just as she was, in tattered clothing, no shoes and no *Picturegoers*. She stared about her and saw smaller fires still burning on the gravel where erupting matter had shot from the main explosion. Helpers were using spades and shovels to beat out embers. Men and women were shovelling glass and rubble into piles, and twisted metal was being loaded onto flatbed lorries.

'Loads of staff and the walking wounded have already been sent home or taken to the War Memorial hospital. You got to let the professionals here get on with their jobs without hindrance.' Eadie was adamant.

'But—'

'But nothing, Joy!' Eadie looked at her fondly. 'You're in no fit state to help anybody. C'mon, the Women's Voluntary Service have set up a mobile canteen near the front gate well away from all this. We'll feel better after a cuppa and we can find out what's going on from them. An' I got family who'll have heard about the explosion and might even worry about me.'

Joy stared at Eadie. She frowned. 'Oh, I'm sorry! If you hadn't come looking for me, you'd probably be home by now.'

'I'm not leaving you until I know you're safe indoors. But Joe'll worry . . .'

'I'm sorry.'

And Joy meant it. She certainly didn't want to make problems for Eadie. Enough screaming and shouting came through the wall, at times, between their homes without the need for more.

'Never you mind, ducky,' Eadie said kindly. 'Anyway, I'm not leaving this place till I've had a cuppa and a fag.' She smiled knowingly and patted her pocket, removed from it a single, battered cigarette and waved it at Joy.

'Where'd you get that? You had to leave your fags this morning in the changing room!'

'I had it given to me in my wanderings looking for you!' Chastened, Joy laughed.

By the time they reached the tent Joy realized that although she wanted to help the very idea was ridiculous. She'd had to hold on to Eadie because she was unsteady and the gravel dug into her feet. It was difficult to walk and she could see pinpricks of blood.

Now, Joy sat inside the large canvas shelter on a wooden crate, sipping the welcome tea and watching through the opening as Priddy's gatekeeper did his best to clear sightseers and worried relatives from outside the main entrance.

The tent was obviously an extension to the mobile tea wagon because the summer weather could be inclement. Joy had no idea of the time but the best of the day had gone. The tea urn sat on the scrubbed pull-down counter and was manned by three helpers dressed in their uniform of long-sleeved, grey-green flannel dresses. Joy saw their sleeves were rolled up, ready for business, most of which, she thought, had already been dealt with. The two women bustling about inside the tent, tidying and collecting crockery, looked tired, their sweat-slicked hair clinging to damp foreheads. Badges with the embroidered red WVS insignia decorated their breast pockets. The third woman was at the helm of the urn, wiping drips.

'Nosy parkers,' voiced a buxom, bossy volunteer, watching the gatekeeper waving his arms. 'Something nasty happens an' people gather like flies. But they're too late. The ambulances left a while since, nothing much to see now. Course some might be waiting for loved ones.' She noticed Joy's punctured feet and said sympathetically, 'Ooh, nasty!'

'Are there many people not accounted for?' Eadie asked her. The woman turned. Eadie was stirring her tea with the spoon string-tied to a nail beneath the counter. She finished and made her way to stand beside Joy.

'A few.' The woman picked up a lipstick-smeared mug and tutted.

'Poor devils,' whispered Joy. There were about ten people inside the awning sharing the steamy atmosphere and holding white enamel mugs. Most, thought Joy, were glassy-eyed and looked troubled. There was little conversation.

'When you leave, the gatekeeper needs you to sign out,' said the woman, emptying dregs of tea from a mug straight onto the grass. 'Keeps a check on the missing, see? Course, Priddy's is shut down now, but the workshops not affected by the blast'll be up and running again in days.' She looked down at Joy's toes and frowned. 'Not that the management will let the grass grow under their feet. They'll have that factory space rebuilt in no time. Couple of months or perhaps sooner will see it full of machinery again and the workers taken back, if they ain't found other jobs. There's a bloody war on, ain't there?' She walked quickly away, back towards the counter where she pulled up the wooden flap and disappeared into the rear of the van with a glance at the woman wiping the urn.

Eadie flicked fag ash, thought for a while, then said to Joy, 'She's right.' She leaned forward and whispered, 'No doubt the management will inform us through the proper channels. But we're going to be without work and who knows for how long?'

'You can't walk about on scorched gravel barefoot, love. You'll do yourself an injury.'

Joy hadn't noticed the buxom helper's swift return because she was watching the crowd at the gate. They seemed to be becoming noisier by the second. She started at the sound of the woman's voice and felt something soft being pressed into her lap. She looked down to see a pair of tartan slippers, complete with red pom-poms nestling in her torn clothing. They were hardly worn and very clean. Before Joy could open her mouth, the woman carried on, 'I always bring them with me because my corns can play me up something terrible. They're all right today, thank goodness, and I reckon you need my slippers more than me.'

'But—'

The woman interrupted, 'They should fit you. They're medium size and that fits anyone, don't it?'

Overcome by the woman's thoughtfulness, Joy felt tears rise but she blinked them away while she put on the slippers. They did indeed fit her. She sighed as their softness eased the soreness. 'Thank you, you're so kind—' she began.

Once again the woman cut her off. 'No, you girls are the tops. Heroines you lot are, risking your lives making bombs and shells to save the rest of us.' Then she ruffled Joy's hair and turned swiftly away, saying, 'When you gets home, you put some iodine on them feet.' As she reached the counter she stopped, turned and winked at Joy, then lifted the flap and disappeared into the back of the van.

'There's some lovely kind people about, ducky, don't you think?' Eadie said. Joy, overcome, could only nod. A long silence between them followed, broken only by the noise outside the tent, the low voices and tea-stirring inside.

After a moment or two, Eadie said, 'Joy, I don't know how either of us is going to manage. We need my wages to keep us afloat. And you and me, we certainly can't live on fresh air, ducky.'

Joy's heart fell. Until now she'd been so grateful that she and Eadie hadn't been permanently injured she'd not thought how today's terrible accident would affect her. How would she pay rent and buy food with no money coming in? And Eadie's finances were stretched even tighter. Eadie, like herself, had no savings.

Eadie thoughtfully repeated the sentence she'd voiced earlier. 'We can't live on fresh air, Joy.' A huge sigh followed.

Maybe it was those words 'fresh air' or maybe because the information on the card in the paper shop was still somehow floating around in her mind, but Joy put out a hand and rested it on Eadie's arm.

'How would you like to go hop-picking? Work in the sunshine?'

And, before Eadie could answer Joy quoted the advert, '"Good remuneration. Accommodation and travel provided. And all in the invigorating Hampshire country air!"'

Chapter Two

'You all right, Eadie love?' Joe's drawn face lit up the moment he saw her and had to step away from behind the front door to allow her to enter. It was obvious to Eadie he'd been on tenterhooks waiting for her, probably peering down the street constantly. 'I heard the explosion from Priddy's.'

She'd hardly had time to remove her key from the lock before he swept her into a hug, squashing almost all of the air out of her lungs. Joe smelt of cigarettes, the tantalizing aroma of freshly made corned-beef hash and shaving soap. Eadie was amazed at the warmth of his welcome, relished it even, until the dreaded guilt slithered over her and she froze.

'I've been frantic with worry.' His voice was low as he moved back, releasing her from his arms. It was, Eadie thought, almost as if he was reading her mind, fearful of overstepping the mark, or perhaps grappling with his own emotions.

He was flustered now, she could tell. Without meaning to he'd let his guard down on his feelings. Joe was her father-in-law, not her husband.

'I was one of the lucky ones,' she said, 'but it was bad.' Eadie couldn't stop the tears that rose with recollections of the explosion and its dreadful aftermath. He let her cry.

After a while she wiped a cheek with a grubby hand and took a deep breath. 'I thought Joy had copped it. I were frantic. Found her eventually down by the creek.'

'Was she . . .?' Fresh worry clouded his eyes.

'Unhurt, thank God. Apart from scratches, confusion and part of a bench that's usually fixed to the floor of our workroom trapping her.' Eadie's voice shook.

Joe led her down the narrow hallway into the living room. Eadie breathed in the familiar smells of polish, and cooking wafting in from the gas stove in the scullery and let out a deep sigh, glad to be home. Joe walked her to the ancient, sagging armchair beneath the window, pushed her down into its worn, velvet softness, then stepped back on the rag rug, looking down at her. 'Where's Joy now?' His voice was gentle, kind. To Joe, Joy was like the daughter he'd never had. He'd have made a smashing granddad too, had Eadie and Will had children. Eadie knew she could rely on him to look in later on her friend to see if she needed anything. All she wanted to do now was to stay safely in her favourite chair and count her blessings.

Eadie had taken the job at Priddy's to alleviate her loneliness after her husband, Will, had joined the army. Children hadn't happened, to their regret, but, as it had to so many happily married couples, the war had forced them apart. Will was sent to France, but in June 1940 he was returned to England, to a hospital in Croydon, South London, that reserved six wards for military casualties.

The Cane Hill Asylum's motto was *Aversos Compono Animos*. It translated to 'I bring relief to troubled minds.' Eadie prayed fervently that, in time, it would live up to its promise for she no longer recognized the man she had married.

As the months went by both she and Joe, when she and Joe were finally allowed to visit him, noticed changes. His babbling slowed, sometimes becoming almost coherent; sedatives calmed him. His crying jags were fewer, so the nurses told her, his sleep had improved, though his nightmares were horrendous, and his complaints of muscular aches and pains had reduced. It was noise Will couldn't stand. Any sharp sounds had sent him shaking and scurrying to hide, causing his blank stare to return. Eventually, though, he had been sent home.

Joe's unflagging help after Will's discharge from the asylum had provided him with a home after his house had been bombed. It also allowed Eadie to remain working at the munitions factory.

Caring practically full time for his son hadn't stopped Joe working: he served behind the bar at the White Swan on Forton Road in the evenings, whenever possible, to help bring in money.

'Where's Joy now?' Joe repeated.

'She's indoors.' Eadie nodded at the wall between their two houses. 'She's all right. I told her to get cleaned up, and then go to bed.'

'Best thing. I'll pop round in a bit with some dinner. She won't feel like cooking.'

Eadie looked at him gratefully. 'She'll appreciate that. Would you?'

He grinned at her. 'No, she can starve!'

It was a throwaway line and it made her smile. Even during the worst of times Joe rarely lost his sense of humour. 'It's a good thing I know you're joking,' she said.

Joe was in his fifties but didn't look his age even though his fair hair was thinning and there were more lines on his face than when he'd first moved into the terraced house. Joy said he reminded her of the film star Burt Lancaster, who became better-looking the older he got.

'I'll go round in a bit but you need settling first,' Joe said, reaching for the packet of Woodbines next to the ashtray on the table. He shook out a couple of cigarettes, put them between his lips and lit both with a single Swan Vesta match. Then he handed one to Eadie.

She took it gratefully, a smile touching her lips. It was the party trick he performed especially for her, stolen from Paul Henreid in the Bette Davis picture *Now, Voyager*. Eadie blessed him for trying to make her feel better.

After a drag on his cigarette, Joe said, 'Now you need a cuppa. The kettle's ready for tea and I'll boil more water so you can wash in the scullery while I'm next door. You shouldn't be disturbed.'

Eadie took in a lungful of smoke, blew it out and asked the question that had been uppermost in her thoughts since arriving home. 'How's Will?'

Joe raised his eyes towards the bedroom above them. 'I had to give him a sodium amytal to calm him down. He was sitting in the garden when Priddy's explosion set him off. He's asleep now.'

29

'Was he very bad?' Eadie's forehead creased with worry. The blast would have triggered great distress in Will.

'No more than usual.'

Eadie shook her head. She knew sometimes Joe played down the strength of Will's episodes when he coped with them alone. He did it to lessen her worry. 'I hate him having that stuff, hate it for blunting his emotions.'

'So do I.' He paused. 'But that's preferable to his outbursts when he hurts himself or others.' He stared at her. 'But he's home with us and that's what counts.'

'I don't know what I'd do without you.'

'You don't have to,' Joe replied. 'You and I work together to do the best we can for my lad, don't we?'

She didn't answer, just watched as his tall, sinewy body made for the scullery door.

Eadie stifled a yawn. She was very tired. Tired of the Luftwaffe that sent its planes over almost nightly to blitz Portsmouth's dockyard, and the bombs falling on Gosport when the crews missed their targets. Tired of the rationing that meant eking out small amounts of meat with bread or potatoes. Tired of the blackout. Tired of wondering whether she and her loved ones would survive this blessed war . . . But most of all she hated what the war had done to Will.

Her husband was an enormously brave man who'd had no

control over what had happened to him at Dunkirk, but its aftermath had rendered him incapable of rational thought. Eadie was fortunate in that her husband had been returned to her. But Will was not whole: he was in pieces. He'd been through hell and sometimes he went back there.

If he continued with the drugs and therapy, she had been told he would, in time, overcome his neurasthenia, or shell shock, as Joe called it.

Eadie doubted she'd ever become reconciled to Will's violent outbursts or his changed appearance. His weight loss hadn't affected his strength – if anything his grip was more powerful than it had ever been – but his eyes rarely held hers, giving her no inkling of his true thoughts, and his beautiful blond hair had turned white.

The chink of crockery from the scullery told her the tea was on its way. Sure enough, Joe appeared carrying a cup and saucer, the contents steaming. Her mouth watered. Joe didn't speak but grinned at her as he left it on the table within her easy reach. She beamed at him. 'I could close my eyes and sleep for ever in this comfy old wreck of a chair.'

'You'll feel better after a wash and a good meal,' Joe responded, and Eadie watched his back as he vanished into the scullery again.

Later, she'd tell Joe she'd been laid off from Priddy's

for the time being, though he'd realize that, she thought. It would be difficult to manage without her wages. Not difficult: impossible.

Hop-picking? At first, she'd thought Joy's idea was mad. Picking hops for beer probably came under the heading of war work but what did either of them know about labouring in the fields? Perhaps all the vacancies had been filled.

Joe might argue that it should be up to him to do a job and bring home money. They'd gone through all this before, of course. His manly pride had taken a battering when they had decided Eadie should carry on at the munitions factory and Joe stay at home to care for Will. 'Women don't work when there's an able-bodied man in the house to earn a living,' he'd reminded her, more than once.

His ego had taken a previous pounding when he'd been turned down, on account of his age, by the army, after volunteering to fight. Will had been conscripted.

Eadie sighed. There was hardly a moment when her thoughts didn't return to Will and the love they'd shared before the war. There were periods when Will was almost like the man she'd married but sometimes it was as if some cruel stranger inhabited him and he would lash out at her with his tongue or fists.

Eadie had never worried that Joe wouldn't be able to

handle Will: he'd always been a huge influence on his son. Will's mother, Louise, had died of influenza when he was three. Joe hadn't remarried.

It was always Joe who insisted Eadie go to the pictures or dancing with Joy. 'Get out and enjoy yourself while you've the chance,' he'd say. Eadie never took advantage of his good nature. She liked sitting at home with him in the evenings, listening to the wireless, reading or playing board games. She was easy in Joe's company, and when Will's mood allowed him to take part in normal family pleasures, which it did occasionally, she couldn't have been happier.

Eadie took another drag on her cigarette, leaned forward and knocked the long grey ash into the ashtray. Her hands were filthy. I must look a sight, she thought, gazing at her torn and grubby clothing. 'I'm lucky to be alive, though,' she whispered.

Joe hadn't pressed for more details about the factory blast and its tragic aftermath. She was grateful. As usual, he was sparing her feelings, knowing she would talk about it in her own good time. And if she didn't want to talk, that would be all right with him as well.

'I'm popping next door now. Won't be long. I'm just taking some dinner for Joy. Our meal's keeping warm and there's plenty of hot water in the kettle for you.'

Joe was standing in the scullery doorway. Eadie smiled at him, then heard the back door latch lift, the swish of the heavy blackout curtain falling into place again, and the door closing.

The tea tasted like nectar. She sipped, looking around the living room, at the wooden sideboard with the wonky drawer, the wireless, powered by an accumulator, sitting silently on top. None of her furniture was ever brand new. Most of it, she thought, was now on its last legs. But her home was welcoming, with its faded flowered lino, the rag rugs she had made, and in the winter, it was snug, thanks to the black-leaded iron range.

Then she glanced at her treasures: the two paintings in their ornate gold frames. She'd fallen in love with them the moment she'd spotted them in the window of Sammy's second-hand shop in Queen's Road. The prints hung on wire from the dado rail, facing each other across the room. No other pictures or knick-knacks adorned the walls.

Pinkie, the original canvas a painting by Thomas Lawrence, showed a dark-haired girl standing on rocks with the wind ruffling her beribboned pink hat, its colour echoing that of the wide sash on her white dress. Eadie was mesmerized by the look of yearning in her innocent eyes.

Gainsborough's *Blue Boy*, holding his plumed hat at his

side and dressed in the blue silk and satin attire popular in the seventeenth century, seemed, from across the room, to return Pinkie's gaze. Eadie saw such sadness in his eyes.

She would stare at the paintings, fantasizing about the couple. Did they long to be together? Were they possibly two young people feeling the first stirrings of attraction, love even, but forbidden to meet, even to think about the fulfilment of their dreams? It mattered not one iota to Eadie that the two original portraits were painted in different decades. She was simply astounded that they evoked such emotion in her.

'One day I'm going to find out all about the pair of you,' she whispered. Did the paintings in some way remind her of her own first love, the man sleeping upstairs? Without a doubt she was nostalgic for what used to be and the happiness she had once taken for granted.

Eadie sighed, got up from the chair and went into the scullery for a strip-down wash. She set her cup and saucer on the draining board, smiling at the clean towel, her nightie and her favourite Pears soap, which Joe had left ready for her. He'd set the corned-beef hash on a low gas in the oven and the scullery exuded a warm and peaceful atmosphere. She began to strip off her soiled clothing.

It felt good to wash away the afternoon.

When she'd towelled her hair almost dry Eadie set about rubbing arnica cream into the cuts and bruises caused by the blast. She hoped Joy had taken her advice and soothed her own lacerations.

Eadie, now refreshed, tidied the scullery, then walked down the passage to her bedroom, the front room of the house, to turn down her quilt and put on her dressing-gown. She dabbed on a little eau de Cologne from the tiny amount remaining in the bottle to cheer herself up. After today, she felt she deserved it.

Eadie no longer shared a bed with her husband. Will, prone to nightmares that left him in despair and often violent, had the front bedroom upstairs, while Joe slept in the back, on hand to subdue Will if the need arose.

Eadie spent as much time with Will as she could. Now she climbed the stairs and gently pushed open his door. The dull light from the stairway illuminated the room without waking him, but was bright enough for her to see. She glanced at the dressing chest beneath the window with its locked drawer containing Will's medication. Joe and she had the only keys.

She looked down at her husband. Will seemed peaceful, breathing evenly. Eadie could still see traces of the young man who'd stolen her heart. Was she wrong to feel such rage that war had taken him from her? In the quiet of her own room sometimes she wept that she was now denied the lovemaking that had left them even more gloriously in love than before. Its intensity had sometimes scared her. She remembered when they touched, when his arms enfolded her and their unclothed bodies had pressed together, how glorious it was. Then she'd cried out with the wonder that occurred inside her body. Even more so when it had happened simultaneously to them both.

Eadie put out her hand to smooth back Will's hair, which had fallen across his forehead, but as her fingers moved forward, she drew them back, denied even that small intimacy. She daren't wake him. The possibility of causing trauma must be curbed at all costs.

She was lonely. Eadie knew that, no matter how busy her day-to-day life, she ached to be loved.

'Eadie!'

She hadn't heard the back door open and Joe enter but now she heard his voice whisper-call her name.

Pressing her fingers to her lips, Eadie turned towards Will and blew him a make-believe kiss. 'Night, night, my love,' she said softly, then went downstairs.

'That was just what I needed. I hadn't realized I was so hungry.' Eadie set her knife and fork on her now empty plate and rose from the kitchen chair. She faced Joe. 'Is Joy really all right?'

'The girl's fine.' Joe tutted. 'She smells like a chemist's shop with all the ointments you told her to rub into herself.' He paused. 'When I left, she was going to bed. It's where you should be . . .'

'I'm too wound up to sleep,' she said, then asked, 'Do you think Will can ever get properly better?'

Joe cleared his throat. 'I just hope the doctors at Croydon, now they've given him electric-shock therapy, hypnosis and pumped him full of drugs, believe that sending him home to a family atmosphere will do the trick.' He stared at her. 'What's brought this on? Every so often you ask me the same question. If you need to talk, Eadie, love . . .'

She knew he would patiently reply to everything, even if she had asked a similar question before. 'You came back from the first war without a scratch.'

'Our coping mechanisms to two very different wars aren't at all similar, Eadie.' His eyes held hers. 'We're just ordinary men, love.'

'I know. But sometimes, in his lucid moments, he shares stuff with you . . .'

'If he doesn't want you to know, it's because he doesn't want you hurt any more or he's not willing to remember . . .'

'But—'

'Look, Eadie, we know what we've heard on the wireless and read in the newspapers but only those brave souls who were there really know what happened at Dunkirk back in 1940 and the massacres that took place in the run-up to it. It was a miracle any of our men and allies survived. Trapped on beaches up to their waists in seawater, waiting to be rescued by small boats piloted by their owners from England because our larger naval ships couldn't get near them in the shallow waters . . .'

He paused, then went on. 'Dunkirk was a miracle for the men who survived. The Luftwaffe mowed our trapped men down like sitting ducks. It was a bloodbath. More than three hundred thousand men were rescued, though. The remainder, left among the dead on the beaches, were sent by the Germans to prison camps.' Joe's voice trembled. 'They said the sea ran with blood. Somehow, though, my boy is still among the living.'

Joe bent his head and cupped his forehead with his hand. Eadie saw his shoulders rise and fall. He was crying. The man who for so long had been strong for her had a breaking point and he was near it.

Eadie rose and stepped around the table. Impulsively she put her arms around him, resting her face against his hair. Joe held on to her. She felt the warmth of him and, though she knew it wasn't the right moment, she couldn't ignore the sudden pleasure that filled her, like the heat from a burning fire . . .

'I'm sorry,' she said, pulling away. Her voice was curt. Sorry for what? For her sudden inappropriate desire or of being shamed by it? 'I shouldn't keep making you relive what he went through.' Her heart was beating fast as she added, 'What Will's still going through . . .'

Joe lifted his head and regarded her. She could see in his eyes that he'd felt her need, returned it even. He gave her a shaky smile. 'Perhaps one day all the terrible truths about the war will emerge. In the meantime, we count our blessings . . . Be a good girl and put the kettle on. I could do with a cuppa, and a fag, couldn't you?

Eadie watched the smoke rise from Joe's cigarette in the ashtray and curl towards the ceiling. Earlier, she'd cleared the living-room table of plates and washed up the pots while Joe dried them.

'Joy told me about the hop-picking job she saw advertised,' he said, placing a saucepan on the scullery shelf.

'You've taken your time coming out with that nugget of information,' she said.

'Only because I've been thinking about it and what it could mean for you.'

Eadie gave the wooden draining board a final wipe, then draped the cloth over the tap. She turned and faced him. 'She's no idea how long the card's been pinned up in the newsagent's so all the vacancies could be filled by now.'

'She's going down to the phone box first thing in the morning to find out. Would you believe she's memorized the telephone number?'

Eadie laughed. 'She did seem keen.'

'Said you were as well.'

Eadie shook her head. 'I'm not leaving you to cope alone.'

'Don't see why not. I can manage perfectly well, and you could do with a break.'

'It's not a bleeding holiday! It's work!'

'Probably back-breaking work an' all, but you'd be out all day in the fresh air and I doubt you'll get Hitler dropping so many bombs on farmland.' Another saucepan joined the first on the shelf.

'You trying to get rid of me?' She was standing in front of Joe now, staring at him.

He grinned at her as he picked up his Woodbine. He took a drag, blew the smoke well away from her face, and said, 'For once I'm not arguing that it's my place to bring in the money because any money will be a bonus. Anyway, it'll pay more than my odd hours at the White Swan. If the hop-picking doesn't work out for you, I'll keep my eyes open for a night-watchman's job so I'll still be around during the day. Looting shops after bombing is worse at night.'

Eadie's eyes were still fixed on his. Her jaw had dropped and she quickly closed her mouth.

'All I'm sayin' is, if you fancy it, it's not like you'll be a million miles away, is it? You'll still be in Hampshire, won't you? Go with my blessing. Hop-picking's not a permanent job, is it? It can only be for a few weeks at most.'

Eadie, astounded, could only continue staring.

'Anyway, Joy's getting up early to use the phone box near the Criterion Picture House.' Joe stubbed out his Woodbine. 'Says she needs to go in the paper-shop as well, something about seeing if they've got any *Picturegoers* left.'

It was the sobbing that woke Eadie. Bloody walls are like cardboard, she thought, as she wearily struggled into a sitting position. Automatically reaching for her dressing-gown at the bottom of the bed, she frowned. The sounds, for once, weren't coming from Will's room but from next door, Joy's bedroom. The anguish in the sobs cut into her heart, like a knife.

Her eyes, adapting to the darkness, settled on the alarm clock while her feet felt beneath the bed for her slippers. It was three o'clock and there was every possibility that it might not be long before Joe and Will were disturbed. She couldn't let that happen.

Silently she padded downstairs, through the familiarity of the darkened living room. Pausing by the scullery door, she unhooked from the nail Joy's spare key. Not that she expected Joy's scullery door to be locked but as a precaution. Slipping it into her pocket she felt the reassurance of her Woodbines.

Joy's darkened home, a mirror image of her own, was easy to navigate and, once upstairs, she gathered the weeping girl into her arms. 'Hush, ducky! You're safe now. Eadie's here.'

'What?' Joy's eyes were wide open but unfocused. Fear clouded them until she recognized her friend. 'Eadie?' she cried. 'What you doin' here?' Perspiration clung to Joy's skin.

'Ssh! You're having a nightmare.' Eadie pulled Joy closer into the softness of her woollen dressing-gown so the girl's words were hushed. 'Keep on going the way you are an' you'll waken the whole street.' Joy struggled away.

Eadie watched as comprehension once more appeared in Joy's eyes. 'I was flying again! Then I was on the grass, like before, by the stinkin' creek. Afraid! Oh, Eadie!' And then

Joy really was sobbing but now it was a different sound, one of quiet relief.

Eadie held on to her, glad that Joy's fear was being washed away by her realization that the nightmare was over and she was safe.

The ticking of the alarm clock and Joy's steady breathing showed Eadie that normality once more reigned. Pushing her away from her arms, she asked, 'You all right now?'

Joy nodded.

'That's the first nightmare over and done with but I don't suppose it'll be the last. What you went through today wasn't no picnic, ducky. Take heart that the bad dreams will leave one day.'

'Will you always be with me?'

'I'll try, ducky!' Eadie's hand smoothed the girl's sweat-damp blonde curls. She grinned at Joy. 'But only if you promise to do something for me.'

'Anything,' Joy said. 'What do you want?'

'Now everything's back to normal I'd like you to go downstairs and put the kettle on for a nice cup of tea.' Eadie pulled her cigarette packet from her dressing-gown pocket. 'And I'd kill for a match for me fag!'

Chapter Three

'Tell me, what did they say?'

Joy stepped from the telephone box and allowed its heavy door to swing shut behind her. She stared at the frown lines creasing Eadie's forehead. Her friend's inquisitiveness had got the better of her. 'Hang on! I've written the details down and . . .' She waved a piece of paper. The noise from a number-two Provincial double-decker to Fareham disgorging its chattering passengers at the Forton Road bus stop swallowed the rest of her words.

'What?' mouthed Eadie.

Joy waited until the pavement was reasonably clear of people, then replied, 'Let's take a walk and sit down in Forton recreation ground. It'll be quieter there. I'll explain everything then.'

Eadie nodded, and Joy slipped an arm through hers. They

crossed the busy road near the recently bombed butcher's shop where the sign propped up outside its boarded-up window stated, 'Business As Usual', and walked towards the nearby play area.

Rubble lined the kerb, a legacy from the previous air raid, and Joy could smell the ever-present marzipan-like fumes from bombing that hung like a burial shroud over Gosport. She tightened her grip on the last copy of *Picturegoer* the newsagent had had left. Its front cover showed Anne Baxter, looking lovely, her hair under a flowered scarf. The magazine, she thought, was well worth the threepence she'd paid for it and she looked forward to reading it later.

Joy waited while Eadie stepped up, over concrete, all that remained of the iron paling that once surrounded the public playground. The council had long since removed metal railings as salvage to help the war effort.

'I'm not sitting on the grass,' Eadie said. 'Let's walk over to the swings.' She turned to Joy. 'Did you wake again last night after . . . ?'

Joy knew she was referring to the fearsome nightmare. She shook her head. She didn't really want to think about it. 'I slept like a baby,' she said. 'I wouldn't have done if you hadn't come round . . .'

'I'll always be there for you. But you know that, don't you?'

Joy nodded. A meaningful look passed between them that needed no words.

The long grass had recently been cut. 'The kids have been making dens.' Eadie pointed to structures cobbled together with branches topped with the dried grasses. 'Little tinkers!'

'You don't mean that. You once told me you'd have loved a house full of kids.'

Joy reached the roundabout and hoisted herself onto its wooden base. She put out a hand and helped Eadie up so she could sit beside her. The playground was deserted.

'I would have done, ducky, if the Fates had smiled on me,' Eadie returned. 'Children bring their love with them, don't they? But I wasn't meant to be a mum, was I?'

Joy saw sadness settle on Eadie's face and felt bad because she'd unthinkingly wounded her friend. 'I'm sorry. I didn't mean to hurt you . . .'

'Forget it, Joy love. What's meant to be will be.' Eadie smiled brightly and once again Joy was reminded of how attractive Eadie was when she wasn't wrapped up in Priddy's shapeless dungarees and the white turban that leached all the colour from her face. She had obviously washed her hair last night and now it hung about her shoulders in shiny waves of red and gold. In the early August sunshine, swinging her legs as the roundabout lumbered in a slow, circular motion, Eadie looked ten years younger, thought Joy. She had a look of Maureen O'Hara about her and the puffed-sleeve green jumper enhanced her emerald eyes. She watched as Eadie dug into the pocket of her skirt and took out her Woodbines.

Joy marvelled that, despite the trauma of the accident at the munitions factory yesterday, she and Eadie were not only lucky to be alive but showed little physical damage despite being tossed about like shuttlecocks in a game of badminton.

Joy would for ever bless the WVS helper for giving her the comfortable slippers. Without them she certainly wouldn't have been walking so easily today. She'd woken this morning to find a huge bruise had bloomed on her leg where the lump of wood had fallen but decided a few more applications of arnica would take care of that, just as it had soothed the minor skin lacerations she and Eadie had sustained.

'You gonna tell me what happened in that phone call, then?' Eadie asked, striking a Swan Vesta and cupping her hand around its flame so she could light her cigarette.

'S'pose I'd better since you came knockin' on my door so bleedin' early this morning,' Joy answered, unfolding the paper she'd written on in the telephone box.

'I didn't want to miss anything, did I?' Eadie grinned at her.

'Right, they're taking workers,' said Joy, assuming a serious tone. 'Train stops at Fareham, it's a hop-pickers' special, runs on a Sunday. Whole families go. Transport will meet the train at Petersfield to take us to the Southerns' farm at Selborne. We'll be allocated a hop hut for three, possibly four weeks' work . . .'

'Oh! I thought the job would last longer.'

'You listening or interrupting?' Joy glared at Eadie, who didn't answer but blew smoke thoughtfully. 'We'll get a special ration book each.'

A smile lit Eadie's lips. 'Why's that, then?'

'We're classed as agricultural workers and need more rations.'

'I like the idea of that,' Eadie said. 'So, when do we get paid?'

Joy laughed at Eadie. 'You thought I wouldn't ask about money, didn't you?'

Their eyes locked.

'Well, we collect our wages at the end of the job.'

'But we'll need money before then, ducky.'

'The farmer's wife said we can ask for subs, Eadie.'

'They must keep some record of how much picking we

do, or subbing from our wages wouldn't be allowed,' Eadie mused. 'How do you know you were speaking to Mrs Southern? It is Southern, isn't it?'

Joy nodded. 'Because the woman said, "My husband pays at the end of the season."'

'Fair enough,' Eadie said, crushing her Woodbine into the metal handrail. She brushed the ash off so the light wind took it away and slipped the remaining half-cigarette back into the packet. 'When and what time does this special train reach Fareham?'

Joy handed her the piece of paper. 'It's all written down here.' She waited as her friend's eyes scanned the information.

'Bloody hell!'

Joy thought Eadie's exclamation sounded like an explosion.

'You never said we start tomorrow!' Eadie expostulated. 'It's a bit soon, ain't it? A nine o'clock train!'

For a moment neither of them spoke. Then Joy said, 'We didn't know until yesterday we'd need alternative employment, did we? Last night your Joe told me he could cope at home if you decided to pick hops with me so I don't see the problem.'

'The problem is I never expected to leave home so soon.' Eadie passed the paper scrap back to Joy.

'And if I hadn't phoned this morning and talked to the

farmer's wife, we mightn't have a job to go to at all.' Joy felt a bit put out.

Eadie took the cigarette packet back out of her pocket. 'This calls for another puff to calm me down. But I suppose you're right,' she admitted, removing the half-smoked cigarette.

'There's something else . . .'

Eadie struck a match and lit up. 'What?'

'Mrs Southern asked me if we'd done this work before and I said, "Of course we have." Then she said, "Be at the station with everything you need."'

Eadie dropped the match and her cigarette. 'Blast!' She caught the cigarette before it hit the base of the roundabout. 'Everything we need? I suppose she means changes of clothes, soap, towels and such. Maybe she'll soon find out we know nothing and send us home again.'

'We're not stupid. If we can work in an armaments factory, we can pick bloody hops, can't we? I stretched the truth a bit because I didn't want to miss out on us getting the work. We need money, don't we?'

'All right, all right!' Eadie took a drag on her cigarette and gave a satisfied sigh that it was still alight. She grinned at Joy. 'Anyway, she'd know by some of those daft questions you asked that we're complete novices.'

There was a moment of silence when the two friends just stared at each other. Sometimes, thought Joy, it was as if they knew each other inside out.

Then she stood up and, holding on to the metal bar, began scooting on the concrete so the roundabout picked up speed and went faster and faster and Eadie, clinging on for dear life, shouted, 'Stop it, you daft cow! Stop it!'

'There's Maureen.' Joy waved and shouted across Forton Road to the down-at-heel woman wearing a turban and pushing a worn canvas pram.

'Don't tell her we've got some work already.'

'Why ever not?'

Joy called Maureen's name again. She didn't like to think the other woman had purposely ignored her but she felt she had. Turning once more to Eadie, she asked again, 'Why not?'

'We've not had official notice Priddy's are shutting down production in our workshops yet. It'll look like we're jumping the gun, being disloyal to the factory bosses.'

Joy stared at her. 'We can't tap fulminate of mercury into shell cases in the middle of a bleedin' field, can we? Our workroom got blown up, remember?'

Eadie sighed. 'I just don't want everyone knowing our

business. You don't know who Maureen might tell.' She whispered the last words as Maureen neared them.

'What you really mean is we'll look damn fools if everyone knows where we've gone and we get sent straight back to Gosport because we haven't got a clue what we're doing.'

'Ssh!' Eadie hissed.

'Hello, you two,' Maureen said grudgingly, bumping the pram up onto the pavement and kicking its brake into position, all the while trying not to look directly at either of them. Self-consciously, she stuck two fingers beneath the turban trying to pull the material further across the side of her forehead to hide a fresh bruise, pretending she was scratching her head. 'I've just come from Priddy's. They don't need us back until there's somewhere safe for us to fill shells.'

'That's logical,' Joy said. She bent and stared into the pram, then frowned.

Maureen said, 'According to Jennie in the office, the work we've been doing is being outsourced.'

'What does that mean?' interrupted Joy.

Eadie sighed. 'It means another munitions factory will take over doing our jobs so production can carry on. Priddy's won't close all its workshops, thank God. The shells will be sent, probably by the railway on site, or shipped by sea, somewhere else to be filled with explosives. We could be out of work for quite a while. Winning this war is the important thing, not our jobs.'

They heard a soft burble from the baby.

'I need to work.' Maureen bent down into the depths of the pram to return the dummy that had slipped from her child's mouth. Joy was able to see more clearly the purpling bruise on her skin.

'We all need to work. Did your Mick do that?' Joy couldn't help herself, though why she'd bothered to ask she had no idea. Weren't all the mysterious black and blue marks that appeared from time to time on Maureen due to her husband's cruelty?

Maureen's hand flew to the side of her head. 'What d'you mean?' The blush blooming over her face answered Joy's question.

'Why don't you leave him?' Joy's voice was soft but Eadie chimed in.

'Did he have a go at you because you lost your job?'

Maureen's eyes filled with tears. 'He doesn't mean it. He's always so sorry afterwards.'

Eadie bent down and looked at the sleeping child. Watching her, Joy's heart constricted. Would Eadie notice what she had spotted?

'He's a bonny little chap.' Eadie stared up at Maureen. 'You got another job to go to?'

'No. When and if Priddy's rehire us, it'll be last in, first out.'

'You're probably right,' said Joy.

She watched Eadie smoothing her fingertip on the little boy's hand, heard her gasp with pleasure when he grabbed it, tightly encircling her finger with the whole of his tiny fist.

'Bless him,' Eadie whispered. She was swallowing back tears as she stood up, disentangling herself from the baby's grip.

Joy knew Eadie needed to distance herself from the child because, like herself, she had seen the mauve marks on the little wrist, like some terrible bracelet. 'Is Mick sorry for that an' all?' Eadie's voice was filled with venom.

Maureen didn't answer. Her tired eyes in her thin face momentarily closed in despair but not before Joy saw the wetness appear on her sparse lashes. A huge sigh escaped her as she said, 'If I could get away from him, I would. Having no money's a curse.' Joy saw Eadie staring at Maureen. She hoped Eadie wouldn't cause a scene. She knew if Mick was Eadie's husband and he'd hurt their child he wouldn't live long enough to do it a second time.

55

Eadie transferred her gaze to Joy. 'You still got that telephone number going round and round in your head?'

'What?' began Joy, then the penny dropped. Eadie wanted to help Maureen. Joy scrabbled in her pocket for the pencil she'd used earlier in the phone box, then took out the piece of paper with the notes, tore it in half and began writing, using the side of the pram's hood as a makeshift table.

When she'd finished, she gave the scrap to Eadie, who promptly passed it to Maureen, saying, 'We'll be at this place for a few weeks, working in the hop-fields. Families go.' She looked again at the sleeping baby, saying gruffly, 'Don't feel you got no one who cares.'

Maureen glanced at the paper, folded it in half and slipped it under the pram mattress. 'I appreciate that,' she said, giving Eadie a hug.

Joy could feel all the unspoken words hovering in the air about them. She looked at Eadie. 'If we don't go, we'll get the sack before we start,' she said. 'We're leaving tomorrow, early, remember,' she emphasized, more for Eadie's benefit than Maureen's.

Maureen nodded and her foot released the pram's brake.

They were turning into their street before Joy spoke again. 'Famous last words, eh? Don't tell Maureen where we're going?' Joy knew exactly why Eadie had changed her mind. She couldn't bear to think of that pig of a man, Mick, hurting his tiny child.

'It was easy enough for us to get taken on at Southerns' farm. If Maureen's got the guts she'll try to do the same. She's not stupid. A few weeks away from that brute might give her a different outlook on things.' Eadie had put into words exactly what Joy had been thinking.

'You're a good person, Eadie,' said Joy.

'Tell me that tomorrow morning when I've overslept and we're hurrying to catch the train,' she replied.

Moaning Minnie woke Joy, the high-pitched sound burrowing into her brain, like a maggot into an apple. Her feet felt for the slippers beneath the bed while she slid her arms into her dressing-gown sleeves. Her movements had become automatic on being woken by the screaming air-raid siren.

Downstairs in the scullery she lit the gas beneath the kettle for the flask of tea, and while the water boiled she scraped margarine onto uneven slices of bread. The jar of Shippam's fish paste would make tasty sandwiches to eat in Eadie's Anderson shelter. The package went into the carrier-bag with her handbag, ration book and identity papers next to a new paperback, *A Tree Grows in Brooklyn* by Betty Smith, which one of Priddy's girls had lent her.

Picturegoer, bought today but not yet read, was also jammed in alongside the freshly filled flask. Earlier, before she'd gone to bed, she'd been packing for Southerns' farm, not reading film magazines. Her suitcase now stood ready by the front door. The clothes she planned to wear for travelling to Petersfield, slacks and a twinset with her gaberdine raincoat, were laid ready over her bedside chair.

After switching off the gas and electricity she banged loudly on the dividing wall between her house and Eadie's to let them know she'd take only moments more before she called round on her way to the shelter at the bottom of Eadie's garden. She was still in her dressing-gown. It was ten o'clock, not yet properly dark, and with a bit of luck, if the raid didn't last too long, she could return to bed afterwards.

The moonlight momentarily dazzled her as she hurried through the ever-open garden gate between her house and Eadie's. Looking up into the sky it was difficult to hear the dull buzz of the enemy planes above the shouting coming from Eadie's living room, but Joy soon spotted the swarm of Luftwaffe bombers growing larger the nearer they approached. Even from this distance she recognized the distinctive outline of the twin-engine Dornier, the Flying Pencil, nicknamed for its slim shape. Larger planes were flying alongside them, and she assumed these, too, were bombers. She gasped. There were so many of them.

Then she saw the tiny black specks falling as the planes released bombs that tumbled through the skies.

Joy stood, mesmerized, watching as the bombs hurtled towards the earth. Next came the dull thuds, the crump of explosions as targets were found or missed.

Hampshire, home of armaments factories, army, navy, air-force establishments, and Portsmouth, with its docks, shipyards and port. And Gosport, ready to absorb all the German bomb-aimers' errors, destroying, maiming, killing. Joy was sure this raid was much larger than previous onslaughts.

Her heart was racing. It was time she, Eadie, Joe and Will were in the relative safety of the shelter. Her hand was on Eadie's scullery-door latch when it opened. She stumbled to stop herself falling inside only to be clasped in Eadie's arms. 'Go down to the shelter!' It was a command, not a request.

Eadie's flannelette nightdress billowed about her as she twisted Joy around. Joy could smell the Gibbs dentifrice Eadie had used to clean her teeth.

'No!' Will's roar from the other room startled her. It cut through Joe's soft, placating words.

'What's up?' she managed to ask, before Eadie manhandled

her out onto the concrete path. Joy felt something being pressed at her and, despite the weight of the bag she was already carrying, grabbed hold of the new object without letting it fall to the ground.

'Will's scared. He won't come out. There's nothing you can do. Take this bag. Get down to the shelter. We'll come later.' The door slammed in her face.

For a moment Joy listened to the sound of a man sobbing interspersed with Joe's soothing voice. She couldn't and didn't want to stand there any longer. It was intrusive of her and best that she did as Eadie wished.

She took a deep breath. Already the sky had changed from soft moonlight to a scene of violence. Flashes of orange and yellow stained the atmosphere where bombs had detonated, and the gaseous stink of explosives now filled the air about her. Lugging the bags she stumbled to the bottom of the garden.

Just as her hand pushed open the shelter's reinforced oak door another deafening noise petrified her, causing her to fall to her knees on the packed-earth floor. Joy closed her eyes with relief – it was the anti-aircraft guns from St Vincent naval training base in nearby Forton Road returning fire to the strafing marauders.

She scrambled to her feet, slamming the shelter's door

on the searchlights roving the skies for German planes. After taking a few deep breaths to settle herself Joy dusted herself down and, in the intense darkness, made her way to the paraffin stove. She wasn't cold but the glow from its flames would make the shelter cosier. A box of Swan Vestas, wrapped in a sliver of tarpaulin to keep them dry, sat ready for lighting on top of the stove. Its warmth helped stop the damp rising from the earth. A metal washing-up bowl, a tin kettle and a saucepan, mugs and tin plates were stored on makeshift orange-box shelving.

Joy could hear the whistles and bangs from outside as she picked up objects scattered from the hastily dropped bags. Plenty of tea and sandwiches, reading material and personal items for each of them: nothing was broken. There were even a couple of towels and a bar of Lifebuoy carbolic soap. Eadie always made sure the four bunk beds were aired and fresh water left in clean containers as there was never a time limit to how long it would be before the all-clear sounded.

As Joy left the few personal belongings Eadie had thoughtfully included on the appropriate beds, she realized how tired she was. Not, she felt guiltily, as tired as Eadie probably was.

It wasn't an easy job coping with Will, especially when the bombing agitated him. How she and Joe managed to contend with daily life when Will was like a lit firework, ready to go off with a bang at any moment or dissolve into tears over any fantasy, she couldn't fathom. Or perhaps she could. Joe and Eadie loved him to bits, didn't they? Lines from a sonnet by William Shakespeare materialized in her brain: 'Love is not love/Which alters when it alteration finds.' Mentally she blessed her father for instilling in her a love of reading anything and everything. Shakespeare was indeed a clever bloke. He really knew all about love.

Of course, it wasn't beyond the realms of possibility that one day Will would return to being the funny, playful man who used to mimic most of the comedy characters he heard on the wireless. His Colonel Chinstrap saying, 'I don't mind if I do, sir,' from the show *ITMA – It's That Man Again* – would have her in stitches. Joy hoped the time would not be too far away when his wonderful sense of humour returned to him.

She perched on her bunk and looked around the shelter. Everything was tidy for when the others arrived. She yawned. This wasn't the first time she'd been sent on ahead to relative safety but sometimes, not always, it was only Eadie who joined her.

Joe had been warned by the Cane Hill Asylum doctors that noise from bombing would in all likelihood bring back to Will the horrors of France. Joe had had the bright idea of cleaning out the coal-hole, the large cupboard beneath the living-room stairs. The coal was relegated to the back shed. Eadie protested that it wasn't very safe, but decided second-best was better than none at all. She managed to pick up a broken camp bed at a jumble sale and Joe mended it. He also rigged up a light in the walk-in cupboard, candles for when the electricity had to be turned off.

After much persuasion Will, though he hated being closed in, would sometimes, during a raid, allow Joe to lead him inside the larger sheltered area beneath the stairs. Never with the door closed on them, though. Joe slept on cushions beside his son's camp bed. Eadie, sometimes unwilling to leave her husband and his father, stayed in the house. Of course, there were times, not frequent, when Will would willingly accompany them to the garden shelter. Always, but always, when the siren announced a raid either Joe or Eadie went upstairs and unlocked the drawer for Will's medication. It was a precaution, a safety measure, but not a necessity.

Joy rose, took the flask from her bag and poured tea. She set the mug beside her bed, eased off her slippers and, after glancing at the front page of her film magazine, wriggled inside the blanket.

Every so often shrapnel rained down, hitting part of the

stout door. The corrugated shelter was dug deep into the ground, at least three feet of earth covering the roof. But still Joy could hear the *whomp* of exploding bombs. What would Gosport look like tomorrow? she wondered. Every time there was a raid the town was remodelled. But she couldn't think about that: she needed to be positive. To think about earning money.

Would she and Eadie get to Fareham station in time to catch the train to Petersfield? Would the train even be running? What would the future, the next few weeks at least, hold in store for Eadie and herself?

Once more she looked at the front page of *Picturegoer* and stared at Anne Baxter's face. What must it be like to be as beautiful and as talented as her? To live in Hollywood?

The magazine slipped from her fingers.

Chapter Four

'Wake up, Sleeping Beauty!' Eadie placed the mug of tea on the floor next to Joy's bunk. She took a couple of sniffs and looked about her, frowning.

Joy stirred, opened her eyes and, after a moment or two, asked, 'What time is it?' followed immediately by 'Shut that door!' Weak sunshine was pouring into the air-raid shelter bringing with it a stiff early-morning breeze and the sulphurous smell of last night's shelling. Eadie chucked yesterday's cold tea out onto the ground. Leaving the door open, she said, 'I don't know how you can sleep through the all-clear. And it's really stuffy in here. Drink that while it's hot.' Eadie watched as Joy slurped it. When it was finished, she held out the mug for Eadie to take from her.

'I'm not your servant, ducky.' Eadie gave her an

old-fashioned look. 'Wake up properly and get up! We got a train to catch.'

Joy's mouth opened like a surprised child's. Then, as though remembering, she pushed back the blanket. 'I was out like a light last night . . .'

'So I see. You forgot to turn off the paraffin stove. It's a good job the oil ran out. With no ventilation in here the fumes could have killed you.'

Joy looked guiltily at the heater. 'I never thought . . .'

Eadie sat down on the bunk beside her. She picked up Joy's hand and held it, feeling its warmth seep into her skin. 'You're usually so careful, ducky. Whatever possessed you to be so thoughtless?'

Anxiety filled Joy's eyes. 'So careless. Jesus! How many times have I slept in here alone?' A huge sigh escaped her.

'With all that's happened in the last few days, we're both probably a bit out of sorts and forgetful. Promise me you'll take care?'

Eadie wasn't sure whether it was the danger of what might have happened to Joy, the trauma of Will's resistance last night to allow his safety to be her and Joe's priority, or even the awful after-effects of the accident at Priddy's, but words poured from her that she'd no intention of saying. 'I lost your mum. I couldn't bear it if I lost you as well.'

Eadie gasped as Joy's arms snaked around her, clutching her so tightly that practically all her breath was squeezed out of her. 'I'm sorry. I'm so very sorry,' Joy cried, in a muffled voice.

Eadie felt tears rise. She tried to make light of it by pushing Joy away. 'You just wait till I tell Joe how you tried to end it all in our air-raid shelter!' She shook her head and laughed to show Joy she was forgiven. 'Anyway, get out of that bed. It's early but I thought you might have household chores to finish up before we leave.' Then she added, 'Joe'll have your key and keep an eye on things for you.'

She watched as Joy, still in her dressing-gown, slid from the bunk.

'How did it go with Will last night?' Joy asked, gathering her personal stuff together into the bag she'd brought down to the shelter.

'The same,' replied Eadie. She didn't want a discussion about it: today was another day. She was dying for a fag but wouldn't light up until she'd finished tidying the shelter and was out in the fresh air. 'We can take these to eat on the journey.' She sniffed at the wrapping on the fish-paste sandwiches.

'Is the street all right?'

Had any of the neighbours' houses been hit? That had

been one of Eadie's first thoughts on waking, aching, on cushions in the coal-hole after discovering that she, Joe and Will were still alive. 'Yes,' she answered. Then, 'Look, I can sort all this out. Get off home next door. First post's due. You might get a letter from that air-force chappie!'

'Chance would be a fine thing!' Joy frowned. 'I never said earlier but I could do with an aspirin. I've got a headache.'

Eadie was folding the blanket on Joy's bunk. She paused. 'You'll get no sympathy from me, ducky. That's your own bloody fault.'

With their suitcases stored in the luggage space beneath the bus's stairs, Eadie tucked Joy into the window seat, paid the blonde conductress their fares and settled back in the aisle seat to survey last night's destruction caused by the Luftwaffe.

Immediately she wished they'd gone upstairs. She'd momentarily forgotten it was 'No Smoking' downstairs, especially as the fug from the smokers above drifted enticingly down. Not that it made a difference: she'd thrown away an empty packet before she'd left home. There were twenty Woodbines, an unopened packet, in her suitcase but none in her handbag.

The damage to homes and shops caused by the bombing

was needless, she thought, and broke her heart. But as the bus trundled onwards to Fareham, making only a few detours due to road and water-main damage, she marvelled at the stoic nature of the affected people. Shop windows were being boarded up; pavements swept of rubble. A smile lifted the corners of her mouth as she spotted a queue forming outside a seemingly undamaged butcher's shop. Women in headscarves, baskets over arms, some with pushchairs, chatted amicably while waiting hopefully. Then she saw a line of nappies flapping in the breeze next to a garden path adjoining a house. A house that was now a pile of rubble. Eadie sighed. Someone had lovingly planted those nasturtiums to flower now with their bright orange, red and yellow blooms and someone had stood at that house's sink, washing the towelling squares. What had happened to them? To the child? Eadie felt the lump rise in her throat that heralded tears. Hastily, she swallowed it. Stop it, she told herself.

She marvelled that people managed to carry on, regardless of what happened in their lives due to the war. Eadie was like everyone else: she wanted life to go back to how it was before the war started. Most tried to keep their spirits high and infuse hope in those about them.

Resilience, solidarity and the usual British spirit helped.

She smiled, remembering the notice-board outside Bert's Café in the town, near the ferry. A message was chalked on it: 'In the event of a German invasion we shall close for half an hour.' That was Gosport humour at its best, she thought. Today wasn't a day to be maudlin. Today was the start of an adventure for her and Joy. She'd left her home and her husband in the capable hands of her father-in-law. Joe's final words came to mind: 'Promise me that, for the time you're hop-picking, whenever a thought about us comes into your mind, you'll immediately brush it away. You need this time for yourself.' Will and Joe had sent her off with their love and a kiss and she would return that love by earning as much money as she could.

The overcrowded bus trundled at a steady rate, stopping every so often to allow passengers on and off, though more seemed to be getting on than leaving. Eadie was glad they'd left home with plenty of time to allow for delays and detours. The early sun was stronger now and she could imagine Will, dressed and breakfasted, perhaps sitting in the garden, reading or listening to the birds chirping.

Sometimes she wondered just how many of the written words Will was able to assimilate. He'd been a great reader once, like Joy, but she'd noticed his book often stayed open on the same page for a long, long time.

'Can you see the headlines on that newspaper?'

Eadie was shaken from her thoughts by a dig in the ribs and Joy's voice. She turned in her aisle seat and saw her friend leaning forward and staring over the shoulder of the young soldier sitting in front.

'Can I borrow your paper for a moment, please?' Joy was treating him to a winsome grin. Since Joy with her blonde waves and curls resembled a younger version of the actress Lizabeth Scott, Eadie knew that the young man wouldn't refuse her request. Eadie saw it was the same newspaper that Joe had delivered daily to the house.

The young man handed the paper to Joy with a smile.

Joy held out the front page so Eadie couldn't miss the headlines: 'Shell Shock Not Cowardice?' and below, in smaller letters, 'General George Patton to Apologize'.

After a while Joy asked, 'Read it?'

Eadie nodded, but said, 'Wait a bit.' She read the article, taking in all the words, her temper rising, and pushed the paper back to Joy, who tutted but immediately smoothed it out.

'Thank you,' Joy said, returning the now neatly folded newspaper to the man, who shyly nodded his thanks to her. To Eadie, she said, 'That's a turn-up for the books, isn't it? Please don't upset yourself.'

71

Eadie was trying not to raise her voice but such was her anger that the written words were growing larger and larger in her mind. 'General George S. Patton, Commander of the Seventh United States Army, slaps two soldiers under his command during the Sicily campaign.'

'How can he not believe in shell shock? It's a medical condition,' she hissed. 'And to strike those men when they were patients in an evacuation hospital away from the front line beggars belief!' Eadie was trying hard not to explode but after the awful night she'd spent with Will her patience was at an all-time low.

'It's because he saw no physical injuries on the men—' began Joy.

'There doesn't need to be outward injuries for a man's mind to be damaged,' Eadie broke in. 'But to say the men were simply cowards, using the hospital to escape the war! And that men like them, unwilling to fight, should be tried by court-martial and shot! That's a terrible claim for him to make.' Her anger was consuming her. Eadie took a deep breath. She was willing herself to calmness. She breathed out slowly.

'General Dwight D. Eisenhower's asked him to apologize,' Joy told her.

'Thank God for that! But it doesn't excuse the man! He

should come here and meet my Will and all the other broken men I met in Cane Hill Asylum.'

The soldier in front, who couldn't help but overhear her, turned round again and said loudly, 'That general has no bloody idea! I agree with you wholeheartedly.'

The conductress's voice unwittingly ended that conversation before it started: 'Fareham station!' Eadie and Joy scrambled up to join the rush of people and children intent on hauling bags and packages from the luggage space beneath the stairs.

'It's a free-for-all to get off the bus, ducky,' gasped Eadie. She was glad to be leaving the vehicle, the newspaper and the conversation it had provoked, when a thought struck her. What if Will saw the headline? What if he read the article? How would it affect his disordered mind?

Eadie nearly stumbled, stepping down with her suitcase and handbag, but caught hold of Joy just in time.

'All right?' asked Joy, when they were standing, with their luggage, on the pavement.

Eadie nodded. 'I think I'd better keep my mind on what we're doing and where we're going.'

'Surely all these people can't be going camping. I mean, who can afford to go away on holidays round here to escape the bombing?'

Eadie was pondering Joy's question as they followed the crowd across the road towards the station. She knew her friend associated trains with holidays and days out. She, however, was beginning to think differently: 'If they are, they're taking their beds and kitchens with them!' She spotted three ragamuffin children carrying quilts and clothing tied up in blanket bundles almost as big as themselves. One of the lads had two large saucepans hanging over his shoulder, with string tied through the holes in their handles. Women carried bags, with packages hoisted on their backs, while clutching the hands of kiddies. Eadie counted two tin kettles fastened to the handle of a child's pushchair. One kettle fine, she thought, but two?

For a single moment Eadie thought she must be dreaming that weird scenario but the noise from the surge of people queuing at the Railway Information and Tickets window told her otherwise. She joined the unruly line, pulling Joy to a stop. Joy seemed happy to release her heavy suitcase.

'He's harassed,' Eadie said, pushing her in front so they wouldn't become separated and nodding towards the small window where a middle-aged man in a peaked cap was endeavouring to count bodies, take money, dole out change and tickets all at the same time.

Above the din Eadie heard a whistle and an earth-shattering rumble as a train belching smoke slowed and screeched to a stop on the track. The station filled with foul-smelling smoke making it almost impossible for anyone to breathe as people poured from its carriage doors. Eadie watched avidly, spotting the driver and a guard leaving the now immobile train to head towards the station's main buildings.

'That's it!' Eadie heard the excited cry from the waiting crowd. 'Train's in!'

Coal fumes, brake dust, grease, body odours, cigarettes and cheap perfumes hung on the air at the railway depot as Sunday workers and service personnel with kitbags jostled past the waiting queue. She craned her neck to look beyond the platform for the station's café, where possibly the train driver was headed and which Eadie could just make out beyond some metal gates. 'I wish we had our tickets,' she said. 'Still, the train won't leave without the driver, will it?' Joy shook her head.

The enticing smell of fresh toast tickled Eadie's nose. Visions of strong tea tantalized her. More than anything, though, she craved a fag. 'Miaow!' She felt a sharp pain rake across her ankle.

'Ow!' She looked down just in time to see a white paw

shoot back into a small hole in a decrepit wicker basket, alongside her own suitcase. The basket was wound about by layer upon layer of string to keep the cat safely inside.

'Sorry about that, missus,' said a boy, holding the hand of a younger girl with gloriously blonde curls. Her nose needed wiping and her tongue protruded as the boy spoke. He saw, shook her violently and protested, 'Use yer 'anky, our Ivy!'

Eadie watched, amazed, as the tiny tot lifted her dress, took out a clean white handkerchief from her knicker leg and blew her nose, then calmly replaced it. Stifling a laugh as the child patted her dress straight, Eadie looked down at her ankle where a thin trail of blood had reached her foot. Quickly she bent and smeared it away before it marked her slacks.

'What you got in that basket? A wild animal?' She looked at the lad, who was probably about ten and had the longest eyelashes surrounding the bluest eyes she'd ever seen.

'Nah! It's Spitfire, our cat. We can't leave him at home. He's only got us. He sleeps with our Ivy 'ere,' he said. 'Me sister can't sleep wivout him.' Eadie glanced again at the little girl: she had similar beautiful eyes. She could just make out the same flaxen colour of the boy's hair even though it was mostly covered by an enormous grey peaked cap, none too clean and at odds with the rest of their scruffy but well-washed clothing.

'Move up, missus,' the boy said. 'You'll be lettin' people push in!' He shoved against her so she was forced to propel Joy forward. Joy bent and clutched her case's handle after grinning good-naturedly at her.

Eadie, dragging her case, continued to inch along. The lad shifted the basket forward with his foot, without letting go of his sister's hand. The cat accepted the move in silence.

'Where are you going?' Eadie asked him.

The lad looked at Eadie as if she was daft.

'We're catching the 'op-pickers' special what goes at nine!' He stared down at his sister, caught her eye and the look that passed between them made Eadie think she'd asked him some absurd, obscure question. This lad was as sharp as a barrel of monkeys, she thought.

She tried again. 'You reckon all these people are catching the same train?' She nodded at the crowd, then at a weary woman carrying a child on one hip, while from her other arm dangled an overflowing holdall.

The boy frowned at Eadie. 'Nah, most of 'em just likes carrying heavy stuff about!'

It took Eadie a second to realize he was teasing her. At about the same time she grasped that she and Joy had made a very big mistake in allowing the farmer's wife to believe they'd picked hops before. That thought simmered in her head for a moment. Then she asked, 'So, you camp out at the hop-fields?'

'Not 'xactly,' he said. She breathed a sigh of relief. 'We gets given huts to live in.' Her heart began thumping fast. A hut? 'That's why we brings our own stuff for bedding an' to cook wiv,' he added.

Eadie stared at him. His blue eyes gazed at her expectantly as if at any moment she might say something else he thought silly. After a while he looked down at her suitcase. 'Ain't you goin' hoppin', then?'

Eadie pulled herself together. She gave him a half-smile but didn't answer. It ran through her mind that if she and Joy had known what was actually involved in the job of hop-picking they'd have come better prepared.

She didn't blame Joy for telling Mrs Southern they'd picked hops before. Joy had realized a prospective boss would rather employ experienced field hands, but she and Joy needed the money. They'd pooled their meagre resources to fund train and bus fares.

Her thoughts were shot away by a long, drawn-out howl from the basket at the boy's feet, followed by frantic scrabbling at the hole in the wicker-work. The cat wanted to escape, and so did Eadie. But where could she run? Not home to Gosport and admit defeat to Joe, that she'd not found out enough about the job and its living conditions before she'd embarked on it. The only sensible thing to do was to see what happened when they reached Selborne. She decided she wouldn't worry Joy with the information she'd acquired from the lad.

'Ain't you goin' hoppin', then?' the boy repeated.

'Are you?' Eadie asked. The boy nodded, at the same time slapping the little girl's finger away from her nose. She pulled a face at him.

Eadie continued quickly, 'Where's all your stuff, then? Your mum, your dad?'

With an air of great confidence, the lad replied. 'Ain't got a mum. I'm keepin' our place in the queue while our dad loads our stuff in the guard's van. The guard's a mate of me dad's, see? He'll be 'ere in a minute. If he ain't, I got to get the tickets. He trusts me,' he said. 'I got the money an' all.' Eadie thought if his chest swelled any more with pride at being entrusted with such a task it would pop.

Joy, in front of her, squashed in on all sides but obviously anticipating another move forward, kicked her case along, turned her head and said, 'Thank God we're nearly at the window. You all right?' She didn't wait for an answer. 'What

I wouldn't give for a cuppa right now. An' the smell of that toast is something else.'

'All I want is a fag,' said Eadie, stepping sideways so her feet wouldn't be trodden on as a tall man elbowed himself in beside her. A faint vanilla and cedar smell came with him. 'Oi! Watch it! Mind my toes,' Eadie cried.

'Your wishes are my command,' the man said, 'with minding your toes and a fag.' His hand delved into the inside breast pocket of his dark blue herringbone wool waistcoat, beneath which he wore a white shirt with the sleeves rolled up. His hair was parted on the side but the blond curls were tumbling onto his forehead. His blue eyes, with long lashes, proclaimed him, without a doubt, to be the children's father.

Eadie had to clench her teeth to stop her mouth falling open in astonishment as the man flicked open a packet of Player's Navy Cut and held it towards her.

'Thank you,' she managed, in a strangled voice, as she took one. For some unknown reason her hand was shaking and her heart thumping so hard she was sure everyone might hear it as time, space, people and station noise withdrew, leaving Eadie to feel as if only she and this man existed.

Click! The magic moment vanished as in his other hand he held a silver lighter, which flamed as he flicked it. His eyes never left hers as he watched her draw on the cigarette.

For some unfathomed reason Eadie's print of *Pinkie* flashed into her mind, with the *Blue Boy*'s haunted eyes.

The cigarettes and lighter disappeared into his pockets and he bent and scooped the small girl into his arms, lifting her high to sit on his shoulders, giggling.

'Aw! Dad! We're nearly at the ticket window and now you're back I won't be able to buy the tickets!' Beneath the too-large cap the boy's face had set into a disappointed frown.

'Why's that, then? You lost the money I gave you?'

The boy's mouth opened in amazement as if he couldn't believe his father would say such a thing.

'I'm teasing you, Tim.' The man laughed and a smile immediately flashed across his son's lips. 'Get the money out, lad. We're next at the window after these two charming ladies.'

Chapter Five

'Ta! I like fish paste,' said the woman, biting into the sand-wich Joy had offered. 'And call me Pat. I saw the pair of you waiting in the queue to buy train tickets. Didn't you get one in the post? Regular hoppers gets special tickets that you show to the station master.'

'We didn't know we were starting till yesterday,' Joy said. That made her think of Maureen. Back at the railway station she'd kept an eye open just in case the woman appeared. She'd not mentioned it, in case Eadie railed at Maureen's lack of gumption in leaving Mick. Joy preferred their new venture to begin as seamlessly as possible. Will's return home, welcome though it was, had left Eadie a little dis-connected from her. Being together, away from Gosport, could only be a bonus for Eadie and Joy, a break she knew Eadie welcomed.

Her friend's voice broke into her thoughts. 'Bit late to post anything, Pat,' explained Eadie, biting into the apple the woman had given her.

'Mrs Southern's a good sort. She won't see you go short. Mind you, some farmers won't allow train vouchers for kids. I've seen kiddies rolled up in mattresses slung over their dad's shoulders to save the pennies for their fares.'

'It's our first time, you see,' Joy put in. She'd already discovered Pat could talk for England and didn't always listen to what the other person was saying. But perhaps she could glean some information from her, especially as she and Eadie knew nothing about hop-picking. Her head swam with the woman's constant chatter while her four red-haired children argued and fought in the carriage that had seating for eight and contained eleven, including four possible hop-pickers, who were trying to ignore the mayhem. Bags and other luggage were strewn everywhere. Joy couldn't wait for the train to reach Petersfield. She knew it wasn't a long ride and she badly needed fresh air and space.

'If nobody wants that, I'll 'ave it.'

Before Joy had a chance to answer, the last fish-paste sandwich had been grabbed by the grubby hand of one of Pat's lads, Mikey. Joy was glad to see the back of it, regretting she and Eadie had packed as much as possible into their suitcases, including food and flasks. It had taken enormous effort to extricate her suitcase buried beneath a pile of tied-up bedding. She'd been worried the intense heat in the compartment might cause the smelly filling to go off and contaminate her clean clothing.

'I'm glad they've all gone,' she said to Eadie. 'I could kill for a cuppa.'

'Don't even think about it,' warned her friend. 'There's no way I'm diving into that lot for flasks.' She motioned to a large pile of belongings teetering over the edge of the luggage rack, almost hiding her own suitcase. 'There'd be tea everywhere, ducky. And I'm dyin' for a fag!'

Joy stared into Eadie's eyes and smiled. She knew they were both remembering the blond man who'd taken an instant fancy to Eadie and given her the last cigarette she'd smoked.

A boy's shout broke into Joy's thoughts: 'Give over, our Marlene. Leave Mikey's sandwich alone!' Pat wriggled her ample body for more room on the seat, gave up, then said, 'When the train gets to Petersfield, there'll be transport to take us to the farms. Maybe lorries or 'orses an' carts. Stick wiv me else you'll end up somewhere you shouldn't. Nearly lost Mikey when he was smaller . . . When we gets to the farm you'll be allocated hut and line numbers. Course I'll get the same hut as before because I'm a regular.'

Joy was almost losing the will to live as Pat's voice droned on and on. Thinking about the blond man with the two kiddies reminded her of Jim and the letter he'd promised her. Any letters sent to her home address would be forwarded as soon as Eadie let Joe know their farm address. Joy allowed herself to remember that night at the Connaught dance hall. Jim had seemed such a serious-minded, shy man, not at all the type to lead her on. She was convinced something must have happened to the young airman to stop him writing to her. An unexpected warmth stole over her remembering his smile . . .

'Of course you don't want an end line to pick. End lines is open to the elements and don't usually 'ave as many 'ops on as middle ones.'

Joy could see Eadie smiling at her while Pat's monotonous voice carried on. Joy smiled back, immediately lighter in spirits. Through the window she could see green fields, the orange berries clinging to rowan branches, the sunburst yellow of cornfields already harvested. Here and there, she spotted the brighter mauves and pinks of late-flowering shrubs. Joy could imagine the atmosphere outside smelling so sweet, so fresh, and not at all like the sulphurous, almond-tainted air that hung over Gosport. She closed her eyes.

'We're 'ere!'

The train jerked, lurched, squealed to a halt and Joy opened her eyes to see and smell foul grey steam from the train's boiler entering the carriage through a half-open window. She felt small hands groping, searching for misplaced belongings beneath and around her seat. Children were arguing over found and hidden objects. A shoe. A ball. A hairless doll. A splintered wooden model of a Spitfire plane was grabbed from near her shoes.

Then, amazingly, Eadie was hunkered down in front of her.

'Fancy you sleeping through that lot.' Eadie's fingers tucked a long strand of hair back behind Joy's ear. 'C'mon, ducky, we've got to move. Train's going on and we don't want to end up at the next station!'

Joy rose shakily to her feet and stood in the now vacant carriage looking at the detritus discarded by Pat's children. She couldn't believe she'd fallen asleep in the middle of all the noise. The handle of her suitcase was shoved into her fingers and she was pulled out of the train's open door just in time to blend in with the crowd hurrying towards Petersfield station's exit.

'Yoo-hoo! This way!' Pat's strident voice caught her attention and Joy peered ahead at the bodies disappearing through the metal gates. She could see Pat frantically waving at them while Mikey, beside her, was practically invisible behind the bedding bale.

'She's going to try to save us seats on the transport,' huffed Eadie, hurrying beside her. 'For God's sake, don't let her out of your sight.'

That's easier said than done, thought Joy, running to keep up with Eadie, who seemed determined not to be relegated to the rear of the fast-moving crowd.

And then they were outside the station where horse-drawn carts, lorries and wagons were lined along the street, already overflowing with prospective hop-pickers, their children and belongings. Joy noticed nearly all the women wore hats in various shapes and styles, some flat caps, like their menfolk. A long line of travellers had already set off walking. Joy supposed they were going to nearby farms and didn't need or weren't assured of transport. She gasped as she caught sight of the cheeky lad, Tim, from Fareham's ticket queue. He was carrying a bundle nearly as big as himself and walking beside his father, who again had young Ivy, securely sitting high on his shoulders. The wicker basket hung from one of the man's hands and a suitcase swung from the other.

'There's your fancy man,' Joy hissed. She wasn't sure if Eadie heard her above the hubbub of laughter and shouting. Her attention was swiftly taken by the ample figure of Pat, yelling and waving from a fast-filling cart. A tall, solid shire horse stood calmly awaiting the carter's instructions.

'Come aboard!' shouted Pat, her children huddled about her. Joy saw the wizened driver nod at Pat and shout to a young lad in dungarees, who jumped down from the wagon and came, smiling, towards them.

'You for Southerns' farm?' Joy was immediately struck by the drawn-out vowels the lad used. His voice was soft, musical almost, not at all resembling the harsh London-like slang of Gosport people. Joy nodded at him.

'Put your foot on a wheel and hoist yourself up,' he said, relieving her of her heavy suitcase as though it weighed nothing and pushing it into a shelf-like space beneath the cart. Joy stared at him, then at the height of the wagon. 'You're quite safe,' he said. 'Hold on to the wooden rail. I won't let you fall.'

She found herself pushed in tightly beside Mikey and his bundle. His red-haired, freckled twin brothers, aged about five, snuggled at his feet. Mikey gave her a gap-toothed grin. Shortly after, Eadie was crammed in opposite her, next to an elderly woman with grey hair, and Marlene, Pat's girl. Both Eadie and Joy profusely thanked the young lad before he climbed, red-faced, obviously not used to being appreciated, onto the front of the wagon next to the driver.

'When we gets to the farm, I 'spect the farmer's wife'll have a word with you,' Pat said, from Mikey's side. 'There'll be loads to do when we arrive. In case I forget, I'll see you both at the fire tonight, all right?'

Joy saw Eadie open her mouth to speak, no doubt to shout thanks above the hubbub to Pat for all the help she'd given, but already Pat was elaborating on how the hop-picking was an annual holiday for most people, especially the children. Eadie smiled at her. No doubt Pat's remark about seeing them at the fire would become clear later.

The wagon began to move. A cheer rose from its occupants and the driver grinned.

Joy had never before sat on a cart with a huge horse contentedly pulling its burden over street cobbles. She made herself comfortable beside Mikey and looked about. The grey horse was making loud clip-clopping sounds with its huge feathered hoofs that sounded reassuring to Joy. Its mane was well brushed, and a length of hair above its eyes had been plaited and tied with a bow of red ribbon. The great animal was undoubtably well loved.

Joy lifted her face and felt the sunshine warm her skin. She breathed in deeply, then let out the sweet air slowly. A sudden ray of happiness washed over her. She and Eadie were taking a step towards the unknown. It felt good.

A few days ago, she was lying next to Gosport's Forton creek, wondering whether she was dying, and today she and Eadie were at the start of something good. Joy could feel it in her bones. It was a new beginning. She and Eadie had been remarkably lucky to escape uninjured from the blast at the munitions factory when others hadn't. She looked across at her friend and received a knowing smile in return. Sometimes, she could have sworn Eadie was able to read her mind.

Joe would miss Eadie. Joy had caught the sudden unhappiness in his eyes that morning when they'd left. He hadn't wanted Eadie to go. Oh, he'd never have admitted it, quite the opposite. He always wanted her happiness, no matter at what cost to himself. Joy wasn't stupid, though. She had sensed the older man's love for his daughter-in-law, and his need to show it. But Joe would never cross that line to harm Eadie's reputation, and would never betray his son. He loved Eadie, he loved Will. Nothing short of death or destruction would change that. And Eadie? Eadie deserved to love, Joy deliberated, and be loved in return.

Joy's thoughts were disturbed by Marlene's giggles. Marlene had engaged Eadie in playing cat's cradle with a length of string. Her long red hair blew about her pretty face as, concentrating hard, she transferred the string from

Eadie's fingers to her own. Joy thought her to be about twelve. Eadie was enjoying every moment of the game. She was so good with children, thought Joy.

'Wanna play?' Marlene shouted, as she caught Joy staring. Laughing, Joy shook her head. There was precious little space to move with so many pickers crammed together on the cart.

Petersfield's a pretty place, she thought. Quite a few majestic buildings, unscathed, so far, by bomb damage, though perhaps what she could see from the wagon as it trundled through the town didn't tell the whole story. One thing she noticed immediately was how clean the place was. She caught a lull in Pat's voice and took the chance to ask how far it was to the farm at Selborne, 'Five or six miles,' Pat answered. 'All countryside,' she added.

'So, the pickers who didn't get transport, have to walk?' Joy was thinking about the blond-haired man and his two children. She wondered which farm they were aiming for.

'The walkers usually get picked up when some of the wagons return to the station for stragglers,' Pat added. Then, 'I 'ope you got some washing soda in them cases of yours.'

Joy looked at her in amazement, then shrugged. 'Whatever for?' She kept soda crystals on the draining board at home because a small handful softened the boiled washing-up water. She'd never dreamed of bringing any away with her.

'Soda's best for getting the brown stain off your 'ands from the 'ops. They'll be brown as anything when the season's over. Scrub your 'ands with soda water. That'll do the trick.' Without pausing, Pat asked, 'Got your 'ats? It gets very 'ot in the fields.'

'So that's why nearly all the women, men too, are wearing hats or turbans,' Joy said. 'It's protection from the sun, isn't it?' She tried to think if she'd packed any scarves. They could fashion turbans from them.

'Got bottles for your tea?' Pat was in full flow now, and speaking loudly so that Eadie, and probably everyone on the wagon, could hear. She was reminding them of necessary articles they needed for working in the fields.

'Bottles?' Eadie looked confused. Joy saw she'd given up playing cat's cradle with Marlene, no doubt because it was difficult to concentrate as Pat was including her in the conversation.

'Nothin' like a nice swallow of tea what's gone a bit cool when you're sitting in the shade somewhere after bein' in the 'ot sun.'

'We've brought flasks,' Eadie said proudly. Joy remembered the tea in the suitcase. It might still be warm when they reached their destination. Then she thought of her

Picturegoer magazine, which she'd included in her packing. Perhaps she'd be able to look at it tonight in bed, if she had a bed to sleep in.

'Don't the children get in the way?' Eadie called to Pat, who guffawed. Joy saw her friend was holding a lit cigarette. Eadie grinned and nodded towards the elderly woman next to her, who'd obviously offered it because she, too, was smoking.

'Since the women mostly do the pickin', who'd mind the little 'uns at home when the old man's at work? They 'ave to come, don't they? Anyway, kids pick as well. Course you got to watch what they puts in the sack, no leaves, mind. But, you see, a lot of the Londoners pick 'ops because in the winter some of their kiddies get bad chests. All that London smog, see. Well, once you're on a farmer's land, he's got to take care of his summer workers so he'll maybe call out the doctor for a sick child. At home the mother perhaps couldn't afford to pay for a doctor. Free medicine as well, you see? Good for kids to come hopping. All the fresh air. Mind you,' Pat was on a roll, 'farmers prefer the London pickers because they're regulars, come every year, like. They picks clean and fast and that's what's needed, a clean, fast picker. Romanies too, they're good pickers . . .' Her voice tailed off as she pointed at the hedges to either side of the narrow road. 'Can you see in the bushes there? See the hops growing wild?'

Joy peered at the shrubbery interspersed with small trees. It was nearing the autumn now and although wild flowers still poked their heads above the long grasses and flourished in the hedgerows, she wasn't familiar with their names, recognizing only their colours and shapes.

'See the five-pointed leaves with the yellowing, hanging cone-shaped flowers clinging to the bushes? Climb anything, hops will. See their tendrils?'

Joy peered hard. She thought they looked exotic, quite beautiful. 'Are they really hops? How did they get there?'

'They're wild ones. Blown seed maybe, who knows? Farmers here have grown hops for years and years. Mind you, the wild ones smell just as strong as the cultivated ones. The stink can knock you out. I've known pickers faint in an enclosed area on a hot, humid day. Smelling salts under your nose soon brings you round. I don't suppose you brought any *sal volatile* with you, either?'

Joy shook her head. She was beginning to think there was a lot more to picking hops that she'd ever thought.

'Don't worry, I got some,' said Pat. 'Most of the regulars brings smelling salts.'

'I don't think I'm ever going to remember everything, Pat,' said Joy.

'Course you will, love. An' what you don't know, you'll find the rest of the women can 'elp you with. Everyone mucks in together. One good thing is there ain't that many men 'ere to swagger about an' get in the way. It can be a bonus to talk to other women. Tell 'em your troubles and listen to theirs. Nobody understands a woman like another woman.'

Joy looked at Pat. Her tired eyes said it all: beneath her bluster Pat had had a hard life, which had left her with a heart of solid gold. Joy felt for Pat's hand, squeezed it and whispered, 'Thank you for looking out for us. We do appreciate it, you know.'

Pat stared at her, her eyes suddenly washed bright with unshed tears. Joy smiled. Pat opened her mouth but before she could say anything a loud shout of 'We're here!' and the cheers from the wagonload of pickers eclipsed all other sounds.

Joy, excited now, stared about her. She expected to see a farm, animals perhaps, dwellings nearby. Habitation so far had been limited to a few pretty cottages partly hidden among the trees. Even the village the cart had trundled through was there and gone in a flash.

Now, for as far as she could see, fields contained never-ending lines of green vines reaching towards the heavens. Thick with a profusion of golden cone-shaped flowers the vines flourished on tall wooden poles threaded with strings. It was an amazing sight.

'See the hop-fields?' Pat waved an arm. 'Those all belong to the Southerns.'

'See them? I can smell them.' A yeasty, peppery aroma blew on the breeze. 'How on earth do we manage to reach the tops of the vines to pick them? They're over twelve feet tall!'

'They're called bines, not vines,' Pat said gently, 'and the bines will be cut down as needed, mostly by men walking on stilts—'

'You're teasing me!' Joy interrupted. 'Stilts?'

'Yes. The stilt men are the farm workers, not pickers, and in the spring, they tie strings to the poles for young hop-plants to climb. The bines grow and in the summer the stilt men use bill hooks to cut the strings so the bines fall and we can strip them of hops. You'll maybe see them soon enough. Though sometimes they've finished their work before we start ours.'

Joy wondered if Eadie had heard Pat's words but she was deep in conversation with Marlene. She'll never believe me when I tell her we might be seeing grown men on stilts, Joy thought. 'There's such a lot to learn,' she said.

'Don't worry about it, love. After you've been 'ere a week it'll all be like second nature to you both.'

Joy wasn't sure about that. 'Eadie and me are used to munitions, to working in a factory for the war effort.'

Pat cut her off. Her face had darkened, her voice hard. 'You don't think making beer is necessary for the war effort? Picking hops is the beginning of brewing beer, for the good of the country! After the growing, that is!'

Joy realized she had unthinkingly upset her.

Pat was agitated, determined to have her say. 'What about them brave lads in Spitfires managing to bring their planes home after fighting for us, and thinking about a nice glass of beer? Don't you think they deserve a drink? What about us celebrating when we've won the war?'

Joy was pleased that, like her, Pat refused to believe that Hitler would dominate the British, but she hoped the woman would stop her rant before her voice rose so high that everyone found out she and Eadie were first-timers at hop-picking.

But Pat was determined to have the final words. 'I'm just sayin' we're doin' important work.'

Joy grinned at her. Pat immediately returned the grin.

The spat was over before it had properly begun and would be forgotten.

Chickens clucked and squawked as the horse and wagon turned into a huge yard. The long, low stone farmhouse was homely looking. Smoke curled lazily high in the sky from one of its many chimneys. The sun glittered on polished windows, and two black-and-white cats were lying curled together in a sunny doorway. They didn't move until the wagon rolled to a stop.

Adjoining the main house, wooden and brick buildings seemed well cared for. Damp concrete showed that the yard had recently been hosed down.

'They've got some land girls,' said Pat. 'Some of the Southerns' workers joined up to go and fight. They didn't have to, farming community being exempt, but they did. The girls have been working here for ages.' Again, Joy wondered how Pat garnered her information.

From where Joy was sitting, she could see part of a large kitchen garden, green with produce, behind the buildings, an orchard and fruit bushes. A tractor blocked a great deal of her view. At least, it might be a tractor. She knew farms used tractors but she had never been up close to one. She thought the farm had a lovely feel to it and caught sight of Eadie grinning at her while trying to extricate herself from chattering Marlene. It was obvious Eadie, too, was happy with their destination, so far.

Two healthy-looking land girls in brown dungarees stood watching the people and children climb down from the cart. One, a fair-haired, tall girl, was petting the shire horse and talking to it. Both girl and horse appeared happy and at ease with each other, as if they were firm friends. The carter had lit a clay pipe and was sitting in his driving seat contentedly puffing out clouds of smoke. The dark-haired girl, clutching a large notebook and a carrier-bag, moved away from the horse and began engaging with the hoppers. Some, with or without the help of the farm lad, had retrieved their goods from underneath the wagon and now stood about, waiting.

'First thing you got to do is let them know you've arrived, find out which hut you're sleeping in and which number your working line is.'

'Looks like those young women know what's what.' Joy nodded towards the land girls. Then she called down to Eadie, who was already off the cart, 'We'd better stay together.'

Eadie mouthed back, 'Get down here with me, then.'

Pat reminded Joy as she slid from the cart, 'I'll leave you two with her,' she motioned towards the young woman with the notebook who was making a beeline towards Eadie, 'and I'll look for you round the fire, later.'

'Hello, welcome to Southerns' farm at Selborne. I'm Jean. Can I have your names?'

With their suitcases at their feet, Joy explained about her phone call to the farmer's wife. 'So, we haven't any paperwork and it's our first time at this farm.' She was very careful not to say they'd never picked hops before.

'I've a note of that here,' Jean said, showing Joy two cards that had been tucked between the pages of her notebook. 'Hop-cards for tallying. Now, do you want a line each or are you working one line between you?'

Joy was suddenly horrified at the prospect of being parted from Eadie and said quickly, 'One line between us,' at the exact time Eadie uttered the same words. Jean smiled. She wrote first on one card, then on the other, and handed the cards across to them. Then she scribbled in her large note-book. Her hands were ringless, her skin tanned by the sun. Again, Joy noticed how healthy the girl looked.

'That's your line number sorted, along with your basket numbers. You've both picked before, I understand.' It wasn't a question.

Eadie merely smiled, but Joy nodded effusively at the girl.

'Smeaton's in the village is the grocer's shop where you're

registered.' Jean searched in her carrier-bag, then handed each of them a thin, papery booklet. 'Extra coupons,' she said, 'to supplement your own ration books. Please sign here.' She supported the notebook while Joy and Eadie borrowed her fountain pen to comply.

'We all hope you'll be happy with us. Any questions or problems, come and find me or knock on the kitchen door for Mrs Southern. It's customary, as you're both aware, to receive full payment when you leave, but you can ask for subs, a subsidy on the money you've earned, so keep a note of all transactions. Anything you want to ask?' Jean eyed their suitcases.

Joy was very aware that they looked like holidaymakers, not workers. She shook her head.

Eadie gave Jean a grin and said, 'You've been very helpful. I think you've summed up everything we need to know for the moment. We'll be ready in the morning. Er . . . What time is it again?'

'Seven,' Jean said. 'You'll hear the bell. Just join the other pickers outside the huts. You're all working in the same place. Finish at six.'

'Of course,' said Joy.

Jean waved an arm, the one not clutching her notebook and bag, in the direction of a grassy path that led in the opposite direction to the farmhouse. 'You're both in hut thirty-seven. The number's chalked on the door.' She smiled again, then turned to talk to another woman waiting. She was holding a pram filled with cooking utensils, bedding and a sleeping child.

Jean suddenly turned back and said to Eadie, 'Oh! Sorry, I forgot. Your sister arrived late last night. She's been settling into your hut.'

Chapter Six

'C'mon, Joy, hurry up. I need to have a word with my so-called sister!' Eadie's suitcase seemed to weigh more with each step she took along the grassy path at the edge of the field. Her ankle still smarted from the twist she'd given it stepping into a hole. 'I bet that's a rabbit warren,' Joy had observed helpfully, as Eadie had picked herself up, sworn she was all right, then continued towards the long line of hopper huts she could see ahead.

Since then, neither had spoken.

Eadie was angry with herself for taking out her bad mood on Joy, who wasn't to blame for Maureen arriving at the Southerns' farm and installing herself in their hut by posing as her sister. Eadie, who could no longer stand the silence she'd instigated, turned to Joy. 'I'm sorry, ducky. I shouldn't be cross with you but you're the only one here to take it out on. I should have known when I asked you to write down the farm's telephone number for Maureen that sooner or later she'd see it as an escape route, if she really was determined enough to leave that awful man of hers. I just never expected she'd invite herself to share our hut.'

Eadie knew she was rambling while Joy, heavy suitcase in hand, stood watching her, her face wreathed in empathy

And then, suitcase flung aside, Joy had her arms about her, words tumbling from her mouth like a waterfall. 'You were doing her a favour. Anything to help her get away from that beast of a bloke hurting her and her kiddie. Oh! I saw the bruise on that baby's wrist. Mick's a bloody animal.'

She stepped back and looked at Eadie, who'd broken in with 'But I never really expected her to turn up here and share with us . . .'

And then Eadie was listening to herself making excuses and hating what she was hearing. Of course Maureen had clutched at the telephone number and the chance to escape from her volatile husband. She'd done it like a drowning person would clutch at a straw. So why was Eadie so put out that Maureen had believed the very last words Eadie had spoken to her?

'Don't think you got no one who cares.' That was what

she'd said to the woman. Making Maureen believe she could seek help, not only as a workmate but as a friend. Making Maureen believe she could leave Mick because she really could summon up the courage to do so.

'She might look at her life differently after working and sharing with us for a few weeks.' Eadie felt uncomfortable at Joy-ever-the-peacemaker's words. 'It could be the making of her,' Joy added.

'You really think so?' she asked.

The conversation was disrupted by a sudden flurry, a rustling in the nearby hedge as a bird, disturbed, flew towards the azure sky. Its blue-black feathered wings glittered in the sunlight.

'Oh, did you see its bright yellow beak? I've never been so close to a blackbird before.' Joy shook her head in wonder. Then she cupped her eyes with a hand to follow its progress before returning to her conversation with Eadie. 'If nothing else, being away from Mick will give her space to think. Maybe you'll feel differently about her later.'

After a silence filled with meaning, Eadie said, 'In other words, I'm to stop feeling aggravated and think about Maureen instead of myself?'

'Yes,' said Joy.

One little word with a huge amount of meaning behind

it, thought Eadie. But of course Joy was right. Eadie was being mean and unreasonable and she knew it.

Sometimes she forgot how lucky she was.

For a few weeks she was able to flee from the relentless bombing because Joe was at home in Gosport taking on her share of caring for Will. She had a good family life, not without problems, but certainly no drunken man was beating her senseless, was he? Nor was any bloke mentally grinding her down, causing her hair to fall out in handfuls because she was worrying about the safety of her child. Unlike Maureen.

'I'm jealous her being with us will spoil things.'

Eadie's words had come out in a rush. Joy stared hard at her. After a little while she said, 'That can't happen. My mother loved you like a sister. I do, too. I don't know what I'd do without you. Your family is my family.'

Eadie saw the brightness of tears in Joy's eyes. 'I'm sorry,' she said. 'I'm being a right cow, aren't I? It's just that I never imagined being saddled with Maureen.'

Understanding swept over Joy's face. After a short pause she confided, 'I'll admit I was put out too, when Jean announced we had a sister sharing our hut. Especially as at Priddy's I had so little to do with her. I felt sorry for her because of her circumstances, I suppose . . .' She paused.

'But if we can both help Maureen, then that's a good thing, isn't it?'

Joy was right. Of course she was right.

Eadie picked up her suitcase. 'You're younger than me so why are you so bloody clever?' She realized again how lucky she was to have the young woman in her life.

Joy shrugged her shoulders and began walking. Then she stopped, turned to Eadie. 'She'll have brought the baby with her, won't she?'

The baby! Eadie's initial jealousy at discovering everything wouldn't go according to her plan was now replaced by thoughts of the child. Oh! It would be lovely to spend time with the baby.

'Nah! Maureen'll have left him at home with his dad!' she quipped.

Joy stared at her. 'That's not funny,' she said. But she smiled anyway.

And it suddenly felt good to Eadie to laugh with Joy as they walked.

Then Joy stopped and pulled at her arm. 'Look!' she commanded.

Eadie followed her line of sight to see three grey rabbits scampering through the grass before they disappeared earthwards. 'Don't see many of them running around in Gosport,' Eadie said.

'No, they'd be in pies,' Joy returned.

And then the huts were in front of them.

'If the insides are anything like the outsides, it doesn't look good,' Eadie said, staring at the corrugated-iron boxes without windows. Some had sheets of planking covering the rotting timber on the wooden doors. Moss grew in the grooves.

'Wonder what ours is like.'

Eadie could hear the disappointment in Joy's voice.

'These are the low numbers. Wait till we find thirty-seven,' Eadie said.

So far, they'd not set eyes on any other workers apart from those who'd accompanied them on the cart to the farm. But then she and Joy had been dealt with almost immediately by Jean. Other hoppers couldn't be far behind, could they? She remembered Jean saying Maureen had arrived last night so it stood to reason that others were already installed somewhere. Surely she and Joy couldn't have strayed off course.

'Wait up,' she said. 'I need a bit of Dutch courage before I go any further.' Eadie sat down on the grass and flipped up the catch on her case. After fumbling around and depositing clothing on the warm earth so she could delve easier, she pulled out the flask.

'Ta-da!' Eadie unscrewed the top and poured the tea into the flask's mug which she passed to Joy. 'It's still hot, ducky. Here's to our hop-picking days,' she said, with more brightness than she felt.

'Where's yours?' Sitting on the path beside her, Joy took the tea.

'I'll have a fag first.' Eadie waved her Woodbines trium-phantly. Within moments she'd lit up and was feeling better. Crickets were chirruping. A light breeze tousled leaves in the hedgerow.

Eadie could see the bines in the next field, standing like rows of enormous soldiers all waiting to be cut down, massacred in their prime. She stretched her neck to see how large the field was. The rows of bines looked endless.

She glanced back at the shabby huts. Of course, they were in the right place and the huts were to be their homes for the next few weeks. Wasn't there always the possibility that the insides didn't reflect the outsides?

They drank one flask of tea and started on the second. Eadie thought how satisfying it was chatting to Joy about Pat and the people they'd met since leaving Gosport early that morning. She pushed away thoughts of Joe and Will. It was too soon to start worrying about them. Now she knew the correct address of the farm, which was printed on paperwork Jean had handed to her, she'd send Joe a short letter, telling him exactly where she was. She smiled, remembering the blond man with the two kiddies: looking into his eyes had made her feel like a much younger version of herself. 'A cuppa, a fag and sitting in the sun with my best mate,' she said. 'I can't think of anything better.'

'Maybe not,' answered Joy. 'But I wouldn't mind betting that Maureen's expecting us.'

Eadie had already risen and was repacking and fastening her suitcase. 'C'mon, ducky,' she said. 'We can't sit around all day. Things to do.' She put out a hand to help Joy scramble to her feet.

And Eadie felt so much better, walking alongside the huts, more so when she could hear voices, children laughing, like they were playing a game somewhere in the distance. And now there were signs of habitation: a line of washing strung between a couple of trees, and somewhere, Vera Lynn was singing about bluebirds, accompanied by tuneless voices. 'That's got to be a gramophone,' she said. 'I hope they've got more than the one record.'

Home-made pushcarts, just boxes on wheels with handles, and elderly prams stood outside a few of the corrugated-iron living spaces. Some contained a profusion of household goods, others had furniture, string-tied for safety and not yet unpacked. Inside one battered pram, a child slept, star-shaped, in the shade of the pulled-up hood.

Eadie sensed people moving about inside some of the huts. But even when their doors were open, she averted her eyes, not wishing to be found inquisitive by whoever was inside. She spotted the charred remains of old fires, the earth burned black and situated well away from the huts. Some of these were enclosed by bricks for safety. Obstacles littered the pathway, making it difficult to walk in a straight line to check the chalk-marked numbers on the wooden doors.

'Just a minute,' Joy hissed. Eadie tried to pull her away to stop her looking inside a hut that had its door wide open. 'I'm not hurting anyone,' Joy persisted. 'It's empty.'

Then, suitcase dumped on the grass, Joy was inside. Eadie sighed but, unable to help herself, followed.

Without windows and only the sun shining in from outside it took a while for her eyes to grow accustomed to the near darkness even though all the corrugated walls had been newly whitewashed. She found she was standing in what was possibly a twelve-foot-square space. The wooden floor had been swept. An iron bedstead with sagging springs stood in the middle of the floor. At its foot was a folded piece of rough fabric that Joy was already shaking free.

'It's a huge bag,' she said, refolding and replacing it. 'Wonder what it's for.'

'No idea,' said Eadie. 'But I'm beginning to see why so many workers on the train carried rolled-up mattresses.' Looking around her, she added, 'Even little kids had bedding in their arms, didn't they? There's no cupboards, no electricity and no water here.' She thought then of the kettles and kitchen equipment she'd seen carried by hoppers.

She looked down at her suitcase containing clean clothes that she now knew were utterly useless for field work. Why, oh, why had she gone along with the lie that she and Joy were experienced hop-pickers? What was it Will used to say before he joined the army? 'Truth costs nothing but a lie can cost everything.' Well, he'd been right about that, hadn't he?

If the hut they were supposed to be staying in was anything like this one, how would they manage? Three adults and a baby! Eadie sighed. Whatever had they got themselves into?

She had no intention of sharing her fears with Joy.

Joy's idea of earning money at hop-picking was a damn good one. If only they'd known what they'd needed to bring with them!

'One bed's no good for a whole family,' muttered Joy, 'Though maybe only one person is coming to stay in here.'

'Any more would have to share or sleep on the floor,' suggested Eadie. 'Though we've all got used to sleeping in funny places,' she added. 'Air raids have taught us how to do that, ducky.'

'Let's get out of here.' Eadie couldn't ignore the desperation in her friend's voice as Joy added, 'I'm beginning to wish we'd never come.'

'Well, perhaps number thirty-seven's a bit more habitable,' said Eadie.

They hadn't gone far when an elderly woman sitting on a stool outside the closed door of a hut said, 'Afternoon.' From inside they could hear sweeping on wooden boards.

'Hello,' they chorused. Eadie wondered how much work she could be capable of as there was nothing to her. Her hands were like twigs, her feet enclosed in worn boots. Dressed in dusty black, her face was cobwebbed with wrinkles but her eyes were like two bright blue buttons.

'New, are you?'

Eadie nodded.

'Thought so,' she answered hoarsely, and the eyelids came down. After a couple of seconds, Eadie realized she had ended the conversation. Eadie glanced at Joy, then at the sleeping woman, and the corners of her mouth lifted in a smile.

As they walked on, Eadie said, 'At least we've met one of our neighbours.'

Joy, however, was concentrating on the chalk numbers. 'This is it,' she said. 'Number thirty-seven.' The door was ajar.

Eadie could hear a woman sweetly singing 'I Don't Want To Set The World On Fire'. Her voice was soft and tuneful.

'What do we do?' she hissed to Joy. 'Knock? Barge in?'

'Neither.' The door was pulled wide and Maureen stood in the doorway. She had on the same grubby dark green woollen dress she always wore and the eternal turban hiding her damaged hair. Her broad smile couldn't conceal how hollow-cheeked and worn out she looked, but her arms went first around Joy in a hug, then enfolded Eadie. 'I've been waiting for you. I'm making tea!'

Eadie felt herself being pulled inside the hut.

Maureen was still talking. 'I made soup because I thought you'd be hungry after the journey.'

Eadie could smell it. It was making her mouth water. She hadn't realized until that moment just how hungry she was. 'It's only vegetable,' apologized Maureen. However, she still hadn't finished speaking. 'Before anything else, I need to thank you, Eadie, for allowing me to get away from Mick. It's only been a day but already I feel like I'm getting my life back. And it's so wonderful not being frightened every time the baby cries because if I can't quieten him Mick'll get angry.' Her words came in a torrent.

'Stop!' Eadie cried. It was as if Maureen was so grateful to them she needed to say as much as she could and as quickly as possible. Eadie didn't want to be thanked. Especially not when she'd been thinking such negative thoughts about Maureen. 'I can't think,' she said, closing her eyes. She took a deep breath but when she opened her eyes again, she gasped.

This whitewashed hut was brightened further by a soft light coming from an oil lamp perched on top of an upended orange box. Sharing space with it, she saw an alarm clock and a tin kettle. From its long spout steam curled, the water inside obviously recently boiled. Three enamel mugs were piled beside it. In the middle shelf section, she noticed a quarter of a pound of Brooke Bond Dividend tea and a small jug of milk. A cottage loaf shared that space. The bread looked crusty and wholesome, unlike the grey loaves Eadie was used to queuing for in Gosport. The bottom of the crate housed an assortment of unmatched crockery and a packet of candles. Standing next to the makeshift cupboard there was an unlit oil stove upon which a large battered saucepan full of soup threw a heavenly smell into the room.

'You're looking at our kitchen,' Maureen said proudly. 'Daren't shut the door when the stove's on cos of the unhealthy fumes. Safer to cook outside on a fire, only I've not had time to hunt for kindling . . .'

Eadie was deeply touched by the woman's thoughtfulness but the words wouldn't come. Her eyes settled on the bed, pushed to the corner. An iron bedstead, similar to the one she'd seen in the other hut. But there the similarity ended. The rough fabric sack had been filled tightly with straw and a sheet, worn but clean, covered it. A couple of grey blankets were folded neatly on top. Beneath the bed a second palliasse, another straw-filled mattress, echoed the top one. Eadie was filled with gratitude at the woman's efforts to make the hut into a home and now deeply ashamed that earlier she'd not wanted Maureen to be there.

'At last we know what those huge bags are for,' Joy said. 'But where did you get the straw?'

Eadie felt she could curl up on either of the two comfortable-looking beds immediately.

'Farmer Southern always fills a couple of the far-end huts with it,' Maureen said. 'A neighbour showed me. I thought you two could have the bed and I'll pull out the other one. Better I take the floor . . .'

'But . . .' Joy began.

Maureen shook her head. She fingered her turban to make sure it was still in place. Eadie noticed her bruise had changed colour slightly.

'I'd much rather, Joy, easier for me to get up to see to the little one.'

Eadie understood the logic in that. She glanced around the hut. There were two cardboard boxes against the other wall, one with terry-towelling nappies folded neatly on top. Eadie guessed the boxes contained Maureen and the baby's personal paraphernalia. Her heart warmed at the sight of a knitted, grubby, one-eared rabbit, which looked well-loved.

'Where is he?' she asked, quickly adding, 'Your little boy?'

Maureen smiled at her. 'A neighbour's girl, Alma, has Billy. It was my dad's name, William, Billy. She's fallen in love with him. I expect you met her grandmother sitting in the sunshine. Alma's pushed the pram up to the stand-pipe to refill the buckets with water.'

Eadie nodded. 'I wondered about water,' she said. 'Are there lavatories?'

'There are, but you use them at your peril,' Maureen said. 'They're earth closets, in the next field, and stink to high heaven. Going behind a hedge is better.' She moved the hot pan of soup onto a tin plate on the floor so the bottom of the pan wouldn't scorch the wooden boards, then foraged in the pocket of her apron, lit a match, and set the kettle to boil anew on the stove. 'The vegetables couldn't be any fresher. I picked them myself, very early this morning, from the Southerns' garden.' She put a finger to her lips. 'Ssh! You didn't hear me admit that, did you? I told Mrs Southern some of the veg needed to be thinned out!'

Eadie opened her mouth to speak, thought better of it and closed it again.

'And I'll bet you're not the only picker that's helped themselves!' said Joy.

'It's wartime. Farmers don't like it but they know hoppers are going to steal anything that's not nailed down, fruit, veg, potatoes – after all, the wages aren't great, are they? Me? I'd rather ask the farmer for pecked apples and fruit lying on the grass. He'd sooner give it away than have it stolen.' Maureen grinned. 'There'll be food tonight. Potatoes baking in the embers of the fire and the publican doesn't stint with the margarine for the filling!'

Eadie wasn't sure how she felt about Maureen's confession of stealing but she jumped in quickly, hearing about the fire that Pat had mentioned. 'You've done wonders with this hut, Maureen. I looked in an empty one, and was filled with despair.' She perched herself on the edge of the bed. 'Tell us about the fire?'

She saw Joy was watching her and no doubt wondering, as she herself was, how Maureen had so much knowledge of hop-picking. Surely she must have worked as a field girl before.

'I'm not saying much about celebrating the first night at the hopping-fields. Just you two pretty yourselves up and take a walk later down to the Spotted Cow and find out.' She spooned tea leaves into a brown earthenware teapot.

The Spotted Cow must be a public house. 'Sounds good to me,' Eadie said. 'But aren't you coming? Is it because of the baby?'

Maureen smiled. 'Oh, no. Babies are welcome . . .' Her voice tailed off.

Eadie caught Joy's eye. She had no need to communicate in words to her friend that Maureen felt too drained and shabby and would rather stay in the hut than brave the empathy of others.

It didn't seem right that because life had dragged brave Maureen down she'd practically lost sight of her own identity. Especially when she'd obviously put such hard work into making the hut a home for them all.

Another of Will's sayings flashed into her mind: 'Tell the truth and shame the devil.' She took a deep breath and said to Maureen, 'We've not been hop-picking before and there's nothing practical in our cases. We let the farmer's wife think we were old hands.'

Joy broke in, 'You've picked hops before, though, haven't you, Maureen? You knew exactly what we needed.'

Maureen nodded. 'These huts are only for sleeping and for shelter from bad weather. But when there's a family it's good to make them nice. Before I was married, my family used to pick hops in Kent,' she said. 'But I had a pretty good idea neither of you had because I've never heard you talk about it and I remember when, you, Joy, started working at Priddy's you'd come straight from school.'

'What I'd like to know is how you managed to bring all the extra things with you,' Joy said. 'Billy, his stuff, equipment for the hut and everything. We only had suitcases and I was soon fed up carrying mine.'

'Mick paid for taxis. Mind you, he doesn't know it yet!' Maureen poured boiling water into the teapot, stirred it, then faced them. A wicked grin spread across her face. 'Well, I expect he knows his money's gone by now, but he has no idea where I am, so who cares?'

Eadie thought the silence that followed could have been

cut with a knife. Joy sat on a three-legged wooden stool and stared at Maureen.

'C'mon,' she said, 'you can't stop there. What do you mean?'

Eadie looked happily at the mug of strong tea set on the floor before her . She was eager to listen.

'You two cheered me up no end when I saw you yesterday. I was on me way home, not that I wanted to go there, mind, when Charlie Dunlop, Dunnie, as Mick calls him, stops me all excited like and tells me Mick's paid him back the half-crown he thought he'd seen the back of. Mick'd had a win on the gee-gees. He said the bookie's runner in the White Swan wasn't none too happy at paying out on a thirty-to-one win.'

Maureen paused to gulp her tea, after which she said mis-erably, 'I 'ave to 'and me wages over to him without question an' if I'm lucky he doles back some to pay the grocer what I've ticked up so I can start again.' Maureen sniffed, then said, 'You don't want to listen to me moaning. Anyway, when I gets in, he's well and truly plastered and sleeping it off upstairs.' She laughed heartily. 'I'd 'ave loved to see him gettin' up them stairs – usually he passes out in the livin' room. Well, I sees on the top of the chest of drawers the remainder of his money. Four nice clean white fivers an' some change. Never seen so much money! I thought, Eadie's given me a telephone number, so sure as God makes little green apples it's a sign for me to get away.'

At this point, she drank more of her tea, then went on, 'Oh, don't think I haven't wanted to leave, many times, but without money it's impossible. So, while he's lyin' there, stinkin', I goes down to the phone box, after hidin' those lovely fivers under the pram's mattress, of course. I asks Mrs Southern if I can come here right away and she agrees. Next I phones Ferry Taxis cos they use the big black cabs. I tells 'em to meet me at the Criterion Picture House. Then when I gets home I rushes round like a blue-arsed fly, collecting stuff and sorting out Billy. I've got sod-all clothing and hardly any personal bits and pieces – well, I can't 'ave, when Mick drinks like a fish, can I?' Maureen moved to Eadie and put her arms around her. 'But I got you to thank for setting me free.'

Eadie was blushing. 'Nothin' to do with me,' she argued, pushing her away because she was embarrassed. 'You just saw you was worth more than being a punching bag! Lucky your pram's not one of them posh high Royale ones. It'd never have fitted in any old taxi, would it? An' when you got to the station, you got the train all right, did you?'

'To Alton, not Petersfield,' Maureen said, stepping back. 'The guard helped me get everything into his van.' She giggled. 'I was so grateful I gave him a tip! Imagine me, giving out a tip! Anyway, I got another taxi to 'ere. It's so lovely havin' the money to do what you want. Drinks on me tonight! I insist on sending you both off with beer money. Sorry for pretending to be your sister, Eadie, but I didn't want to be on my own . . .'

Maureen had recounted her story, even made her and Joy smile, but inside, Eadie knew, she was close to breaking point. 'It took a lot of guts to leave,' she said. 'You're very brave. Especially with the little one.'

'It's a wonder Billy survived underneath that pram-full of stuff,' Joy said.

'Oh, he wasn't in the pram.' Maureen's eyes widened. 'I carried him close to my heart in a sling I made by tearing a sheet in half,' she said. 'Billy's the only good thing to come out of my marriage to that workshy bast—'

Eadie put a hand on Maureen's arm. 'Don't upset yourself. Mick's not worth it and you're with us now.' Eadie smiled warmly at her. She'd meant every word she'd said. 'Tell you what,' she added, 'why don't you sort that soup out? Me and Joy are starving an' it smells so good. Afterwards we can go through our suitcases and work out what we're going to wear tonight.'

'I only got what I stand up in. I told you I'm not coming . . .' Maureen's voice was very small.

Eadie could see she was embarrassed at having nothing to wear, so she squeezed Maureen's arm. 'After what you've been through an' the explosion at Priddy's, we should stay really good friends, like them three men in that famous French book where they say, "All for one and one for all." That means sharing everything. Now what's that book called . . .?'

Joy piped up, '*The Three Musketeers.*'

'That's it, Clever Clogs!' Eadie said. 'So what I brought with me belongs to you, Maureen . . .'

'Don't forget my suitcase!' said Joy. 'Actually, Eadie's got more meat on her than you or me, so my clothes might fit you better.'

'Cheeky!' Eadie said.

'But I've not got anything to share.' Maureen looked as if she was going to cry.

Eadie waved her hand around the hut. 'You call this nothin'? I'd say for the next few weeks this'll be Heaven but there's only one thing missing . . .'

'What's that?' Maureen looked pained.

Eadie said, 'You still haven't served up the soup, woman!'

Chapter Seven

'You look so different.' Joy couldn't help taking admiring glances at Maureen as they sat together on a wooden bench, the pram beside them, outside the Spotted Cow. Empty glasses, plates and two barely touched half-pints of beer were nestled beneath the seat. It was a warm evening made warmer by the dying flames from the bonfire lighting up the night sky, well away from the hostelry. Families sprawled together on the grass or sat at tables, laughing and smoking, chiding children, who ran carelessly among them. The air was redolent with the meaty smell of cooked rabbit and the malty aroma of beer. From inside the packed half-timbered building, a pianist encouraged voices to swell into the night.

Joy remembered how earlier it had taken a great deal of persuasion from them both before Maureen allowed Eadie to style her hair into a front Victory Roll. It meant brushing her long, thinning locks forward over her head to conceal the bald patches.

'We're going to get rid of that turban tonight, woman,' Eadie had pronounced firmly after she'd stubbed out her cigarette in a cracked saucer pretending to be an ashtray.

'But there's so much grey!' Maureen had wailed.

'So what? You earned it, be proud of it!' Joy knew by Eadie's firm tone there was no stopping her. She was determined to help Maureen find her self-esteem.

Eadie had made Maureen sit up straight on the stool while she tied most of her hair on top of her head, then proceeded to pin the rest into rolled coils on the crown, teasing each curl until it looked thicker than it was. Watching Eadie's fingers transform Maureen's hair had been magical. When Eadie had finished, Maureen's thin face had been recast.

'Now you look like Katherine Hepburn! Those wonderful cheekbones!' Joy hadn't been able to stop herself exclaiming any more than Maureen had been able to conceal the tears that threatened when she surveyed herself in Eadie's compact mirror.

'Make-up,' said Eadie. 'You need make-up.'

'I haven't got any,' Maureen had whispered.

'Maybe not, but our Joy has!' Eadie said. 'Give us your Pan-Cake first.'

Joy had foraged in her suitcase and out came the small cotton drawstring bag in which she kept her treasured cosmetics. She valued them highly as, due to war shortages, make-up, especially lipstick, was rarely available in the shops.

Eadie dabbed the pressed powder from the small round container carefully onto Maureen's forehead bruise, obscuring it, then blended a little beneath her eyes to lighten the shadows.

Maureen had sat quite still on the stool while Joy had spat on the mascara in the blue plastic case and brushed it on her lashes after a dab of blue shadow on her eyelids. A bright coating of Elizabeth Arden's Victory Red lipstick completed Maureen's new look.

Then it was Eadie's turn to search in her case and triumphantly wave a red cotton dress with patch pockets and buttons down the front. 'Try this on,' she demanded. 'It's tight on me but I think it'll suit you to a T.' And it did.

Joy stepped back holding the small round mirror so Maureen had a marginally better view of their achievements. Her mouth trembled and her chin quivered.

Eadie had shouted, 'Don't you dare cry and spoil our handiwork!'

'I do look different, don't I? You'd never guess I was the same woman, who . . .' Maureen's voice had been small, pensive. 'I look like the young woman who first attracted Mick!'

Joy was just in time to lunge forward and stop her hands raking the carefully layered curls and destroying Eadie's ministrations. 'What are you doing?' Joy had cried.

Maureen's eyes were filled with anguish. 'I don't want to attract a man! I never want another man in my life! I want to be myself!' She'd collapsed back onto the stool and sat staring, trembling, unseeing, at the white wall of the hut.

Joy, shaken, had gathered Maureen into her arms, holding the thin, quivering body tightly.

Eadie, practical as ever, had moved into action. Swiftly relighting the stove after shaking the kettle, she turned and snapped, 'When's that young girl due back with Billy?' Clearly she wanted to soothe Maureen before her child was returned.

'Not yet, there'll be a long queue at the stand-pipe.' Maureen's voice was little more than a whisper spoken into the depths of Joy's embrace. Eadie nodded towards the teapot.

'When the water boils, Joy, shove another spoonful of tea on top of the leaves.' She stepped towards Maureen and Joy, separating them but leaving Maureen on the stool. 'Now, you listen to me, you silly, brave woman, and listen bloody good! What on earth do you take us for?' She hadn't waited for an answer but carried on, 'Now you just tell me how you felt when you first looked into that mirror and saw a different you.'

Joy watched Maureen's face as she struggled to take in what Eadie was saying. After a long while her eyes connected properly with Eadie's and she answered so quietly that Joy had to listen really hard. 'Different. Like nothing showed of the harm that's been inflicted on me.'

There was a moment of silence except for the water roiling in the kettle on the oil stove.

Joy watched as a small smile lifted the corner of Eadie's mouth. 'So that was your first thought, eh? And was your second thought, I hope I look pretty enough to attract a man tonight?'

Maureen's voice exploded: 'It was not! Don't be bloody daft! I sort of marvelled that, after everything that's happened, I was still me. Still me!' She repeated the last two words precisely.

Joy watched as Maureen sat back on the stool and digested their conversation.

Eadie began to laugh. The sound bubbled up from inside her, spilling into the hut, and Joy realized exactly what Eadie had done in attempting to transform the dowdy browbeaten woman into the vibrant female she once was.

129

'You're a clever cow, aren't you?' Maureen said. 'So, this is my first lesson in putting the past behind me? That looking good and making the best of myself gives me the power to say, "I am me. I have control"?'

'That's what I believe.' Eadie smiled at her. 'A lot of women go around with scrubbed faces, not bothering to make the most of what the Lord has given them. They say that pleasing themselves makes them feel good. Fair enough. That's up to them. But if it gives you a lift to make the most of what you've got, why not? And let's face it, Maureen, you're a stunner!' Eadie shook her head. 'But it certainly doesn't mean you're making the most of yourself because you want a man!'

Maureen had closed her eyes. She sniffed. 'Will you go on helping me look nice while we're here on the farm?'

'What did we say? One for all, all for one?' Joy chimed in. Maureen, overcome, allowed her face to fall.

Eadie shouted, 'Don't you dare bloody cry!'

Maureen had laughed and hiccuped, then lifted her feet, showing the scuffed black lace-up shoes that had seen better days. 'Don't suppose either of you got a pretty pair of shoes to fit me so I can walk to the Spotted Cow tonight?'

Eadie had looked at the size of Maureen's feet. 'Blimey,

you don't want shoes, woman, you wants the cases they come in!'

Now, hearing a whimper from the pram at the side of the bench, Joy turned to Maureen. 'Billy's awake.'

'Give him a cuddle if you wants.'

Joy lifted the warm, damp bundle from the blankets and noticed that the pressure mark inflicted on the baby's wrist by his father was barely discernible. Big eyes stared at her. 'He's wet.'

'So would you be if you'd had an exciting day like him.' Maureen delved into the depths of the pram and found a couple of nappies. 'I expect you're hungry too, my little man,' she said to Billy. Then, to Joy, 'Hand him over, girl.'

'If he was older, he could have shared the jacket potatoes from the fire embers, spread with marge that we wolfed down earlier,' Joy said.

Maureen grinned at her. 'Before you two arrived today, Alma's granny told me the owners of this pub always provide cooked rabbit and potatoes on the night before picking begins.'

'Must cost them a pretty penny,' Joy said. 'And it was all delicious.' She licked her lips, remembering.

Maureen shrugged. 'The rabbits are free and they probably do a deal with Farmer Southern for the potatoes. It's a good idea, especially as this is the nearest pub within walking distance and a lot of beer'll be sold during the picking season.'

Joy passed her the placid baby and marvelled while Maureen deftly unpinned and pinned nappies all the while talking to the small person. He was a pretty baby, she decided, with dark hair that Maureen had fingered into a quiff and eyes the colour of toffee surrounded by long lashes. She watched as Maureen, ministrations complete, unbuttoned the front of her dress and cradled Billy, who quickly latched on to her. She spread the other clean nappy across her breast and settled back unconcernedly. Joy smiled at her, remembering how Eadie had earlier called her brave. Joy doubted that if she had married and the union had turned as sour as Maureen's had, she'd cope as skilfully as Maureen appeared to be doing.

Her thoughts turned to the young airman, Jim, who'd been so eager to write to her. There was no point, she told herself, in dwelling on what might have been. After all, it wasn't as though boyfriends had been scarce in the past. Her main stumbling block with men was that she was probably too choosy. And working long hours in the munitions fac-tory had left her with too little time for more than the odd picture-house visit, which she adored, or an evening out with Eadie, Madge or other women friends from Priddy's to dance halls. Besides, she liked her own company, loved her books, going to the pictures on her own or with Eadie, and following domestic pursuits. In fact, hop-picking had opened her eyes to a whole new life she hadn't known existed –and it hadn't really started yet! She tried to pretend to herself that not hearing from Jim didn't matter. But she was lying to herself.

Whenever there was a lull in the pub's piano-playing, Joy could hear violin music. She heard it now. Emotional and passionate. She had no doubt it came from the Romany folk camped nearby. The men were darkly handsome, some with bright neckerchiefs; many wore hats tipped at a rakish angle. Their women were dressed in brightly coloured skirts, gold in their ears and on their fingers. Earlier she'd watched two young children brushing one of the horses, a second patiently awaiting its turn to be groomed. Later she'd seen the children, a boy and a girl, riding those horses bareback.

'I thought Eadie might have returned by now,' Maureen said, her hand protectively shielding Billy's head as a couple of kiddies thundered past to the next field where the Romany caravans had set down for the picking season. 'You've got to admit she was taken aback when that blond bloke came across and started speaking to her when we first arrived here tonight.'

'We'd met him and his two kiddies at Fareham station on our way here,' Joy said. 'Never dreamed the little family was heading here, though. He was walking from Petersfield station.'

'Mostly the same pickers return year after year,' said Maureen. 'Eadie was going to walk up to the postbox near the farmhouse, said she'd written a quick line home. I saw them walk off together as I went into the bar to buy drinks.'

It wasn't so surprising that Eadie had walked willingly away with the man, Joy thought. Even she had noticed a heightened awareness between the pair in the station as he had lit a cigarette for her. Joy wished now that she'd mentioned it to Eadie but there hadn't really been time or the right opportunity, Maureen had moved Billy to her other breast to feed and he was sated. A bubble of milk showed at his tiny mouth as Maureen, all buttoned up now, held her boy against her shoulder while she rubbed his back.

'C'mon, you,' she said. 'I know you're tired and full but you can't go to sleep until you've given me a nice big burp!'

Joy, with a smile on her face, listened to Maureen talking to her son. She too, was tired. She brushed potato flakes, real or imaginary, from her high-waisted green trousers, then bent down and searched beneath the bench, bringing up the two half-pint mugs of beer. She sipped one, trying hard not to spill any on her pale green blouse. Maureen eyed the second as Joy set it down on the bench.

Joy laughed, hearing Billy burp.

'There's a good boy,' cooed Maureen, rising and stepping over to the pram where she carefully laid him down and covered him lightly with his blanket. 'I could certainly do with my drink now,' she said. 'It's not gone flat and horrible, has it?'

'Not at all,' Joy said. When Maureen sat down again, she and Joy drank in companionable silence, watching and listening to the people about them.

'When Eadie and I arrived earlier this place was like a ghost town, hardly a soul about. Now look at the crowds,' Joy said.

'I'm glad you persuaded me to come tonight. It's been nice chatting to people. I like the way they seem happy to be here.'

'That's probably because they're looking forward to a night's sleep without having to rush out to an air-raid shelter. I doubt any bombs will fall on the huts tonight. A lot of these workers are Londoners who've had it bad.' Joy took another mouthful of beer, swirling the malted yeastiness with her tongue. 'I could really get to like this beer,' she said.

Maureen warned, 'Don't get to like it too much. It's my old man's downfall.'

Joy nearly spluttered into hers. 'You have to look forward, not back,' she said.

Maureen set her empty glass on the grass beneath the bench. 'I am, Joy love. And I'm thinking, with the early start tomorrow for the first day of picking, that my bed's calling me. You stay, if you want . . .'

But Joy didn't.

Chapter Eight

Moonlight had enabled Eadie to enter through the hut door, but once it was closed, she'd stood still until her eyes adjusted to the blackness. She'd breathed a small sigh of relief as she dropped her clothes onto the floor and tugged her nightdress over her head. She could only think Joy had been perceptive enough to leave it draped across the foot of the bed. Thank goodness she'd not woken the baby coming in so late: she really didn't want to incur the wrath of Maureen, asleep on the palliasse on the floor. She slipped into bed, mindful not to wake Joy, who thoughtfully had chosen to sleep next to the corrugated wall. She winced at the crackling sound the straw made in the mattress as she got comfortable.

The ticking of the alarm clock pierced the silence, which was punctuated by the sounds of Maureen and Joy's steady breathing and Billy's occasional gentle snuffle. The scent of Johnson's baby powder and Joy's perfume lingered in the air. She could smell on her skin the vanilla and cedarwood of Vinnie's Old Spice shaving soap. She smiled.

Earlier in the evening she'd parted company from Joy and Maureen, ostensibly to catch the last collection from the postbox near the farm. From out of nowhere, it seemed, the man she'd met on Fareham station appeared. She'd been like a pin to a magnet when he'd offered to accompany her and she'd not seen her friends since. She knew she'd have an awful lot of explaining to do in the morning.

'What have you done with Tim, Ivy and Spitfire?' had been her first words to him.

'Fancy you remembering the cat's name as well.' He'd immediately taken her arm, which she hadn't at all minded. 'The kids are round the fire, Eadie, being looked after by a large, very friendly lady named Pat, who has youngsters of her own, and the cat's shut up inside our hut and will be until he's used to the place.'

He'd worn a light-coloured shirt beneath a dark blue waistcoat and smart matching suit trousers. The blue made his hair seem even blonder and she'd wanted to smooth the wayward curls back from his forehead.

Would she have worn something more glamorous if she'd known she might meet the good-looking stranger again? Probably not. The button-through emerald green dress with the waist peplum was a favourite of hers. Joy said it enhanced the red in her hair but she liked it because it was comfortable to wear.

'I've met Pat,' she'd said, wondering if he could hear her heart, which was thundering in her breast. 'I don't remember you asking my name in the train station, though.'

'You mightn't have given it to me, if I had.' His eyes held hers. 'I asked Pat about you.'

'That's a bit cheeky.' He had an air of cockiness about him, which she liked, and his blue eyes made her think of warm summer pools she'd have loved to dive into.

'I didn't think so. It's Fate that we've both turned up here, at the same farm. Especially after that spark of magic jumped between us when I lit your cigarette. Which reminds me . . .'

He stopped walking, felt inside his inner waistcoat pocket and took out his packet of Player's Navy Cut cigarettes.

'You believe that, do you?' Eadie asked.

'Don't you?' He gave her a questioning look. 'It's never happened to me before.'

Up ahead she'd spotted the postbox and breathed a sigh

of relief. She wasn't sure how far she wanted to go with this particular conversation. It was disquieting.

She didn't give him time to say anything else. Suddenly the letter in her hand felt as heavy as lead. A stab of guilt pierced her heart because she'd written the hasty note to Joe saying she missed him and Will. But at that moment, all she could feel was excitement that something memorable was about to happen and she certainly wasn't going to stop it.

'I won't be long,' Eadie said. It took only seconds to move quickly ahead, in the high-heeled peep-toe shoes she loved wearing, despite the pain one caused to her bunion, and moments to post the letter. As it disappeared into the red pillar-box, she allowed all her misgivings about being picked up by strange men to disappear with it. Instead, she felt bloody marvellous.

Back alongside him she took the lit cigarette. 'Thanks,' she said. 'This is getting to be a habit, you providing me with fags.' She breathed out a stream of smoke.

He smiled, his eyes holding hers. 'And is the magic still there?'

'So far, but time will tell,' she said, wishing he'd talk about something other than the feeling that had certainly knocked her for six. She could only liken it to a bolt of lightning striking her. She allowed him to take her hand and lead her down the lane beyond the farmhouse. Grasshoppers were chirping in the undergrowth and Eadie could feel the warmth of the evening sun on her back. His hand in hers felt dry and strong. She had no idea where they were heading and she didn't care. All she knew was that she was exactly where she wanted to be.

A bird rose from a hedge at the side of the lane and settling on a nearby tree branch began singing as though its heart would break.

Eadie, entranced, said. "I've never heard birdsong so beautiful."

"It's a nightingale. He'll be leaving soon. Somewhere warm, like Africa."

"Nightingales don't live here all year round?" Eadie was surprised.

"No, they're shy birds; arrive in spring, sing their hearts out for a female, sing to protect their territory and their young, then fly away around September time, job done."

"I never knew that," said Eadie.

"He'll be back next April, looking for a new mate . . ."

"And the wooing begins again?"

"And the wooing begins again," he repeated.

At the five-bar gate to the field he slipped up the latch, ushered her inside and followed, fastening the gate behind him. Small fibres from the ripe, whispery wheat clung to her dress as, holding her hand, he pushed through the dry, sweet-smelling stalks. Momentarily, he halted and looked back at her. The unspoken question in his blue eyes spoke volumes, and Eadie smiled: it was what she desired – no, more than that, what she hungered for.

He pulled her close and whispered, 'You're beautiful,' then began caressing her face, all the while searching her eyes until he finally kissed her. It had been such a long time since Eadie had felt the softness of a man's lips on her skin. The heat from the evening and his closeness heightened the smell of the shaving soap she recognized as Old Spice, and she knew that whenever she caught its scent of vanilla and cedar she would be reminded of him and that glorious moment.

His tongue ran along the side of her neck. His breath lingered warmly across her shoulder as his fingers unbuttoned her dress, allowing it to fall. His hands unclipped her brassière and he bent his head to kiss first one then the other taut nipple. She felt his body become alive as he slipped from his clothing allowing her to marvel at his muscled shoulders and the soft blond hair covering his tanned chest. Together they sank into the coarse but yielding featheriness of the wheat.

His lovemaking was gentle, fierce yet experienced. Eadie

was lost in him. Both bodies tumbling, twisting, turning, each of them spurred on by the intensity of their emotions. Her body became locked in perfect rhythm with his. Until she could hold off no longer as he moved faster, stronger and stronger, deep inside her, making her moan as she drowned in wave after wave of pleasure. Eadie felt every nerve, every muscle in her body exploding. And she cried out as his orgasm surged through her.

After a while as she lay sated, he kissed her. She felt his tongue search, explore. Then small kisses, like the brush of butterfly wings on her skin, travelling from her neck, down, over her nakedness, past her hip, along her leg to her ankle and foot, now bare of her favourite red high heels. He paused as he looked at the swelling on her toe and looked up at her.

'You've got a hurt,' he said. His gentle kisses had paused at her bunion. A 'hurt', he had called it. She looked into his beautiful blue eyes. She could imagine him using the word for grazes on a small child's skin. He was probably a very concerned father to his two children. 'I'll kiss it better,' he said. And he did. And Eadie's heart melted.

Lying among the wheat, Eadie again heard the skylark. But this time its song wasn't so joyous. Among the notes she could discern an air of sadness. Strange, she thought, when nightingales symbolized joy and happiness. Was it perhaps because the end of summer was near?

'We both need another cigarette,' he murmured. He pulled away to search among the scattered clothes. Eadie giggled as he held up her French knickers, made from parachute silk. 'Very nice,' he said, and winked broadly at her. He put them aside as he spied the Player's and reached for them.

'Actually,' said Eadie, 'at the moment, there's something I'd like more than a fag.'

He paused during the opening of the cigarette packet. 'And what's that?' he asked.

'To know your name,' Eadie said. She watched as he removed two cigarettes from the half-full packet, put them between his lips and lit both with his silver lighter. As he handed her one and she took a deep drag she was suddenly reminded of Joe lighting a cigarette for her in the same way.

Eadie realized she could no longer hear the nightingale.

'Vincent Scott. I answer to Vinnie,' he said. 'I was born in Portsmouth thirty-seven years ago to costermongers from Charlotte Street. I volunteered for the army at the beginning of the war and was medically discharged last year.'

'Hello, Vinnie,' she said. 'And I do have ciggies of my own, so the next one's on me, unless you're not partial to Woodbines.'

He laughed and took a drag on his cigarette. 'You're a very desirable woman, Eadie. It won't be another fag I'll be wanting when I've finished this one . . .'

They remained among the wheat talking and making love until the sun went down and hunger drove them to walk into the nearby village.

'I don't want to return to the hop-fields, the fire and the Spotted Cow yet,' Vinnie said. 'When we set foot there, I'll have to share you with Pat, the kids and your friends. Then all too soon it'll be morning and full-on working on the bines.'

In the public bar of the Vine, the wireless playing the Jimmy Dorsey Orchestra's 'Amapola', Vinnie and Eadie sat drinking half-pints of ale and eating Spam sandwiches. Every time thoughts of her life in Gosport and people she cared about entered her mind, Eadie pushed them away.

'I'm a salesman,' he confessed. 'Because of the state the country's in at present, many ordinary people can't afford to pay outright for items they need or want. That's household goods, I mean, clothing and such. Stuff people have lost in the bombing along with their homes. As you're aware the government makes available goods bearing the Utility mark. Cheap and cheerful items, if the customer has the ready money to buy them. The Portsmouth firm I work for makes it possible for folks to have what they want now, good-quality stuff, none of the Utility rubbish, and pay for it all in easy instalments. A shilling in the pound commission.' He paused, then carried on, 'So, too, people often want cash so they can sort out family problems that crop up. Same rule applies, a shilling in the pound commission. Just pay regularly, that's all the firm asks.'

'Isn't it difficult to get household goods and clothing, due to war shortages?' Eadie thought about Joy's make-up, and pretty shoes were impossible to buy as the government had decreed Utility heels should be only two inches high. Eadie looked down at her red three-inch-heeled shoes, which meant so much to her.

'There's always ways and means, Eadie,' he said mysteriously. 'And I need to work especially hard to keep a roof over Tim and Ivy's heads. I come hopping because my children can run free here, with no bombs. It's like a holiday, and I get paid for it.' He grinned at her.

'What about their mother?'

'My two get more love from the cat than they ever did from her!' His eyes were the colour of flint now. 'I was discharged from the army on medical grounds and got home unexpectedly. The first thing I noticed was the hair oil on the pillows. Something I never use.' His voice was bitter. 'Her mother was looking after them, not her. Brenda was out every night. She was in a Southsea dance hall with some Yank when the bomb fell . . .' His voice tailed off. Then, as if he remembered where he was and who he was talking to, he said quickly, 'They're my life, those kids.' After a pause he added, 'That's enough about me, Eadie. Tell me about you.'

So she did. About the factory explosion. About Joe. About her husband. 'Sometimes it's like Will has demons in his head,' she said eventually.

Across the table she felt the warmth as Vinnie's hand slid around hers. He was staring at her. She decided he was a good man. A man who idolized his children so much he wouldn't leave their beloved pet cat at home when they all came away to pick hops.

'You must love him a great deal,' he said. 'Your husband.'

Automatically Eadie answered, 'I do. And I care deeply for Joe because without him I couldn't carry on.'

Vinnie smiled at her but the smile only crossed his lips after the dark shadow had faded from his eyes. 'So that leaves me where, exactly?' he asked.

Before she could think of a suitable answer, he'd gathered up the two empty beer mugs. 'I'll pop up to the bar for more drinks,' he said

Eadie watched him disappear through the mass of people towards the counter.

She closed her eyes. Her reply had hurt him when the truth had automatically fallen from her lips. Whatever had she got herself into?

Vinnie was a lovely man. Good-looking enough to take any woman's breath away. He'd certainly sent her head and heart into a spin when whatever it was had shot through them like an electric charge.

But did she really want to upset her life with Joe and Will by having an all-out affair with him? What had they done to deserve the hurt she'd inflict on them both? And was there the slightest shred of possibility that real love even entered into what had happened earlier this evening between her and Vinnie? Lust, yes. He'd wanted her as much as she'd wanted him. And why had she wanted him? Was it because she yearned for the proper married relationship she'd once shared with Will and which now was denied her because of his condition? Of course it was! Eadie felt the heat rise at the back of her neck, thinking of the past few hours. She'd been like a bitch in heat over a good-looking man who'd lit a cigarette for her, hadn't she? But was that really all it was?

She closed her eyes and sighed. Shutting her eyes didn't make it all go away.

She opened them and glanced around the bar. Could she leave without him seeing her flee the pub? But that would be the coward's way out, wouldn't it? What would happen when she saw him at the farm? And see him she undoubtedly would, as they were picking hops at the same place.

Now here he was, placing two more mugs of ale on the table. He smiled. 'So, you're here to pick hops for the money and the war effort? And you've never done it before?' he asked.

Eadie nodded. He was being a gentleman, making small-talk. *Where does that leave me?* He'd already asked her that. She'd struggled to find an answer and he'd moved on before she'd responded. How long did she have before she was forced to tell him that any kind of relationship with him would be a mistake and there'd certainly be no repeat of the lovemaking, wonderful though it had been.

Eadie took a sip of ale and said, 'Yes, I'm going to pick hops so the country can go on drinking this.' She pointed to her dimpled glass.

And that was when he laughed. 'Oh, you're a tonic, Eadie girl! Didn't anyone tell you there's no hops used in the making of ale? That's what you're drinking, ale. Now, beer is different. Hops give beer its lovely earthy, bitter flavour and help preserve it.'

149

'You're making that up!' She was worrying about the future and he was joking with her.

He shook his head. 'Would I lie to you?'

Eadie stared at him. No, she didn't think he would. 'I guess I'm learning new things all the time,' she said.

'Well, I know I am.' Vinnie swallowed a mouthful of ale. 'I'm also guessing you've no intention of making me your bit on the side, your fancy man.' There was now a huge smile on his face.

Eadie opened her mouth but nothing came out.

'I'm teasing you,' he said softly.

She stared at him, then closed her mouth.

'You're a lovely person, Eadie.' His hand left the glass and he placed his fingers lightly on her arm. 'It might surprise you to know that I don't bring my children and my cat hop-picking, in the hope I'll find a gorgeous woman to make love to in a wheat field.' He paused. 'We'll probably find ourselves working together at times and we have a mutual friend, Pat, who loves to talk. I don't want to forget what happened between us but it might be better for both of us if we pretend it never happened.'

'You'd do that for me?' She stared at him.

'Not just for you, for Tim and Ivy. It's nineteen forty-three and we're in the middle of a war but gossips can still hurt people . . .'

She'd been worrying about the effect her fling would have on Will and Joe but she'd not thought what would happen when it reached the ears of the hopping crowd. 'Thank you,' she said softly, wishing she could shut her eyes and it would all go away. Tomorrow would be the first picking day and she certainly didn't want to begin it with the possibility of fingers pointing her out as a tart.

'Don't thank me,' he said. 'You don't know how sorry I am we can't be more to each other.' She felt the pressure of his fingers on her skin, and when he removed them, she sensed the loss. 'Drink up,' he said. 'I don't want to compromise you, so better we're not spotted together. Hopefully it'll stay reasonably light for you to make your way back to Southerns' farm. It's not far and I'm sure you'll be safe. I'll follow later.' He'd fumbled in his pocket and produced his lighter, saying, 'Take this. Sorry it's not a torch but it'll do, if you need it.'

She'd left him then. He was right: it wasn't far back to the farm and she'd not needed to use the lighter until she was well past the Spotted Cow's fire, now a smouldering mess in the field: even deep in the country the blackout had to be observed. Several people shouted drunken goodnights to her as she walked the path to the hut. Fearful of rabbit holes, she was glad of his lighter's flame when the moon disappeared. When the lighter would work no longer, Eadie realized it had probably run out of fuel, but with their hut just steps away she had felt even more indebted to Vinnie.

Now, lying in the darkness, listening to the steady breathing of Joy beside her, Maureen and her child asleep on the palliasse on the floor, Eadie wondered what tomorrow would bring.

Chapter Nine

Joy woke to the delicious smell of bacon frying. Opening her eyes she saw she was alone and the gorgeous aroma was wafting in, with weak sunshine, through the open door of the hut. Eadie's voice calling, 'Peekaboo,' proved her friend had made it home last night and the baby's laugh told Joy the two of them were enjoying themselves.

She rolled off the bed, slid into her slacks, blouse and a jumper she'd left ready, and stepped into the doorway.

'Sleeping Beauty's just woke up,' exclaimed Maureen, prodding, with a fork, fried bread sizzling with the bacon in a large pan over a wood fire.

'Look, Billy, there's your auntie,' said Eadie, waving towards Joy.

'Morning, everyone,' Joy announced. 'The smell of that food's making me realize how hungry I am. Wherever did you get that lovely bacon?' She had ventured nearer the flames and was looking at the lean rashers with the rind nicely crisping.

'That's payment in advance for hoeing Mrs Southern's kitchen garden,' said Maureen. 'I offered, she accepted. Sit down on the grass and eat. We need a good breakfast now and a sarnie for later when it's dinnertime. Pickin' hops gives you an appetite.'

Joy stared at Maureen. There was something different about her. Then it dawned on her that she wasn't wearing her usual headscarf. Her hair was brushed forward over her head and tied into a sort of bun with a piece of faded yellow ribbon. The result was very fetching, thought Joy.

'Did you do your hair?' she asked.

Maureen coloured. 'Is it silly? I've tried to hide the bald patches.'

Joy smiled warmly at her. 'It looks lovely,' she said. 'I'm proud of you for wanting to make the best of yourself, I really am.'

Maureen said shyly, 'I hoped by not wearing that turban the sun might help my hair to grow back.'

Joy sat down next to Eadie, who had Billy sitting on her lap. 'It probably will,' she said.

Joy had already grabbed the cottage loaf and a sharp-looking knife. Maureen passed her a tin plate.

'Where did you get to last night?' Joy asked Eadie.

'That's for me to know and you to find out, ducky.'

Joy glared at her.

Eadie looked at Maureen, who was carefully turning the fried bread so it became golden on both sides, and whispered, 'Ask me again later.'

Joy nodded and went on slicing the bread. At the side of the fire on a flat stone, the teapot was keeping warm. She could hear Glenn Miller playing 'String Of Pearls', not loudly but clearly enough to make the outdoor breakfast a sociable affair.

'Where's the music coming from?' Joy asked.

'That tawny-haired girl, Marlene, belonging to that big woman, Pat, has a wind-up gramophone.' Maureen waved her fork along the line of huts, where other hut dwellers were also cooking outside. 'Marlene and Alma,' the fork moved in the opposite direction, 'have palled up and swap records,' she said. Joy gathered from the way the fork had swung that their hut was in the middle.

'Alma's the girl who likes looking after our Billy?' Joy asked.

Maureen nodded. 'You finished with that bread yet?'

Joy said, 'Almost.'

'Well, when you've made up the bacon sarnies we'll be taking with us, you'll find a nice clean bit of sheeting in a biscuit tin, middle shelf of the kitchen area in the hut. Now we've a paper shortage, and no wrapping paper because of this damned war, so that'll do to put our daily dinners in.'

Eadie looked at Joy and grinned. 'Cos you're the youngest, it looks like you're the runabout. That'll be your daily job from now on. Making up our dinners. There's something special about eating food out in the fresh air.' Eadie wiped the last of the fat from her plate with a piece of bread. She set the plate in the grass, stretched contentedly, then reached for her Woodbines.

'Don't get too comfortable, either of you. There's loads to do before picking,' Maureen chided, already on her feet again.

Joy was surprised by how little time they wasted, clearing up, readying themselves, preparing Billy and filling his pram with flasks of tea, bottles of water and food for the day.

The hut dwellers were going about their business when a loud handbell rang out at seven o'clock. Then, it seemed, everyone was talking, laughing, armed with bags of necessities and moving in the same direction along the path, away from the huts and towards the first field to be picked.

Joy had no idea where they were going but assumed someone in the lead did, so, with Maureen pushing the pram, Eadie and she joined the caterpillar of noisy folk.

Already the sun promised to be scorching when the pickers arrived at the designated field. Rows upon rows of hop bines grew in fields about them as far as Joy could see. She and Eadie, followed by Maureen, pram and baby, were shown by a handsome Romany man, with curly hair, to their lines. The twelve-foot bines had been trained up strings that had already been cut at the top for easy access. The rows seemed to Joy to stretch into infinity. She suddenly remembered Pat regaling them about stilt walkers who were needed to cut the very top wires. She thought that would be a fine sight to see early in the morning. Though perhaps the stilt workers, due to their dangerous job preferred to work in seclusion before the workers arrived.

'I'm your foreman,' the man said, after ascertaining their names and checking his notebook for the line number. Joy and Eadie were to share one. Behind them, Maureen had one to herself. 'My name's Elijah – call me Eli. I'll be around all the time. This is your bin.' Joy saw a huge empty sack supported on a numbered wooden frame. 'You swing the bin into position next to you both, pull down the thick top of the cut bine, tear off the bunches of hops and throw them into the bin. Strip the rest of the bine, making sure you don't leave any hops behind, cutting or breaking the other strings as necessary. Move the bin as needed. No leaves or stalks in the bin. The measurer won't take 'em. Tidy the line as you go.' He spoke tersely and didn't make eye contact. Joy thought he had the whitest teeth she'd ever seen and he'd obviously put on a clean blue shirt for the start of the hopping.

Then he turned to Maureen and the very same words poured from his mouth before he moved on to the next line and another worker. It had happened so quickly and Joy was pleased she'd kept her wits about her.

'Speed is of the essence,' she said to Maureen, who was foraging warily beneath the mattress in the pram.

'Don't you forget it,' Maureen answered. In her hand, wrapped in an old piece of towelling were small, sharp-looking knives. She handed one to each of them. 'You'll find these useful,' she said. Then she searched again, very carefully, because Billy was sleeping like an angel, and brought out a brown carrier-bag containing three large potato sacks, one of which she tied about her waist to protect her worn but reasonably clean dress. 'Picking's a dirty job,' she said. Joy and Eadie copied her. Joy's sack very nearly reached her ankles.

'This early in the morning the bines are dew-wet, cold and messy. Later the numbness in your fingers will disappear as the sun warms everything through. There are tiny thorns covering the stems but in a couple of days you won't notice them tearing into your skin. Back in the hut I've Vaseline to put on your hands. It'll soak in and smooth them while we sleep. Picking will be slow work at first but you'll soon get used to it. And as the sun dries the hops, you'll smell that lovely, bitter aroma. Anything else I can tell you?'

'I've just understood more from you than I did from Eli,' Eadie said, searching her pockets for her cigarettes.

'He's got a field full of pickers to sort out quickly and that means keeping his eyes and ears sharp and treating everyone the same. But he'll look in on you every so often and I'm right behind you, so don't worry.' She paused. 'One other thing, if you hear Billy, don't offer to help with him. He's already sleeping much better than he did at home. I'll feed and change him, as and when. Your help will only hinder yourselves and me. Me and him'll soon get into a little routine and all three of us are here to earn money. That means picking as fast as we can.'

'Cor, she talks like a teacher!' said Joy. But she heeded Maureen's words and hauled their bin close beside her and

Eadie. Tentatively she pulled a cut bine downwards and as it dropped a shower of dew fell like cold rain all over her.

'Bugger!' Joy cried. Eadie began laughing at her. She pinched the end of her cigarette and returned it to the packet so she could smoke it later and grabbed a bine. Joy was wiping her face and hair with a corner of the sacking apron when the same thing happened to Eadie.

'That's a bloody good start,' Eadie muttered, mopping at herself. Then she sighed. 'Hopefully the sun'll soon dry the dew.'

Joy grinned at her, then looked longingly at the flask tucked into the grass at the bottom of the first bine, along with a bottle of water.

'Don't even think about it, ducky,' warned Eadie. 'We've got to eke out the water and tea. Dinnertime we'll see if there's a stand-pipe close by.' Soon she was shaking the dew from long strings of hops and leaves with one hand, picking bunches of the cone-like ripe hops with the other and tossing them into the bin.

It was slow work to begin with, and despite the irritation to her scratched and bleeding fingers, Joy was happy to see their bin fill as they moved it along, hauling down the bines and stripping them of their fruit. The air began to warm up, drying the bines, and a general hum of good-natured chatter could be heard. Every so often Maureen called to them, asking if they were all right, and Joy caught sight of Eli pacing the length of the huge field and keeping an eye on things.

Now and then, Joy heard snatches of off-key singing as workers gave voice to well-known songs. Early-morning grouchiness was wearing off and spirits rising, as the sun climbed higher in the sky. Joy discovered she was getting into a sort of picking rhythm where she was able to separate the bunches of hops and think of different things at the same time.

Eadie still hadn't told her where she'd disappeared to last night. She knew she would eventually. It wasn't something Eadie wanted Maureen to share so it must be personal. She glanced at Eadie, who smiled at her as she threw hops into the bin. A friendly nod passed between them. Joy decided that after Eadie had posted Joe's letter last night she was now wondering how soon she'd receive a reply.

'We're not the fastest pickers but we're certainly not the slowest,' announced Eadie, as she passed the bottle of water to Joy. She drank thirstily, gave back the bottle, then walked to the head of their line to see what was going on. All the bins had been moved to where their pickers were currently working. From their staggered positions they now showed the more experienced pickers.

Quite a few of the women picked together, Joy noticed. The Londoners were extremely quick and very noisy, often breaking into song. She supposed many of them returned year after year but especially now, if only to escape the constant bombing London was receiving.

Earlier Joy could have sworn she'd heard Pat's strident voice calling for Marlene, but Eadie said she was mistaken.

A very elderly Romany woman's bin was halfway along the line. Joy gasped. Eadie, beside her, said, 'She's got the kids picking with her.'

'An' there's enough of them!' Joy said, as she watched the energetic youngsters tossing bunch after bunch of hops into the bin. 'And they're all ages!' she added, watching the wizened woman, dressed in voluminous black, her hair twisted in plaits across the top of her head and decked out in gold, expertly pulling and cutting the bines. Every so often she'd yell something that Joy couldn't understand to the eight or so healthy-looking youngsters. Their Romany language probably, Joy thought, and the children listened carefully, then did her bidding. A little girl, about three or four years old, Joy guessed, with gold in her pierced ears, was happily picking up the fallen hops, depositing them in the bin, then clearing the ropes of bine to one side, keeping the line tidy. The woman saw she was being watched and gave Joy and

Eadie a courteous nod. Joy noticed a high-backed cane chair nearby in case the woman needed to sit awhile. They waved back enthusiastically.

'I hope she didn't think we were spying on her,' Joy said.

'Which we were!' added Eadie.

'No good you standing about watching others work.'

Maureen's voice startled Joy as she appeared from her line.

'Stopped for a drink,' said Eadie.

Joy saw Billy draped sleepily across Maureen's shoulder. He had on a dry nappy and a tiny vest. His arms and legs were plump and pink. Joy watched Eadie's face light up at the sight of him.

'I've just fed him,' Maureen said. 'He loves the fresh air. Got to keep the pram hood up, though, gonna be a warm afternoon. He doesn't need too much sun. Which reminds me . . .'

Her child still glued to her, she searched in the pockets of her dress and produced two coloured cotton headscarves.

'One each,' she said. 'You don't want to get heatstroke on the first day. Come dinnertime, which should be soon, everyone'll be wearing their hats.'

Eadie bent forward and put her arms around Maureen. 'I don't know what we'd do without you. You think of everything.'

'Get off! You're squashing Billy,' Maureen said.

Joy saw she was embarrassed but pleased by the show of affection. Maureen seemed surprised at how much they'd picked.

'Before dinner Eli will be back with the measurer, who'll have a wicker basket that holds a bushel of hops. Yours will be "weighed", put in a poke, which is six feet long and four feet wide. When it's full, it holds ten bushels of hops. By the way, these huge sacks, filled with straw, are what we're sleeping on – our mattresses or palliasses, as some folks call them.' Maureen laughed. 'Every time the measurer weighs out a bushel, he'll call its number. Sometimes there's a bookie who'll write down the amounts in a book. You keep a tally as well of how many bushels you've picked. You already know we'll be paid at the end of hopping. And we can sub from Farmer Southern if we need it. But we won't because I've got money enough for most of our needs, and we must pop into the village shop with our ration books to register with the shop . . .'

'Just a minute.' Joy stopped Maureen's long speech because she was horrified. 'You've already done so much to help us but if you think we'd take money from you, you're mistaken.'

As they knew, Maureen had helped herself to her husband Mick's racing winnings to escape from him, but neither Joy nor Eadie would feel comfortable using any of that money. She looked at Eadie for confirmation and got it. 'Anyway,' she added, 'Eadie and I have pooled what little we have.'

'What happened to the Three Musketeers, all for one and one for all?' Maureen was adamant. 'Doing it my way we'd all have decent wages to come at the end of the season.'

Joy could see from Eadie's face that she was considering the suggestion. It made sense because she had to support Will and Joe. Maureen, at present, had no future plans but she had Billy to care for and no safe home to go back to in Gosport. She was also desperate to show her appreciation to them for helping her change her life.

'All right,' Joy said. She knew then that, whatever happened, the three of them would stick together.

The raucous sound of the handbell announced it was dinnertime.

'Twelve till one,' said Maureen, and proceeded to push the pram with the sleeping child towards the trees where it was shady but well within sight of the lines. She looked tired, thought Joy.

And she'd lost her own sparkle. Joy's hands hurt. They were covered with small cuts, filthy with the juice from the hops, and her skin itched because a myriad of tiny insects preferred her to the bines.

Hoppers were unwrapping food, swallowing tea from bottles and settling for a well-earned rest. Men were pulling off knitted clothing that had warmed them in the chill of the early morning. Chatter filled the air. Joy noticed dogs among the hop-pickers. A smile lit her face as she watched children throw a ball for a barking mongrel to chase. She was reminded of the cat, Spitfire, in the basket carried by the blond man, brought hop-picking because his little girl couldn't bear to be parted from it. Her smile widened.

Maureen handed her a bacon doorstep that Joy had put together earlier that morning. She was glad now she hadn't stinted on the size of the slices of bread. Eadie passed her a mug of strong tea and her spirits rose once more.

'So, you were pleased by the measurer's tally this morning? You should be,' Maureen said. 'That's a good number of bushels for first-timers.'

Eadie piped up, 'Don't forget we're supposed to be old hands at this picking game!'

'You're not the only ones who've never been in a hop-field before. Why d'you think Eli gives the same patter to everyone? As long as Farmer Southern's hops are picked, and quickly, before the rain sets in, he won't grumble.'

'I need a wee,' admitted Joy.

'Off you go, then,' Eadie said, cigarettes in hand. 'Find a secluded bush somewhere.'

When the handbell rang again at one o'clock, Joy rose from the sweet-smelling grass where she'd been lying, thinking how amazing it was that a rest in the shade, satisfying food and drink had made her feel brand new again. She looked at Eadie, flat on her back with Billy draped across her chest, fast asleep. 'C'mon, you, give that baby back to his mother.'

Maureen was already on her feet, bustling about after refilling the flasks and bottles with water from the stand-pipe at the edge of the field. Now she lifted the sleeping child off Eadie and returned him to the pram. Joy put out her hand and pulled a yawning Eadie to her feet.

For Joy the afternoon passed in much the same way as the morning, except she'd never felt so weary in her life. At Priddy's factory she'd thought nothing of sitting for hours and hours filling shell cases with highly dangerous explosives, even volunteering for overtime. But here she was a picking machine. A sweating, aching automaton who craved shade from the sun, water to drink and an end to the pain she was feeling in every part of her body.

'All right?' Every so often those two words would pass between Eadie and herself and the answer was always a smile and a nod. There were no grumbles from Eadie: she wasn't that sort of person.

Joy could see the fresh sweat that glistened on Eadie's skin before it was covered with dust from the earth kicked up by their feet. Cigarettes were Eadie's salvation: every so often she'd light one and furtively blow out a few puffs of smoke before extinguishing it and returning it to the packet for later. The farmer didn't allow smoking in the fields. A fire hazard, Maureen had said. Eadie would be more than careful, Joy knew, holding the cigarette in the palm of her hand, waving away the tell-tale smoke before anyone could smell it.

Joy remembered the copy of *Picturegoer* back in the hut. She'd still not found the time to open its pages, which promised so much delight for her with information she craved about the film stars and the pictures they were in. She knew if she was now in the heavenly cool of that twelve-by-twelve-foot corrugated box, she wouldn't have the energy to read. She'd simply sleep on the straw mattress for eternity.

Joy guessed when the measurer and Eli came round to weigh their pickings that the bell would ring soon to signify the end of day one. 'I don't have the energy to be excited,' she said. All the same, pride swept through her when the number of her and Eadie's bushels was shouted out and recorded. A huge wink from Eadie confirmed her delight.

'That's it. That's me finished.' Maureen appeared after the bell had chimed, pushing the pram. Already she'd collected their flasks, bottles and clothing discarded during the heat of the day.

It was nearly seven o'clock and Joy relished the light wind that had risen. She wanted nothing more than tea, made in a teapot, a good wash and a sit-down.

Eadie took one look at Billy and a screech came from her, loud enough to wake the dead. 'Look at him! Look at Billy! He's sitting up by himself!'

Joy stared at the little boy. He was lopsidedly wobbling but he really was sitting up in the pram, totally unaided.

'Oh, my little love,' she said, and took a step towards the pram. Billy's mouth was open showing off his one tooth. Joy could only think Eadie's loud voice had startled him for he promptly fell sideways and began to cry. Maureen laughed as she propped him up.

'You're not hurt, my sweet,' she cooed at him. Then, to Eadie and Joy, 'He's been trying to sit up all afternoon,' she said, a broad smile covering her face, which was now lightly browned by the sun. 'It's his party piece!' She had a final look around to make sure no equipment would be left behind, and said, 'Home time, girls!'

Joy could see that the crocodile of people wending their way back to the huts had lost the morning's impetus. Despite the tiredness that engulfed her, her spirits rose even higher when the hut came into view. People were shouting, 'Goodnight,' or 'See you tomorrow,' or 'You going up the Spotted Cow?' as Eadie pushed open the hut door.

Maureen's next words surprised her. 'I'll feed and change Billy, then go up to the farm to honour my promise of hoeing their kitchen garden. We shouldn't be long. But it would be a big help if you two can get stuff ready for work tomorrow and peel a few potatoes. There's a tin of corned beef in a bag, there.' She pointed to the box that served as the kitchen area. 'We can have corned-beef hash tonight.'

Eadie was first to speak: 'Jesus, woman, aren't you tired?'

'Of course I am, but a promise is a promise . . .'

Joy said, 'Fair enough, but after you've fed Billy, why not leave him here with us? We can sort him, then put him to bed. It'll give you a bit of a break.'

She'd not really known Maureen until the last few days. At Priddy's factory she had thought her withdrawn, uncommu-nicative. She'd always kept herself to herself, never removing her turban and always hiding her body when she was getting into her regulation dungarees in the changing room. Maureen and Eadie sat next to each other filling shell cases, and Eadie had said Maureen's husband was handy with his fists. Away from work there had been no socializing between the three women.

Joy was now looking at Maureen in a different light. It was as if she'd left that cowed, taciturn self in Gosport. Here, in the hop-fields she was an extremely hard worker and always eager to help people. Perhaps, Joy thought, Maureen had always been a gregarious woman. She wondered then if it was possible her husband had knocked every bit of confidence out of her, and her escape from him had allowed the genial, kindly, smart woman to return.

'Well . . .' Joy could almost see the cogs whirring in Maureen's brain '. . . are you sure?' Her eyes were full of tears, as if no one ever did kindly things for her. She sniffed. 'I could lodge our ration books with the shop, Smeaton's, while I'm out.'

Eadie was already at the suitcases rooting around for them.

Joy said, 'Won't the shops be closed?'

Maureen answered, 'Nah! Hopping times their hours change. They don't want to lose out on trade. Village shops can make more money in these few weeks than the rest of the year.'

Eadie made tea on the oil stove while Maureen fed her child. When the little one had finished, she passed him to Eadie saying, 'You wind him. He's yours now.'

Then she rubbed a wet flannel over her face. She'd already cleaned her still blackened hands to feed the baby, and said, 'I'll have a proper wash in the stream when I get back. I'm only going to get dirty again in Mrs Southern's garden, aren't I?'

Joy said, 'Stream? What stream?' All afternoon and evening Joy had been dreaming of a wash in cold water and wondering how she could get hold of enough without using up all their precious fresh drinking water.

'Oh! Didn't I tell you? At the back of the hut there's a stream. It meanders down to a pool at the back of the farm-house, in a field where the farmer keeps all his cows. I love swimming, but I'd not get in there, no matter how hot the day was. The water's useful for cleaning but not for drinking. It's not pure. A trip to the stand-pipe's safest for that.'

'That'll do for me to stand in to cool off,' Joy said happily. It seemed to her that, every minute, things were getting better and better.

*

Chores finished, potatoes almost boiled, Billy sleeping like an angel, Joy sat on the bed, her freshly washed hair wrapped in a towel, smoothing Vaseline on her sore hands and watching Eadie brush her red hair with long, even strokes.

'Are you going to tell me what you were doing last night?'

Eadie put down the brush and stared at her. The smell of eau de Cologne wafted in the air. 'Only if you promise never to tell anyone.'

Joy grinned at her. 'Try me,' she said.

Eadie took a deep breath. 'A gorgeous man was making love to me in a wheat field. Afterwards we went for a drink in a pub.'

Joy laughed. 'Not the Spotted Cow?'

Eadie could see Joy didn't believe her. 'No, the Vine.'

Joy stopped laughing. 'My God! Are you telling me the truth?'

'Would I lie about something so serious, ducky?'

Moments passed. 'Do you realize what you're saying?'

'I'm not seeing him again.'

'I thought you cared about Will. And Joe thinks the world of you.'

'Caring's not enough.' Eadie covered her face with her hands. 'I'm not seeing him again,' she repeated.

Joy's mind was in turmoil. Whatever had possessed Eadie

to go against everything she believed in? Her marriage meant everything to her. It was hard to believe that she would even look at anyone else. Eadie was so straitlaced when they went dancing: if a man held her too close, she refused a second dance with him. Eadie's confession had shocked her. Eadie had come hop-picking to keep a roof over Will and Joe's heads and put food on the table because she cared so much for them. It didn't make sense . . .

And then it did.

She remembered the blond man waiting in the queue at Fareham station who couldn't take his eyes off Eadie. The man with the children, coming hop-picking. The man walking along the road towards this farm.

'You didn't have to sleep with the bloke because he lit you a cigarette,' Joy said. 'I'm right, it was him, wasn't it?'

Eadie removed her hands from her face. Her cheeks were wet with tears.

Joy wiped her hands on the towel to absorb the greasy Vaseline, then went over to her and put her arms around her. 'I think you're marvellous to have stayed faithful to Will all this time,' she said. 'Him being the way he is.'

'It's not going to happen again,' Eadie said, looking into Joy's eyes. Her voice was very small. 'I don't really know what came over me.'

'At the station he looked like he could eat you up,' Joy whispered. 'No one's ever looked at me like that!'

'Well, it's over, over, over, before it really began,' Eadie told her. Then, 'I can't risk Maureen knowing. It might get about and you know how people gossip . . .'

'Maureen was there when you wandered off with him.'

'Wandering off doesn't matter. It's what happened after-wards that does,' Eadie said.

'What about him? Will he brag about it? Some men would.'

Eadie shook her head. 'No, he's a good man. He'd have liked something permanent until I told him about Will. He knows about the awfulness of shell shock. He under-stands . . . I couldn't help myself.'

'You'll have some explaining to do.'

'What d'you mean?' Eadie frowned.

'Last night when we walked up the path towards the Spotted Cow, you carried on to post that letter. Maureen saw him catch you up.'

Eadie pursed her lips. 'Damn'

'You'll just have to make an excuse if she mentions it. She might. She's not daft and she's more talkative here to people than she ever was at Priddy's. After all, we didn't see hide or hair of you till this morning.'

Eadie tutted. 'I'll have to think of something in case she asks.'

'And what about Joe, at home? He cares about you. You going to tell him? You're not usually one for keeping secrets from him. Not something like this. After all, you're married to his son . . .' Joy stepped back from Eadie and took a long, deep breath that she let out slowly. 'I understand why, Eadie. I really do. You and Will used to be so close, always kissing and cuddling . . .' She sighed deeply. A smile crept across her face. She made a fist and gave a soft, friendly punch to Eadie's shoulder. 'He is lovely, though, that blond bloke. I wouldn't have minded changing places with you!'

Chapter Ten

Eadie wondered where Maureen had got to. It was almost dark outside and she'd lit a candle so Maureen wouldn't fall over in the hut and wake Joy, or Billy, who was flat out. He was such a good little soul, she thought.

'I'm hungry and I want to sleep,' Joy had moaned earlier, after they'd both prepared for work the next day. As time passed and Maureen still hadn't returned, they'd cooked and eaten their share of the food and left Maureen's meal sandwiched between two plates.

Joy's film magazine lay open on the blanket. She'd started to read it but fallen asleep. Eadie stepped over to the bed and rescued it in case it became damaged if either she or Joy thrashed about in the night. The straw, filling the palliasse on the floor, ready for Maureen to sleep on, crackled beneath her feet. Last night the baby had slept with Maureen but

Eadie feared he might get trodden on so, for now, she'd left him in his pram.

She'd looked outside earlier and discovered, much to her surprise, that some hoppers were sitting around fires, drinking, chatting. She'd wondered where their energy came from after such a strenuous day in the hot sun. However, after a strip wash she'd felt more like herself and had even managed to rinse out a few items of clothing. Wearing her long nightie, she'd crept outdoors and hung the wet washing over the line. She'd also washed up the dishes and pots she and Joy had used when they'd cooked the corned-beef hash.

Eadie was debating whether to boil a few of Billy's nappies on the oil stove when Maureen's voice hissed from outside, 'Give us a hand! I can hardly manage this lot.'

Sweeping open the door Eadie found her clutching carrier-bags and bulging hemp sacks. Eadie immediately recognized the smell of Imperial Leather soap.

'Ssh! You'll wake everyone up!' She hauled in a couple of the heavy sacks. 'What you got in here? Coal?'

'Better than that! I got fresh stuff to last us a few days. Apples, plums and pears, fallers from the Southerns' orchard. I got extra to give out to the kids. For us there's lettuce, a cucumber . . . Mind them tomatoes!' Maureen's voice rose dramatically. 'Don't squash 'em!' Maureen elbowed her aside as the sack Eadie was man-handling split and some of its contents spilled across the wooden floor. 'Get a saucepan!'

Stunned, Eadie did as she told, then watched as Maureen gathered up ripe, sweet-smelling tomatoes and placed them in the pan, filling it. The smell of soap as she knelt beside her was stronger than ever. Eadie leaned in closer and sniffed Maureen's neck. 'You've had a wash with Imperial Leather!' she accused, her voice rising to a crescendo.

'Whassamatter? What's going on?' Joy asked sleepily from the bed.

'No, I 'aven't. I've 'ad a bath!' shouted Maureen.

Eadie sat on the floor and stared at her. Speechless, she waited for an explanation.

'What's up? What's all the noise?'

'Shut up!' The words came in unison from Maureen and Eadie.

Eadie stole a quick look at Joy, who was now sitting up in bed clearly quite affronted. Then she turned to Maureen and said, 'Well?'

Maureen let out a deep sigh, then said, 'After getting permission to scrabble beneath the fruit trees in Betty Southern's orchard to give some of the pickers' kids a bit of a treat, I got even more dirty and smelly hoeing and weeding her garden than I already was after working today. She asked if I'd like to wash before I 'ad a drink of tea. I said I'd prefer a bath. I was being cheeky, and she said it was fine by her as long as I didn't use more than the regulation five inches of water!' Maureen's words had all come out in a rush. Then she added, 'Well, would you 'ave refused?'

'First-name terms now, are we?' Eadie wondered incredulously. 'Betty Southern?' The name came out sarcastically. She thought briefly, then said, 'No, I wouldn't have refused.'

'Excuse me?' Joy was crawling out from the blanket. 'You've woken me up,' she said sweetly. 'And if you don't keep the noise down, you'll wake Billy as well.' Sitting on the edge of the bed, she looked at each of them in turn. Then she saw the food and gasped.

Joy slipped from the bed, pulled the two carrier-bags clear of the hut door, closed it, then searched inside first one brown bag and then the other, muttering as she rifled through them. 'Bacon, yum-yum . . .'

'That's part payment for more gardening I'm wanted for,' Maureen said.

Joy pulled out a tin can with a handle and a screw top.

'Fresh milk,' Maureen said. Joy set it carefully on the floor.

Loose potatoes came next. They were soil-encrusted but large and without blemishes.

'For baking in the fire,' Maureen said.

Eadie thought Maureen sounded bored with the need to explain.

'A large Cos lettuce, to go with some of the tomatoes,' announced Joy. Then she took out a muslin-wrapped square. She stared at it.

'You don't need to unwrap that. It's cheese from the farm, again part-payment for work that I won't get actual money for,' Maureen said. 'And I'm sure neither of you will breathe a word about me asking to be paid in goods. It might not be strictly legal but I don't think it's any worse than Gosport shopkeepers, who keep stuff under the counter for certain customers.'

Eadie said, 'All's fair in love and war.' She was beginning to see a different side to Maureen. This assertive woman was nothing like the cowed munitions hand, who worked alongside her, taking her husband's abuse for granted.

Maureen smiled at her. 'For me it is, Eadie love. The less other hop-pickers know about my business the happier I'll be . . .' Suddenly she went quiet, gave a little laugh and said, 'But that's a story for another time. You got other bags to look inside yet, Joy. I went to the village first and did a bit of shopping after registering us with Smeaton's.'

Joy had a grin on her face a mile wide. She looked at

Maureen. 'Is this for me?' She was holding a magazine as if at any moment it might disappear into thin air. 'Oh, how lovely. I can't afford this one as well as *Picturegoer*.' The *Picture Show* cover depicted Maureen O'Hara and Henry Fonda in a still from *Immortal Sergeant*. 'I want to see this film when it comes to the Criterion,' she said. She turned to Eadie. 'You and her could be sisters you look so alike.' Then, to Maureen, she said, 'Thank you. You know how I love reading about film stars.' She added, 'Or I would read, if I didn't fall asleep like I did earlier tonight.'

'We're all overtired,' Maureen said. 'The sooner we get into a proper routine the better.' Eadie saw Maureen was talking to Joy, who wasn't really paying attention. Instead she was digging deeper into the bag.

'That's useful,' Eadie said, as Joy brandished an Eveready front bicycle lamp.

'I expect you could have done with that to see your way home in the dark last night,' Maureen said.

'How d'you know what time I got in? You were asleep!'

'Was I? Was I really?' Maureen winked broadly at Eadie. Then she said, 'The lamp's got a brand-new battery. I made sure of that.'

Joy put the lamp on the floor, delved into the bag again and this time when she'd brought out a small article she began to laugh. She threw the packet of twenty Woodbines at Eadie, saying, 'We all know who the fags are for.'

Eadie caught it. 'You're a lifesaver, Maureen. An angel in disguise! Thank you.'

Maureen waved away her thanks. 'So now we come to the last bag. One item only. It's got newspaper round it for a reason, so I suggest you leave it in the bag, Joy, and just make a hole in the paper to see what it is.'

'Well, it's heavy,' Joy said, weighing the bag. Eadie looked at Maureen, who was smiling.

'The paper's quite damp,' Joy added. She frowned. 'It's difficult burrowing through it. My hands are still sore from the thorns on the bines.'

'Oh, shut up moaning!' Eadie reproved her. Joy, kneeling, had pulled the carrier-bag onto her lap. 'Tear off a big piece of paper so I can see what it is as well,' she advised.

Joy was wrenching and tugging, frowning as she did so. She leaned her head closer, practically inside the bag, to get a better look.

'Agh!' Her scream filled the hut. 'It's got a bloody snout and ears and eyes!' She leaped to her feet. The contents of the bag rolled onto the floor, the soft newspaper falling away.

Joy's shriek woke Billy. He gave a scream of fright, then settled for a lusty yell. Maureen was on her feet in moments and swept him from his pram into her arms and was murmuring soft shushing sounds to pacify him.

Eadie had her hand across her mouth, stifling her laughter. Every so often, 'Oh dear!' and 'Dear, oh dear!' slipped out between chortles.

'That'll teach you not to be so nosy, miss!' Maureen said, between giggles. She'd comforted Billy and he was in her arms, looking around inquisitively.

The partly wrapped pig's head stared up at them from the floor. After a moment, Maureen said, 'I went into the butcher's, as you now know.' Another smile tipped the corners of her mouth but she composed herself. 'He offered me that.' She nodded towards the floor. 'Naturally I jumped at buying it. On an outside fire I can boil it up. The meat's delicious. I can fry the ears, make soup—'

'All right, all right!' Joy stopped Maureen's speech on how to cook a pig's head. Eadie could sense her friend was distressed at the joke played on her. 'I suppose you think that was funny!' she added.

Eadie put her arms around her. 'Actually, ducky, it *was* funny. And you should know people only play tricks on friends they love, friends they believe can take a joke.' Eadie stepped away. 'All right, ducky?'

'All right.' Joy gave her a little smile.

Eadie moved towards the much-prized pork item lying on the floor, picked it up and began rewrapping it as best she could. Because of the war every item of rationed food was doubly precious. Once it was safely back in the bag she put it on the orange-box shelf in the kitchen area.

Maureen had moved to the stool and, Billy clinging to her, had unbuttoned her clothing so she could feed him. Eadie was reminded of pictures she'd seen of Madonna and Child paintings. It was clear to her that Maureen absolutely adored her child. She thought that that would be an incredible feeling, to love a small someone who was part of you, who had grown inside your body.

Eadie realized Maureen was watching her. She grinned and Maureen returned the grin with a smile as Billy latched on to her breast. Eadie shook her head. 'You're a bugger,' she said to Maureen.

'Given half a chance I think I might be. When I was in the butcher's, he asked me if I wanted the pig's head chopping up. I told him to leave it exactly as it was, even with the eyes. I said I hadn't got much money but they'd see me through the week.'

Joy huffed. 'That's not funny either.' She opened the hut door a few inches, then went to the oil stove and lit the flame. 'I'm making tea for us, and then I'm going back to sleep, else I'll be fit for nothing in the morning.'

Eadie noticed Maureen's dinner was still untouched. 'D'you want me to warm that for you?'

Maureen shook her head. 'Nah! I'll fry it up over a fire outside tomorrow with the bacon. Like bubble and squeak. We can each have a bit with our breakfast.'

'Does that mean we won't get fried bread?' Joy set out mugs.

'Fried bread's a must!' Maureen answered. She transferred Billy to her other breast. There was a moment's silence while she made herself and her baby comfortable. Then she asked, 'Well, what do you think of your first day's hop-picking?'

Eadie, gathering food from the floor and stowing it away, said, 'Hard, painful, tiring and . . . exhilarating!'

Maureen laughed. 'What about you, Joy, love?'

Eadie saw Joy was concentrating on filling the teapot with boiling water. When it was done, she said, 'It was only a short while ago I'd been blown up and landed by Forton Creek. My body felt scratched and painful. It still does but I don't care because there's no war here. No Moaning Minnie telling us to run for the air-raid shelters. No searchlights, no bombs . . . It's like this farm and the hop-pickers are part of a huge family. I like it!'

'Just as well, then, isn't it?' Maureen said, holding Billy across her shoulder and rubbing his back to get his wind up. 'Yes, just as well you like it because in another few hours we've got to get out in the field and start all over again!'

'Which is why when I've drunk my tea I'm going back to bed,' said Joy.

'And I won't be long after you,' Eadie said. 'I'll stand outside in the moonlight, smoke a fag, and then I'll turn in too.'

Later, in the moonlight, as Eadie listened to the bubbling of the stream running past the rear of the hut, she wondered why she'd never heard it before. It was probably because in the short time they'd inhabited the hut there had been so much going on. She sighed contentedly. It was nice to feel the warm night air on her skin. The moon was a big bright circle in the sky. Unlike last night when she'd needed Vinnie's cigarette lighter to find her way along the path. Of course she'd return it to him. It must have been expensive. She'd looked for him and his children today, and Pat. They were probably picking hops at the far end of the field, she thought. She smiled remembering him. Vinnie truly was one of that rare species, a good man. She was sure of that. Why was she so sure? Because back in Gosport waiting for her were two more good men, her husband and her father-in-law, Joe.

Eadie slid out a cigarette from the packet and lit it with a match. She breathed in the satisfying taste of nicotine. It felt good. She hadn't liked the cloak-and-dagger stuff today, hiding her cigarette like a naughty girl in case she was caught smoking in the field.

Something rustled in a nearby tree. One of the night creatures, she supposed. A bird? A bat? She'd seen bats before, funny little furry things with tiny hands and clingy feet. A long time ago, when she and Will were just married, he'd taken her to Corfe Castle in Dorset. It had been a long walk uphill to the ruins in the dark. But she hadn't been afraid of the many bats there. She was with her husband. What need had she ever to be scared? Will would always protect her.

'Bats symbolize death and rebirth,' he had said. He'd pulled her close, unbuttoning his coat so she could snuggle inside against his warm chest. 'Not death as we know it, but certainly the termination of one thing and the alteration of another.' She'd liked it when Will told her things she knew nothing about. 'Apparently when a bat appears it might suggest you move beyond your fears and embrace the unknown,' he'd added. Well, she'd certainly done a lot of that since she'd watched all those bats hanging upside-down inside the castle's tumbledown walls.

The rustling continued, followed by tiny squeaking noises.

'It's probably a small creature, or creatures, wanting, like us, to go to bed and sleep.'

Eadie turned at Maureen's voice. The smell of baby powder hung in the air around her. 'I think it might be a bat,' Eadie said. 'Did you know bats hang upside-down? It's a symbol for us, telling us it's good to look at things from a different angle.'

Maureen stared at her. 'You're daft, you are,' she said. After a while she filled the silence that followed. 'I just wanted to say how much I appreciated the two of you looking after Billy while I ran errands, and was up at the farm.'

'I love being with him.'

'I know you do,' she said gently. 'You should have had kids of your own.'

'Let's not talk about that,' Eadie said. Brightly, she added, 'That's a lovely thing to do, you bringing back fruit for the hoppers' kids . . .'

'I only had to ask Betty Southern. She's a kind woman. The fruit rots on the ground otherwise,' Maureen replied. 'Or gets stolen.' Again, there was silence.

'Aren't you going to ask me where I was last night?' Eadie stared at Maureen. She wanted to get out of the way all of the questioning she was sure was coming.

'No. Why should I? It's your business.'

Eadie frowned. She hadn't expected that.

'I'm not going to pry into what you do. I'm only too happy that you and Joy have given me a new life away from that . . . Look, all the time we worked together at Priddy's, you listened to me but you didn't pry. I appreciated that.' Maureen gave a smile. 'It's lovely to have a couple of friends to trust, which is one of the reasons I've come out to talk now Billy's asleep.'

Eadie waited. 'The hop-picking will probably last a month or so. It's going well because the weather's good. That's why we've changed fields. Next comes the potato harvest. I'm hoping to stay on as long as there's work here because I'm not going back to Mick, now I've had a little taste of a better life.' Maureen paused, took a deep breath and carried on. 'There's always work on a farm.' She smiled. 'That's why they've got land girls here. I'm hoping to persuade Betty Southern to take me on permanently, like them.'

'But you can't live in a hut in the middle of winter with Billy!' Eadie couldn't help saying.

'No!' Maureen laughed. 'The land girls live-in at the farm. There's plenty of room there now the Southerns' youngest son is the only one of their grown-up children living at home.'

'And that's what you want?' Eadie loved her home and Gosport too much to want to leave for ever, but it was different for Maureen.

'I honestly think I can be useful to Mrs Southern. And I'd like to try. Not just for my sake but for Billy's. The Southerns lost their eldest son. He went down on the *Royal Oak* in Scapa Flow. Apparently, Betty's a shadow of the woman she used to be. She's let things go, not just the domestic stuff but book-keeping for the farm. I can do that.'

'You're a very brave woman,' Eadie said. 'But if I may, I'd like to offer a few words of advice . . .'

A worried look sketched itself across Maureen's face. 'What?' she asked.

'The less you tell of your business to other people, the better.' Eadie was almost knocked off her feet by a hug from Maureen.

'Which is exactly why you're the only one I'm telling,' she said, stepping away again. 'I know Mick won't let me get away with taking his winnings. Sooner or later, he'll come looking, and Billy and me need to be safe when he does.'

'You can't be sure that he'll come,' said Eadie.

'I can,' Maureen answered. 'Mick would never let me, a woman, get the better of him. He won't like being laughed at by his drinking pals.'

Eadie said, 'If Joy and I can help—'

'Actually, you can,' Maureen interrupted.

Eadie frowned. 'How?'

'Because we're in the fields during the day, I've only got the evenings to go down to the farm. Tonight I realized how much work I can get through without Billy. I've never left him before . . .'

'Oh, you'd like us to look after him sometimes? Of course.'

Maureen scratched her head. 'I didn't know how to ask.' Relief flooded her face. 'It won't be every night – I'd miss him too much for that.'

'Of course,' Eadie said. 'We can take him with us if we go to the Spotted Cow. Kids are everywhere here. That's settled, then, Maureen.'

Just then soft squeaking noises were heard among the rustle of leaves and a tiny shape flew high into the air.

'It's a bat!' laughed Eadie. 'He's after insects. A bat,' she repeated. 'I'd say that's a good-luck sign for both of us, wouldn't you?'

Chapter Eleven

'No! No! Eadie! Help!'

'Sssh! Joy, it's all right! I'm here . . .'

Joy opened her eyes to see Eadie's face in front of her. She felt her friend's hand smoothing her cheek. 'I'm here, you're safe.'

Then the tears started.

'I'll make some tea,' said Maureen, padding in bare feet towards the kettle. 'Thank goodness the water's still warm from earlier.'

Joy, now sitting on the edge of the bed, whispered, 'I'm sorry, I'm so sorry.' She looked down at the palliasse on the floor where Billy sprawled, like a star, among the covers, breathing evenly and still fast asleep. 'Thank God, I haven't woken him,' she muttered.

'There's still time,' Maureen said cryptically. She turned

to Eadie. 'You warned me about the possibility of Joy's nightmares returning, Eadie. I didn't know they could be so violent. Same bad dream?'

Eadie nodded at Maureen, then pulled the damp blonde curls from Joy's cheek and tucked them behind her ear.

Joy clung to her. 'The nightmare never changes. I'm flying and then I'm lying, unable to move, on the bank at Forton creek. I hurt so bad and I was calling for you. I know I'm dying and you don't come . . .' Joy buried her face in Eadie's neck where her warmth and the scent of her eau de Cologne, dabbed on earlier that night, comforted her.

'Ducky, I'll always come when you need me,' Eadie whispered.

Joy's panicking heartbeat was slowly returning to normal when Maureen set a mug of tea on the stool. 'Drink that, love,' she said. Then, ever practical, 'You must try to get back to sleep. Another few hours and we've got to be in the fields again.'

'I'm sorry, I'm really sorry,' Joy said again, dabbing at her eyes with a handkerchief Eadie had magicked up.

Maureen put a hand beneath Joy's chin and tipped her face towards her. 'You've nothing to be sorry about. What happened to you in Priddy's factory explosion was bad, really bad, but you got through it. And the dreams will fade in time, I promise you. Now drink your tea.'

Joy picked up the mug and took a mouthful. Its strong taste fortified her. She smiled at Maureen. 'Thank you,' she said. Then, 'That explosion at Priddy's tossed you about as well. Have you had any after-effects?'

Maureen said, 'I get depressed thinking about it. Especially the poor women who didn't live to go home to their families. I think about them dying. I don't have the nightmares Eadie told me you have.' Frown lines curved across her forehead, then a thin smile raised her lips. 'I've got a volatile husband so I've nightmares of a different kind.' She sighed. 'With this damned war it's a wonder any of us can sleep soundly. If we're not worrying about whether we'll be alive tomorrow, we're worrying about loved ones and friends, if they'll return home safely. You just thank God the nightmares don't come every night. That's something to be really grateful for.'

Joy wanted to believe her but her thoughts turned to Will, Eadie's husband. Joy hadn't experienced one iota of the horrors he'd lived through. Would his nightmares ever end?

'You Are My Sunshine' rang out from the pickers across the field as Joy plucked the yellow-gold hops and threw them into the bin. Weeks had passed and two complete fields had been picked bare of hops. Joy didn't need to peer into a tiny compact mirror to know she looked better than she ever had in her life. Her skin had turned from pasty white to golden brown after the days spent in the hot sun, toiling, laughing, and sitting in the evenings around a fire with friends was satisfying and rewarding. Best of all, she'd been sleeping soundly.

Pushing the pram up to the Spotted Cow and sitting outside with a glass of shandy after work was relaxing. Getting to know the Romany folk and being invited to their evening gatherings, when the muscular, dark-eyed men played fiddles and the black-haired, beautiful girls danced, even inviting them to join in, had made Joy see that hop-picking was truly like the holiday folks said it was. She also enjoyed moving from field to field to pick a new crop. It was good to go to sleep tired out from working hard and wake refreshed next morning with a heart so light she wanted to do it all over again.

She glanced to the end of the line where the big bag of plums Maureen had brought back to the hut last night stood propped in the shade against the pram in which Billy slept.

'You sure you don't want to come with us to give out the fruit to Queenie's band of kids?' Joy had to shout to make herself heard above the singing to Maureen in the row behind. The measurer and Eli had already visited, and the bushels of hops had been counted and written down, so at any moment Joy expected to hear the bell clanging, telling everyone it was dinnertime.

The old Romany woman, much revered by her people, was named Regina, which meant Queen, she'd told them one evening, when Joy and Eadie had been invited into her brightly painted red, yellow and green wagon, which she called a *vardo*. She'd been known as Queenie all her life. Her horse-drawn home was immaculate, full of brass ornaments, with hand-made lacy curtains at the windows.

'Nah! I saw enough plums when I was collecting them last night in the orchard,' said Maureen. 'But give Queenie my love. I'll feed and change Billy, give him a bit of cuddle,' she said, 'an' I could do with five minutes' peace away from your chattering and singing. Billie Holiday's got nothing to worry about when you open your mouth!' Joy pulled back the bines between her and Maureen's row, pushed her face through the gap and stuck out her tongue at Maureen.

As Joy carried on picking, she thought about the Romany people. Queenie said the large extended family had been coming to Southerns' farm for years. Some turned up early for the strawberry picking, June being the prime month for that. Often they stayed on after the hopping, helping with the potato harvest into October. She said her people were respected by the farmer: the men kept order if 'weekenders', as they called the husbands who worked during the week and visited their families in the hop-fields at weekends, got drunk in the Spotted Cow and caused trouble. A few muscled Romany men soon sorted them out, she said.

Eli was her grandson. He worked summer jobs for Farmer Southern.

During the freezing weather when work was scarce, the Romany people overwintered together. That was when families met up and stayed in one place. Sometimes farmers wanted the encampments to move on before they had secured another settlement. On those occasions wheels miraculously fell off wagons and the camp had to stay put until the caravans 'could be fixed'. Queenie said she liked hop-picking best of all the work they did.

Queenie especially liked Maureen. Sometimes they sat talking and drinking tea far into the night, long after Joy and Eadie had taken Billy back to the hut. Eadie said Queenie could see something of herself in Maureen.

Sundays were days of rest. Nobody worked in the fields on a Sunday. Joy loved Sundays when they could tidy the hut, listening to Alma and Marlene's popular records blaring out across the fields on the wind-up gramophone: Ella

Fitzgerald, Peggy Lee, Bing Crosby, Frank Sinatra, the
Andrews Sisters, the two girls had all the best songs and
dance music. They'd become good friends and Sunday was
their special day to take out Billy in his pram. Maureen
never asked where they went but when they returned, late
afternoon, and after Billy was bathed, fed and put to bed,
he was out like a light. Maureen said the hop-fields and the
fresh air agreed with him: he'd never slept all through the
night in Gosport.

Sundays gave the three women time to wash clothes.
Joy and Eadie had had no idea what sort of clothing
was needed for field work before they'd arrived at the
farm. Both had now utilized a few of their less-liked
suitcase items. Slacks with the lower legs cut off made
excellent shorts. Long-sleeved blouses with the sleeves
removed, kept them cool in the hot sun. Nobody cared
about fashion, toiling in the fields. Comfort was the priority. Joy and Eadie, of a similar size, swapped cut-about
clothing constantly. Eadie wouldn't let Joy throw away any
butchered scraps of fabric. She'd folded and returned them
to her suitcase. 'It's wartime and you never know when
they'll come in handy,' she'd said.

And now, as the dinner bell rang and the hoppers left their
rows to eat, drink and rest, Eadie lit a cigarette. 'Can you

manage that bag of plums on your own?' she asked. 'I'll be seeing Queenie later, and I'd like to pop down to the farm to see if the postman's been.'

Joy didn't ask why Eadie couldn't do that when they'd finished work for the day because she knew her friend was anxious to hear from Joe. She'd not had a reply to the letter she'd written and was worried.

Joy nodded. Eadie doused her cigarette and returned it to the packet, then picked up a bottle of water and drank. Afterwards, she looked at Maureen and said, 'I remember on my first day working here, I'd never have contemplated walking down to the farm in my dinner hour. I'd have thought I'd die! I was that tired!'

'That's what hard work and sweet, fresh air does for you,' said Maureen, sagely. 'Look what it's done for Billy.'

Billy was sitting up, strapped into his pram, happily making nonsense noises, and waving his tiny fists in the air.

'Take these with you,' urged Maureen, passing both Joy and Eadie huge bacon sandwiches. 'Eat on the go. You can't come back in an hour and work the rest of the afternoon on empty stomachs.'

'Thanks,' mumbled Eadie.

Eadie and Joy were still laughing at Billy's antics as they walked along the edge of the hop-field, carrying the hessian bag of plums between them, while munching their sandwiches.

'You've never carried that heavy bag by yourself, have you?' Queenie asked later. The Romany inflections in her voice were melodic. She gave Joy an enquiring look, increasing the wealth of wrinkles on her sun-browned face.

'Eadie left me at the end of your row of hops, so I've not walked far carrying it. Anyway, the plums are from Maureen. They needed picking before they rotted on Southerns' trees, she said to tell you. She thought the kids would make short work of them.'

As if to prove the point two curly-haired little boys in ragged clothing seemingly appeared from nowhere to dip grubby fingers into the hessian sack. Queenie gently slapped away a hand. 'Wait, *chavies*!' she said. 'Wait until you're offered!' Both stepped back, shamefaced. 'Now take a couple, but nicely, mind!' she admonished. Blushing, but giggling, the dark-haired lads did as they were told, then mumbled a thank-you before running off and disappearing into the hop-laden bines.

'You tell Maureen I appreciate her kindness. Eli will take what's left of the fruit back to my *vardo*, after the other young 'uns, helping me pick, have had their fill.'

Queenie, sitting on the cane peacock chair that Eli made sure was waiting for her in the field each morning, stared hard at her. 'You've a bright aura about you today, Joy.'

Joy frowned. 'What do you mean?'

'I can see with my mind's eye what's impossible for others to notice with their eyes wide open,' Queenie said. 'There's spiritual forces surrounding each of us and yours is certainly shining today.'

'Does that mean you can tell fortunes?'

Queenie sniffed derisively. 'True Roma can see the past, present and future.'

Joy hunkered down in front of her chair. Close up she could see the fine stitching on the black crêpe-de-Chine dress Queenie wore. Panels of velvet were encrusted with tiny glittering beads. Joy wanted to brush the dress's hem, which was dusty from being worn in the field, but felt that such familiarity might not be well received.

'Do you have a question to ask of me?'

Queenie's words shook Joy. A question? She had many questions about many things. Would she survive this awful war? Would her wages from hop-picking enable her to pay bills until she found another job?

Joy opened her mouth and unprepared words spilled out. 'I've been having nightmares.'

Queenie's dark eyes on her felt as if they were searching her soul. 'Your mind will relive the horrors until you are healed.' Queenie's words were concise.

'But when?'

'When the time is right. The process has already begun. Starting today you have much, much to look forward to . . .'

The older woman's voice was lost in the loud clanging of the bell announcing that it was time to return to work. And now children, grubby, noisy, with two barking dogs in tow, were clamouring around Queenie and the sack of plums.

Joy rose to her feet. Even though she'd been in Queenie's presence only a short time she felt as if she had awakened from a deep sleep. 'I must go . . .'

Queenie grabbed her hand. There was a strange moment of silence before Queenie said, 'Think on, Joy love. Remember well what I've told you.' Then she smiled. 'And thank Maureen for the plums.'

When Joy reached their line, she wasn't surprised to see Eadie happily picking hops and throwing them into the bin but she was astonished to hear her singing the Ink Spots song, 'I Don't Want To Set The World on Fire', softly to herself. It wasn't a popular tune the hoppers sang aloud. 'You're happy,' she said, bending down and scrabbling among the bines for the bottle of water.

As she swallowed, Eadie stopped singing, wandered up to her and said, 'You'll be happy an' all when you see what I've got.' Her hand delved into the front of her sacking apron and from it she produced a letter.

'Oh, you've heard from Joe.'

'This one's not for me. It's for you!'

Joy tried to assimilate her words. Eadie waved the envelope high in the air. Her other hand disappeared into the sacking apron at her waist and reappeared with a second opened envelope. 'This one's mine!'

'I've got a letter?' Joy could hardly believe it. 'Who's it from?' She made a grab for it and Eadie whisked it just out of reach, then meekly handed it to her.

'I don't know who it's from, do I? But since you've been waiting for a certain airman to write . . .'

Joy squealed. With the letter in her hand she sank down onto the earth floor, among the bines, to read it.

> RAF Hospital Cosford
> Shropshire
> England

Dearest Joy, if I may call you that?
A wonderfully kind nurse is writing this letter for me, as

*I am unable to hold a pen, but I will in the fullness
of time. My Lancaster found it difficult to duck from the
power of a German 88mm flak artillery shell while
returning from a successful operation in Germany's Ruhr
Valley. I can't divulge more due to military secrets. Suffice
to say I am being patched together by this hospital's team
who are truly magnificent. In fact, all crew are safe now.
You have been in my thoughts constantly since that
night in May when I held you in my arms on that dance-
floor in Gosport.*

*An unexpected mission forced a return to the
squadron at Scampton in Lincolnshire and I've been
eternally sorry I was never able to finish the letter I began
writing you.*

*I remember everything about you, Joy, despite holding
you only for the duration of that last dance. The way that
blonde curl wouldn't stop falling across your forehead.
Your green eyes with their flecks of gold and the smell of
your perfume. The way you barely reached my shoulder and
I wanted to protect you, not just for the duration of that dance
but for always. I'm sorry, I'm rambling on and getting
ahead of myself when perhaps you never gave me
another thought after I begged for your address and then didn't
write. Again, Joy, I'm so very sorry.*

I'm hoping you'll answer this letter or better still come
and visit me, if you can. Please.
  Jim Tremaine

'Joy! Are you all right?'

Eadie's voice wormed its way into Joy's head and she stared at her friend as she rose from the ground.

'I'm more than all right.' Joy thrust the pages at her. 'Read it.' She shrugged. 'I've no secrets from you.' Eadie took the letter in hop-juice-blackened hands and began.

Joy picked the fruit on the bines, then transferred the hops to the bin. Her heart and mind were no longer consumed by the job she was doing but on the contents of Jim's letter.

Her first thought was that although he had been hurt he was recovering. Obviously, he hadn't wanted her to worry about his injuries. Their Lancaster bomber had been shot down over Germany, back in May. He had started a letter to her and been unable to finish it because he'd been in hospital. But he was safe now. It wasn't because he didn't care for her that she'd not heard from him. His letter showed he'd thought of her often, and a great deal. As she had thought about him.

'I thought he'd forgotten about me.' Joy's voice was small.

Eadie handed back her letter. 'That says otherwise!' Eadie's smile practically split her face in two. 'You must write back tonight and arrange to see him. There's money we're owed for picking, plenty to cover your train fare to Shropshire, wherever that is.' Eadie fumbled in the depths of her sacking apron and brought out her Woodbines. 'I'm so happy for you, ducky. Pop into the next row and tell Maureen.'

'I'd rather not, just yet,' Joy said. 'I want to keep it between us two for a little while and think about it.'

Eadie drew in smoke, then released it slowly. 'I understand, love. When I reply to Joe I'll thank him for sending that letter on for you . . .'

'You must think I'm so selfish! I never asked if everything was all right with Joe and Will.' Joy resumed picking.

'As all right as it ever will be while the bombs keep dropping on Gosport,' Eadie said. 'Mrs Saunders's house at the top of the street caught it. Luckily, they were in the public shelter at the time. Nobody was hurt. She's moving in with her daughter in Inverness Road . . .' Joy was listening to the Gosport news as supplied by Joe in his letter but most of it went over her head. Jim's letter was far more exciting.

'Well, what do you think?' Eadie's voice had an edge, and Joy guessed she'd ignored something important that Joe had written. Eadie had smoked half her cigarette, pinched the end and put the remainder into her pocket. Evidence she'd been smoking in the hop-field wouldn't do her any favours.

'I'm sorry. My head isn't tuned in properly. What did you ask?'

Eadie tutted and chucked a handful of ripe hops that looked almost like a bunch of grapes into the bin.

'I asked you if I should tell Maureen her husband went round to see Joe to find out where she is.' Eadie spoke in a low voice so Maureen in the next row wouldn't hear. Joy felt that wasn't really necessary as the pickers had started singing again and 'The White Cliffs Of Dover' blotted out nearly all conversation.

'Oh!' Joy stopped picking and stared at her. 'He didn't tell her anything, did he?'

Eadie shrugged. 'I told Joe in my letter she was here. I saw no reason not to. Joe knows she works at Priddy's with me. None of us socialize. Mick must have been asking around about her factory workmates.'

'Would Joe have said anything?'

'I don't know. I suppose it depends when he received my letter and when Mick went to see him.'

Joy thought for a moment. 'What's happened has happened. Nothing either of us can do about it, now. He's a bad lot, that Mick.'

'So?' Eadie frowned. 'Shall I say something to Maureen?'

Joy shook her head. 'No. Why worry her? It's good to see her happy.'

Eadie nodded. 'Fair enough.' Into the bin went more hops. 'I don't suppose you took it in earlier that I've promised Pat we'll visit her tonight. She walked down from the far end of the bines in the other field while you were visiting Queenie, specially to ask. She wasn't alone. Vinnie was with her. He was going into the village. It made me feel quite funny us being so close after . . . I kept remembering his lovely body entwined with mine and the smell of his skin. And how he made me feel like a real woman after being denied love for so long. I know he was thinking about that night, same as I was. I'm sure Pat sensed something. You know how she can be . . .'

'We don't have to go tonight, if you're worried about Pat asking you questions.' Joy put a hand on Eadie's arm.

'We do.' Eadie sighed. 'If we don't, Pat'll be like a dog with a bone, wondering. She won't have forgotten Vinnie asked her my name after we'd met on Fareham station. Anyway, she said she's looking forward to seeing us. She's got rabbit stew . . .'

'That'd be nice.' Joy could imagine the tender meat, the succulent vegetables. 'Maureen can't come with us – she'll be at the farm.'

'Oh, Pat knows that, but she'll talk about her anyway.' Eadie shook her head. 'People gossip in the hop-fields just as neighbours do at home . . .'

'And what they don't know they make up,' added Joy. 'Try not to worry about tonight. I'll be there to hold your hand,' she said.

Eadie smiled. 'Anyway, it's been a good day so far, for you, hasn't it, ducky?

'Yes,' said Joy, with a grin. Into her mind came Queenie's prophecy about her aura. What was it the old woman had said? Starting today her luck would change. Well, she was certainly right, wasn't she? Perhaps Queenie really could foretell the future. She tossed another handful of ripe hops into the bin.

Chapter Twelve

Eadie pushed Billy's pram along the well-trodden pathway fronting the huts towards number 122, occupied by Pat and her family. Dogs and children ran everywhere. She smiled and spoke to hoppers she knew who were busying themselves at their fires or relaxing outside.

She said to Joy, 'That shower we had as we left work has softened the earth and made the air a little fresher, thank God. Maybe there won't be so many kids messing about in the stream at the rear of our hut. Maureen said Farmer Southern's fed up with shouting at 'em for hanging around that smelly pond at the back of his house.' The pram juddered as it encountered a puddle. Eadie wrenched it free. 'The pram wheels are clogging up.'

'Won't take long to knock the mud off when we get back

to our hut,' replied Joy. 'I'll sort it out, if you get Billy ready for sleep.'

'There's not an ounce of sleep in him!' said Eadie.

Billy was sitting up taking notice of the colourful leaves on the trees, his little arms waving, as if he was conducting an orchestra. Tucked at the bottom of the pram was a large bag of apples, a cauliflower and some carrots, courtesy of Maureen for Pat.

'Look at the berries on that rowan tree. Queenie says the Romany folk make rowan jelly . . .'

'I've made that, Joy, it's not difficult. What's difficult with the war on is getting hold of enough sugar.'

'Such a lovely colour, those orange-red berries. I'd love a lipstick that shade.'

'One day, maybe, when the war's over, ducky.' Eadie smiled at Joy. Then her voice took on a more serious note. 'In that letter I scribbled to Joe tonight, I asked him not to let on to Mick that Maureen's here with us. That's if Mick goes banging on our door again because he hasn't already found out where she is. He was drunk, so Joe wrote, cursing and swearing. Joe sent him off with a flea in his ear.'

'Good! She's better off without him. Maureen's blossomed like a summer flower in the time we've been here, Eadie. So have you!'

Maybe it was working in the fresh air and feeling the sun on her skin, instead of being enclosed in an armaments factory, handling explosives day after day, that helped Joy, too, to look better and feel good about herself. Receiving Jim's letter had put a permanent smile on her face and Eadie was so happy for her. Up ahead she could see Pat bending over the fire, stirring a pot. Pat, sensing their arrival, looked up and waved. A heavenly meaty smell drifted along the path. The Romany folk, Eadie knew, were a reliable source of fresh rabbits, trapping and selling them to the hop-pickers. Often Queenie's people could obtain foodstuffs the village store had run out of.

Pat's ample stomach was covered with the sacking apron most of the women wore to work in the fields. Eadie stared in amazement at Pat's seating arrangements set about the glowing fire. From somewhere she'd managed to get hold of an old sagging sofa that was partly covered with a tarpaulin – to ward off further rain, Eadie guessed. Inventively Pat had also set a plank on top of small stacks of bricks, making a long seat. She needed it with four children. The whole scene looked inviting, thought Eadie.

'That's a damn good idea, that long seat, ducky,' said Eadie to Joy. 'Beats sitting on the grass like we do.' Then she added, 'Here comes Chatterbox!'

Marlene was hurtling along the path towards them, her tawny hair flying in all directions. Breathlessly she asked, 'Can I push the pram?'

Eadie stepped aside. 'Watch the potholes,' she advised, as Marlene took her place. Eadie couldn't see Mikey or the two young ones. 'Where's your brothers?' she asked.

Marlene, her hands already on the pram handle and gazing lovingly at Billy, said, 'The twins are up at the Romany camp. Fascinated by the ponies, they are. One of the girls is looking after them. Mikey's gone down the pond with his mate.'

Joy butted in: 'Farmer Southern doesn't like the kids being there.'

'He's gotta catch 'em first,' laughed Marlene. 'It's nice to play in the water to cool off,' she added, 'even if it is a bit smelly.'

Eadie thought about the cows that stood about 'cooling off' in the pond water, and shuddered.

Pat was now waving frantically at her visitors. 'Cooee!' she called. 'Just in time! The rabbit's falling off its bones!'

Eadie waved back, just as Vinnie, his little daughter Ivy at his side, stepped from Pat's hut. He was carrying a pile of white bowls. She was uneasy at seeing him – twice in one day, when previously she'd not set eyes on him since leaving him in the Vine and walking back to the hut in the dark. Her heart began beating so fast she was sure everyone could hear it. Why, she wondered, when he discovered Pat had invited her to eat tonight, had he turned up as well? Hadn't they agreed not to see each other?

Vinnie saw her, became flustered and stepped sideways knocking against Ivy, who had the biggest white cat Eadie had ever seen, dangling from her small arms. Ivy fell, the cat flew from her near-stranglehold and disappeared into the open door of the next hut. The pile of enamel bowls clattered to the ground.

'Damn!' shouted Vinnie.

Ivy, now sitting on the ground, let out an angry little-girl shout: 'Come back, Spitfire!'

Vinnie crouched, checking Ivy wasn't hurt. He pulled her to her feet and kissed her forehead. Then he gathered up the white bowls with their blue rims and announced brightly, 'Good job they're enamel and not bone china!'

Ivy had scuttled to the other hut still calling her cat. Eadie, seeing no real harm had befallen anyone, walked over to the elderly sofa, pulled back the tarpaulin, let it drop on the grass, then sat down. Joy stood watching, totally bemused.

Marlene was now making Billy chuckle playing peekaboo with him and his grubby knitted rabbit.

Pat, who was still laughing, managed a straight face, and asked Vinnie, 'And your next trick will be?'

'You didn't have to put on a show just because we're coming for a meal,' Joy broke in, going over to Vinnie and taking the bowls from him. Spying a washed tea towel draped over a bush along with some other items drying in the sun, she began wiping each bowl of any accrued dirt. 'I remember you from Fareham station,' she said to Vinnie.

'That's right,' he answered.

From her seat on the sofa Eadie could see Pat was listening avidly to them.

Vinnie didn't look very comfortable talking to Joy.

Pat could be persuasive. Had she got the two of them together because she'd somehow heard gossip about them? Vinnie had asked Pat who Eadie was, hadn't he? That would have suggested he was interested in her, wouldn't it? Stop it, she told herself, you're looking for problems where there aren't any.

Vinnie had been carrying enough bowls for all of them. He knew she and Joy were expected for a meal. He was staying in the next hut, wasn't he? For that's where Ivy and the cat had disappeared to. He had been shocked, though, to come out of Pat's hut and see her. It had surprised him. She thought back to the glorious evening they'd spent together.

Hadn't Vinnie told her then that Pat was looking after his children? Pat had obviously taken him under her wing, which was a kind and neighbourly thing for a good-hearted but nosy woman to do, Eadie thought.

Eadie told herself there was no hidden agenda in Pat inviting her and Vinnie to sit and eat together. She must act naturally and not arouse suspicion, despite her heart beating so erratically at the sight and nearness of him. After all, it had been her decision to end their relationship before it had properly started, hadn't it? The possible fallout and its effect on Joe and Will would be too horrendous even to imagine, had she continued to meet the man she'd inexplicably fallen for.

Why, then, couldn't she stop thinking about that evening?

The intense pleasure they'd shared in each other's bodies? The deep kisses full of acute longing? The way he'd caressed every inch of her? Satiating her desires, which had lain dormant for so long? Making her feel like a woman again?

Looking at him now, she was aware that he, too, was remembering every moment.

She hoped when they chatted it wouldn't be obvious to Pat that she and Vinnie knew each other intimately. Well, she'd soon find out because Vinnie was making his way towards her, under the eagle eyes of Pat, who was still methodically stirring the large pot over the fire.

'Pat,' called Eadie, 'if you look in the bottom of Billy's pram, you'll find some bits and bobs Maureen sent.'

Pat nodded. 'I'm dishing up now. I'll be there in a minute. You be sure to thank her for me.'

Vinnie sat next to Eadie. 'It gave me quite a shock seeing you today again.' His voice was hardly more than a whisper.

'So I saw.' The corners of her mouth turned up in a smile. 'It's the same for me,' she confessed. 'If I'd known you'd be here I could have returned your lighter.'

She spoke as softly as she could to make sure she wasn't overheard.

She wanted to tell him she'd watched carefully for him as the pickers moved from field to field. She'd been eager to catch even a glimpse of him or his children, even though she'd said that on no account must they meet again. She'd searched, too, among the revellers at the Spotted Cow when Joy had dragged her there.

Eadie had a sudden urge to grab Vinnie by his shoulders and smother him with kisses. Of course, she did no such thing. She sat quite still, daring herself not to move closer or to touch him, even though she could almost taste his maleness enhanced by the enticing vanilla and cedar scent.

She was reminded of Gainsborough's *Blue Boy* print and the hunger in the youth's eyes as he stared at his beloved

Pinkie, framed on the opposite wall of her home in Gosport. A couple so near to each other and yet so far away.

'You look fantastic,' Vinnie whispered, then quite loudly, 'How are you liking hop-picking? Bit late, though, in asking, now it's coming to an end.'

'If the occasion arises, I'd return.' Eadie looked towards Pat, who she was sure was unobtrusively listening. Joy was setting out the dishes for her to fill with stew. A large loaf had already been cut to accompany it. 'Field work's different from anything I've ever done before.'

'Cigarette?' Vinnie offered Eadie an open packet of Player's Navy Cut.

'This is where I came in, isn't it?' whispered Eadie. Then, 'I won't, thank you. We're just going to eat.' She and Vinnie were the only smokers.

'Sit down and eat, whoever intends to eat,' Pat called, ladling stew into dishes. She passed food to Marlene, who had pushed the pram closer to the wooden bench so baby Billy wouldn't feel left out. Joy stood near Pat and nodded towards Eadie, signalling she should sit where she was and Joy would serve her and Vinnie. Next to Vinnie, Ivy had snuggled in, clutching Spitfire, who seemed totally at ease with it all. The cat was no doubt expecting rabbit titbits, thought Eadie. She remembered Tim telling her at the station that Ivy couldn't sleep unless Spitfire was near her. She smiled at the little girl, who grinned back. Ivy's smile clutched at Eadie's heart.

'Ivy won't be able to eat a full bowl,' called Vinnie.

'I'm aware of that!' chided Pat.

Vinnie pulled a face at Eadie, making her laugh. She was beginning to unwind and enjoy Pat's hospitality.

Eadie swallowed a spoonful of the thick stew. Not only did it smell heavenly, it tasted wonderful. 'This hits the spot, Pat,' she called. 'Pity Mikey's missing out.'

'I told the little beggars to be back in time to eat,' Pat shouted back, 'but there'll be plenty left for when he and Tim finally decide to come home.'

Staying next door to each other, of course, the two boys, Vinnie's Tim and Pat's Mikey, would have palled up, Eadie thought.

Joy sat on the bench near Pat. 'Will you come again next year?' she asked, putting a spoonful of stew into her mouth. She chewed and swallowed. 'This is really tasty, Pat,' she said.

'I expect so. I come most years. The weeks are passing quickly this time.'

'What happens to the bines after they've been picked clean?' Joy wondered. 'Does the farmer dig them out and plant new ones for the next year?'

Pat paused in wiping her bowl with a chunk of bread. 'God, no! The bines re-grow for about twenty years before they need replacing.'

'Really?' Joy was amazed.

Pat loved explaining things. 'They'll be cut down while the bines are still pliable, until around the first frost. The Romany folk make hop garlands from the bines, supposed to bring good luck, they are. Of course, the wreaths and garlands smell lovely. But back in the fields, the hop plant is making new growth after being chopped to one or two feet from the ground and being smothered in a layer of mulch for the winter. And so the whole process starts again. Like I said, the hops can flourish for maybe twenty years but then the fields are dug and left fallow to recuperate.'

Joy stared at her. 'You're a fount of knowledge, Pat,' she exclaimed.

Pat preened. 'I been comin' hopping for ever, it seems,' she said. 'God willing, it'll go on and so will I. You want some more stew?'

Joy shook her head. 'I'm stuffed,' she said.

'Lovely meal,' said Eadie. 'I've eaten fresher food here than I have at home.' She was making conversation. She'd been too quiet, too guarded, sitting on the sofa next to

Vinnie, fearful of someone, anyone, seeing how his close-ness was affecting her.

As if reading her thoughts, Vinnie whispered, 'Don't doubt my feelings for you. Change your mind, please?'

He was asking her to spend time with him before hop-picking ended. Eadie looked at him, at the face she'd seen so many times in her dreams. Oh, how she wanted to nod instead of shaking her head, ever so slightly, in the hope that Pat wouldn't observe it. Her eyes met his. He couldn't disguise his disappointment. She looked away. It just wasn't in her nature to be more selfish than she'd already been in hurting Will and Joe. Even though being with Vinnie was what she wanted more than anything.

'I'll collect empty dishes, shall I?' Her voice quivered as she rose from the sofa. Bravely smiling at Billy, sitting up in his pram, Eadie said brightly, 'Next year, Billy-boy, you won't be depending on your mum. You'll be eating Auntie Pat's tasty rabbit stew as well . . .'

She'd hardly got the words out when—

'Dad! Dad! A Romany boy nearly drowned!' Tim, his outsize cap damp and low on his forehead, flew from a gap between the huts towards the sofa and threw his arms around Vinnie's neck. His clothes were wet and a stale musty smell came from him.

Eadie picked up Vinnie's empty bowl as it fell from his hands. Ivy looked most disgruntled.

Mikey was close on Tim's heels. He, too, was wet. 'The boy was in the middle of the pond waving his arms about,' Mikey yelled excitedly. 'We thought he was muckin' about because he kept disappearing for stuff we was throwin' in the water. It's really deep in that bit! She just dived straight in, no messin', an' stopped him going under again. She lugged him to the mud an' thumped his chest until he spewed up. Ugh!' He was excited, his words garbled.

'Mikey, slow down!' Pat grabbed hold of her son and gently clamped his arms, which he was excitedly waving all over the place, to his sides. 'Slowly, now, tell us what happened.'

Tim, in the safety of his father's embrace, took over talking. 'It was that Maureen woman what works in Farmer Southern's garden.' He looked at Eadie. 'What lives with you.' Then he turned to Joy and said, 'She can't 'alf swim good!'

'Our Maureen?' Joy's forehead was creased in disbelief. She looked at Eadie, who stared open-mouthed.

Mikey wriggled out of Pat's clutches. He blew out his cheeks. 'I wish I could swim like that!'

'Tim,' said Vinnie, 'slow down a bit.' He stared hard at the lad. 'Now tell me if I've got this straight. Earlier tonight a young Romany boy was saved from drowning in the pond by Maureen, Eadie and Joy's friend?' Tim nodded.

'Yeah!' Mikey chimed in.

'Where's the lad now?' Vinnie asked.

'Got taken to hospital,' said Mikey. 'His dad went wiv him. You know Eli who sorts out the hoppin' lines.'

'But he's all right,' Tim carried on. 'The ambulance man said best to take him because the pond's piloted . . .'

'Polluted, you nitwit,' said Mikey, looking pleased with himself.

'And what about Maureen?' Vinnie stared at Tim.

'Oh! She's all right. She went into the farmhouse for a cuppa,' Tim said. 'We was all told to clear orf and not come back. There's nobody there now.'

Tim added, in a gruff voice, obviously an imitation of the farmer, 'Clear orf back to your 'uts!' He shrugged. 'Can I have something to eat? I'm starving.'

'You can both have some food, but not before you've washed off all that stinking pond water.' Pat had substituted the stew-pot for a large pan of water that was heating nicely.

'Tim stinks,' said Ivy, sliding away from her father. Spitfire was busy with a rabbit bone a short distance from the sofa.

'I agree, Ivy,' said Vinnie. In a soft, caring voice Eadie

heard him say to his son, 'You sure you're all right? Not hurt in any way? You haven't swallowed any of that foul pond water?'

'Nah, I'm just hungry,' answered Tim.

Eadie had watched Pat pour the heated water into two separate washing bowls.

'Cor!' said Mikey. 'You usually makes me wash in cold water!'

'Yeah! Being in that dirty pond you needs to scrub yourself properly.' She handed him a steaming bowl. 'Now, get yourself into the hut and give yourself a good going over.' As he walked away carefully, carrying the bowl, Pat shouted, 'An' wash your hair!'

'Can I trust you to clean yourself properly, hair as well?' Vinnie asked Tim. 'You'll need to remove that cap first!' He was now standing over him with a similar bowl of water.

Tim looked at his father scathingly. 'I'm not a little kid!' he answered, taking the bowl and walking towards their hut with it, careful not to let himself down by spilling any water.

Pat turned to Eadie, who had taken Billy from his pram and was now in the process of removing his wet nappy. She'd moved from the sofa and now sat on the wooden plank. Billy's legs were waving about. The smell of talcum powder filled the air, and Billy was giggling because Eadie kept blowing on his tummy.

'After all that excitement I think I'll brew some tea,' Pat said.

'None for me,' Eadie said, removing the nappy pin from her teeth so she could talk. 'If you don't mind, Pat, I'd like to get back to the hut to see if Maureen's all right.'

'Fair enough,' said Pat, watching her fasten the nappy. 'I know I haven't seen as much of you two, or Maureen and her little one, as I'd have liked but it's not so easy when our huts aren't close and we're working in different fields.'

She went over to Joy and hugged her, then bent and kissed Eadie, who was pulling up Billy's rubber pants. 'You know where I am if you need anything,' she said. 'And thank Maureen for the fruit and veg. Tell her I think she's very brave.'

'You're a good friend,' Eadie said, buckling the baby back into his pram.

Ivy threw herself at Eadie. Her nose wasn't running like it had been at Fareham station. She'd definitely put on weight since then and looked very healthy.

'Do you like Spitfire? He was in the basket before. He scratched your ankle but you only saw his paw, not all of him,' the little girl said. The white cat in question had discovered another discarded rabbit bone nearby and was crunching it noisily.

Eadie knelt down to her level. 'Of course I like Spitfire. But I like you best of all,' she said, putting her arms around the little girl and holding her tightly. Ivy's blonde curls smelt of Amami shampoo. She pushed away her longing for a child just like her.

When Eadie released Ivy, she saw Marlene had turned the pram around and moved it a little way along the path in the direction they were to go.

Joy had already said her goodbyes and was waiting for her.

'Perhaps I'll see you again,' Eadie said to Vinnie, who was standing close by. 'Though I doubt it.' She wanted to tell him her heart was hurting because she had to leave him. She said nothing more.

He leaned forward and whispered in her ear, 'Remember, Eadie, there's no substitute for what you really want.'

Eadie turned and walked quickly towards Joy so no one else would see the tears in her eyes.

Chapter Thirteen

Joy thrust open the hut's door then pushed the pram inside. Eadie went over and lit the lamp.

'The evenings are getting darker, aren't they?' Joy said. Then, 'I expected Maureen to be here.'

'It's near his lordship's feed time so she won't be long,' Eadie said, nodding towards Billy. She shook the kettle, decided there was enough water for making tea and set it to boil on the stove. 'Today might be a special day when she saves a little boy's life but, you can depend on it, she won't let her own lad down.'

She faced Joy. 'I'm going to tell Maureen there's a possibility her husband might come here.'

'I thought we'd decided not to say anything. Aren't you being a hypocrite? You want to keep your evening of passion a secret but think Maureen deserves to worry herself stupid about when her husband's coming to bash—'

'Oh! When's that gonna be, then?' Maureen stood in the doorway, her face inscrutable.

'Bugger!' The oath left Eadie's mouth.

'So, you both know something I don't?' snapped Maureen. 'What happened to the Three Musketeers, "All for one and one for all"?'

Billy began to whimper and Eadie moved towards him.

'I'll see to him, Eadie. He needs feeding,' Maureen said coldly. She went to the pram and unbuckled Billy from his harness. Joy thought the atmosphere inside the hut could have been cut with a knife. It was probably what had made Billy anxious. Maureen swept towards the bed, sat down with her baby and began unbuttoning the front of her dress. He began to suckle hungrily.

On the other side of the room Eadie was making tea. Maureen asked, 'What's all this about?'

Joy said, 'You started it, Eadie. You finish it!' She saw Maureen's damp hair was tied back off her face and she was wearing different clothes from what she'd had on earlier.

Eadie jammed the lid onto the teapot. 'In the letter I had from home,' she said, 'your Mick went round to Joe and Will, on the rampage, looking for you. We don't know whether Joe told him you might be with us.'

'It's not me he wants. It's his money. But if he can clout me one while he gets it back it'll stop his mates laughing at him.'

'We didn't want you worried, Maureen. You've been so happy, like a different person, since you've been here.'

Maureen transferred Billy to her other breast.

'I thought you ought to know, Maureen. Be prepared, like . . .' Eadie sighed.

The stirring of tea in mugs and Billy feeding were the only sounds in the hut until Maureen finally said, 'I'd have probably done the same . . .'

Eadie took her a mug of tea and set it on the floor beside her. Then she put her arms around Maureen and Billy. 'Thank you,' she said. She stood back and surveyed Maureen. 'So, you're a life-saver now? Well done! Are you all right? How's the boy?'

'One question at a time, please!' Maureen laughed. 'They took him to hospital, as a precaution. He must have swallowed half that filthy pond.' She paused. 'The Romany kids are sharp as knives but hardly any of 'em learns to swim. It was Queenie's great-grandson, Vano, Eli's boy.'

'You'll be for ever in Queenie's good books,' said Joy,

after Maureen's words had sunk in. 'Did she give you that new dress you got on?'

Maureen shook her head. 'This is one of Betty Southern's cast-offs. When I took mine to dry off afterwards, it crawled into the dustbin on its own! They wanted me to go in the ambulance, but I told 'em I'd be all right after a wash down. I've had another bath!' She glanced down at Billy, flopped contentedly against her. 'C'mon, little man,' she said. 'You can't go to sleep until you're clean and changed. Will you do the honours, Eadie?'

Eadie grinned. Maureen delivered Billy into her arms, did up her dress, then bent down and picked up her mug of tea. A flurry of rain hit the corrugated-iron roof.

'Sounds like mini pieces of shrapnel, doesn't it?' said Joy.

'Thank God, it isn't,' said Maureen. 'This breathing space without bombs falling is wonderful.'

The wind increased sending tiny fingers of a chilling breeze into the hut. The rain was heavier now.

'Might need to wrap up a bit more tomorrow,' surmised Joy. 'The bines will be soaking and sticky.'

'Have you written back to that airman?' Maureen set down her mug.

Joy shook her head. She looked at Eadie undressing a relaxed, sleepy boy and smiled. 'I'm not going to answer

Jim's letter. I don't know what to say because there's so many questions going around in my head about him being shot down, about his injuries, about everything, really . . . I've decided, if it's all right with you two, that I'll go and see him.' Joy waited for an answer, any answer.

Eadie looked up from pinning a clean nappy on Billy. 'I think that's a sensible thing to do.'

'Does that mean if his injuries are really bad you needn't see him again?'

Joy stared at Maureen. 'That's a bloody awful thing to suggest!' Tears prickled the backs of her eyelids.

'No, it's not. Women do that all the time so they don't get lumbered with looking after blokes back from the war with disabilities . . .' Maureen's voice petered out. Then, 'Oh, God, I'm sorry, Eadie. I didn't think before I opened my big trap.'

Eadie was cuddling Maureen's drowsy child to her chest. She rose, taking him over to the pram, laying him down gently so he wouldn't wake. Then she covered him with his knitted blanket and set the floppy rabbit near him. Finally, she said, 'You're right, Maureen. Women do it all the time to make life easier for themselves. They know whether they can cope or not with their men who come back from fighting with such horrific injuries. I saw men delivered unendurable

pain from their supposed loved ones' lips when I was visiting
Will in hospital at Croydon . . .' She shrugged. 'Actually, it's
probably the best thing a woman can do, to walk away from
a man she can't love again. For both of them.'

Eadie moved to the kitchen area and put her hand on the
teapot to see if it was still warm.

Maureen was across to her immediately and her arms
went around her. 'I'm so sorry! Eadie, forgive me.'

Eadie pushed her away gently. 'Of course I do!' She
breathed out slowly, then said, 'Look, it's been a long day
for all of us. I vote we have another cup of tea, then turn
in. After this rain it'll be an awful day picking tomorrow and
we need all the rest we can get.'

Maureen said, 'I'll put together the stuff we need for
work and breakfast.'

'No,' Eadie answered. 'We'll do that. You've been busy
saving a life while we've sat about eating rabbit stew. You
just sort yourself out. I'm going outside for a fag.'

'Don't be daft! It's pouring.'

Joy grabbed Maureen's arm. 'Let her go!' Joy watched
Eadie slide out of the door with her cigarettes in her hand.
When she'd gone, she looked at Maureen. 'Like us, she's got
a lot on her mind,' was all she said. A gust of rain splattered
against the corrugated front of the hut.

Later, when Maureen was dozing comfortably on her palliasse and Billy was spread-eagled, fast asleep, in his pram, Joy finished filling the bottles with fresh water to drink in the fields. She looked at the enticing bed with her copy of *Picturegoer* lying ready for her to read. Anne Baxter was still smiling beguilingly on the front cover. At this rate, Joy thought, she'd be taking the magazine home unread. More rain fell against the door. She doused the paraffin lamp, lit a candle that was sitting ready and left it burning as she made her way to the door and peeped outside.

'Psst! I'm over here.'

It took a moment for Joy's eyes to discover in the darkness where 'here' was. The glow of her cigarette gave Eadie away. Tucked in the small space between two huts, with a sheet of tin overhead, warding off the rain, Eadie sat smoking on a tea chest.

As Joy slid in beside her, Eadie moved up.

'You've got a little den here, haven't you?' Joy said. 'Are you all right?'

Eadie put a cold hand on Joy's warm arm. 'I am now. I just needed to escape.'

'We all do, at times,' Joy said.

There was a moment when neither woman spoke and Joy, eyes now accustomed to the dark, watched the rain hitting the huts then falling to the ground and running in rivulets down the path. 'I shouldn't have said I wasn't going to write back to Jim . . .'

'Don't be daft! You danced with the bloke once. Neither of you really knows the other. All right, a thunderbolt might have hit the pair of you and persuaded you there could be more to it. But until you really know the bloke you can't make any promises. And don't forget, he's hampered in saying what he really means by needing someone else to write his letters for him. I think you're being very wise in going to see him first.'

'Really?'

Eadie blew out a stream of smoke. 'Really. D'you want me to come with you?'

Joy stared at her. 'You'd do that for me?'

'Well, you don't know where you're going, do you? I don't mean I'll come in and visit. I'll wait for you in a café somewhere.'

Joy said, 'That's really nice, that is! I'd like that.'

'That's settled then. You decide when. Mr Southern surely won't give us the sack for missing one day. After all, it's our own pockets we're hurting by not earning, isn't it?' She doused her cigarette and put the dog-end back in the packet of Woodbines. 'C'mon, we'd better go in. If Maureen isn't asleep, she'll be worrying. I reckon she's had enough excitement for one day, don't you?'

'Actually, there's something else I want to say,' Joy said.

'Oh? What's that?'

'The next time you say, "We'll clear up," you can stay in the hut to do it!'

'That fire was a devil to light this morning,' moaned Maureen. 'Good job we always keep some dry sticks in the hut. You might want to bring a cardigan or jumper to the fields today. It's not as warm as yesterday.'

Joy wrapped the last of the bacon doorsteps in cloth and pressed them into the dinner tin. She shivered. She could hear plane engines growing louder by the second.

Children were shouting! She waited with bated breath for the awful crumps the bombs made when they fell to earth. The planes were closer now, practically overhead. People were cheering! She moved to the door of the hut. Pickers and kids thronged the muddy path, waving, shouting words of encouragement, gesticulating wildly, while gazing and pointing heavenwards.

Joy raised her eyes to the sky. The weak sunshine bouncing off the iconic shapes made their metal bodies glisten. Spitfires – too many for her to count as she stood clutching the tin that contained their bacon sandwiches. Her heart lifted with happiness, with pride. Those weren't damaged planes returning from battle. They were shiny, whole Spitfires being flown to—

'Where are they going?' Joy cried.

A woman in a bright red headscarf was holding the hand of a little girl. Her other hand shielded her eyes against the sunlight. 'I think they're flying to Middle Wallop airfield. Loads of Spitfires there!' Then she and her child were waving and blowing kisses as the small planes passed overhead, the engine sounds fading the further they flew. 'That's a lovely sight to start the day,' the woman said, moving off. Her huge smile endorsed her words.

Joy had to agree. As the people quietened and began to shuffle along to the hopping fields, she wondered if Lancaster bombers flew from Middle Wallop, which had to be, she supposed, a nearby airfield. She thought about Jim. He'd flown his Lancaster from Scampton in Lincolnshire, hadn't he? Had people waved and shouted good wishes to him?

'Hey! Dilly Daydream!' shouted Eadie. 'You coming to work today or are you going to stand in that hut doorway lookin' gormless?'

Maureen and Eadie were waiting for her. Joy closed the hut door behind her.

Joy gasped and lifted the *Portsmouth Evening News* from the train carriage's seat.

A picture of Maureen looking bedraggled gazed up at her from the front page.

'Woman Saves Child,' it proclaimed. In the background there was an ambulance.

'Will you look at that!' she said, thrusting the newspaper at Eadie, who had slipped off her black court shoe to rub her bunion.

She studied the picture. 'It's a good likeness,' she said, pushing her foot back into its torture chamber as the carriage began filling with sailors and kitbags. 'Someone took that photo at the scene,' she said. 'I wonder who . . .'

'Doesn't matter who photographed her!' Joy said crossly, grabbing the paper back and moving nearer the window so a tall sailor in blue could squeeze in beside her. 'Everyone in Gosport buys the *News*. Not only is Maureen's face plastered on the front but so is the name of the farm and where it is—'

'Are there direct words from Maureen?' interrupted Eadie. She looked across the carriage at Joy. Joy's forehead wrinkled.

Joy shook her head as she read through the story again. 'No.'

'Then I'm betting Maureen didn't know it would be published. Someone probably sent the story in. Maureen doesn't want Mick to know where she is. Now everyone in Hampshire who reads that paper knows she's in Selborne . . .'

'Including everyone in Gosport,' Joy said.

'Exactly!' answered Eadie. She tutted. 'At least Joe won't carry all the blame now when Mick comes looking for her.'

Joy sat back in her seat and stared out of the window at the countryside. There wasn't much point in trying to carry on a conversation with Eadie because there were too many servicemen, other adults and children in the carriage now, laughing and talking.

Cigarette smoke stung her eyes and her sense of smell was being attacked on all sides by sweat, perfume and musty, grubby kitbags slung on the overhead luggage racks and taking up space on the floor, which was already covered with detritus. She tore the front page from the newspaper and slipped it into her handbag beside the letter from Jim. She tucked the rest of the newspaper behind her on the seat.

She and Eadie had risen this morning while it was still dark. After previously arranging a lift to Petersfield station on the Southerns' cart, which was delivering meat, they'd boarded the first of the two trains necessary for the long journey to Albrighton, Shropshire. From the pub in the village square a bus would drop them at Cosford RAF hospital.

All the time she and Eadie had been planning their journey, Joy had been excited, eager, now she knew Jim was alive, to see him. At present, sitting in the bus that meandered through pretty country lanes, passing half-timbered houses that looked as though they'd been drawn in a book of fairy tales, Joy had become apprehensive.

'Suppose, after talking for a while, we decide we don't have anything in common.'

'Joy, ducky, that's why you're seeing him face to face. It's too easy to allow a relationship to grow on paper when you have no real idea of how the other person reacts to you. And vice versa.'

'I'm just edgy, I suppose.'

'I'm sure if Jim knew you were arriving, he'd feel exactly the same.' Eadie, sitting beside her, covered Joy's hands with her own for consolation.

The bus pulled into a clearing near a long, tree-lined driveway. The name of the hospital was barely visible behind bushes at the side of the road.

'You make a mental note of return times from the driver,'

said Joy. 'My head's all over the place.' Then, she asked, after alighting from the vehicle, 'Do I look all right?'

'You look like a golden girl with that suntanned skin. Your hair is prettier than Lizabeth Scott's and that blue dress fits you where it touches. What more do you want?'

The driver tooted the horn as he drove away. They were the only passengers who had left the bus.

Eadie waved towards the imposing stone house at the end of the enormously long drive. 'You should be asking me if my bunion will be killing me by the time we get there! And there'd better be somewhere for me to get a cuppa and a sit-down with a fag while you're chatting with Jim.' Eadie pushed her arm through Joy's.

Huts were tucked into verdant lawn areas alongside the building, rose gardens too. The scent, blown on the breeze, was heady in the heat of the sun.

'My eyes are filled with colour,' said Eadie. 'It's a beautiful setting for a hospital.'

Joy saw, way up on the grass, umbrellas shading wooden loungers that were dotted about the grounds. Some were in full sun, others beneath trees. Most contained reclining patients. Blue-clad nurses were in attendance. It was a peaceful scene.

'Perhaps I should have written back,' she said. 'Perhaps we shouldn't have just turned up.'

'Don't be daft! It's a hospital! Visitors are encouraged,' Eadie said. Just then a vehicle horn beeped behind them. Eadie clutched at her chest with one hand as if she was experiencing a heart attack and pushed Joy to the side of the driveway with the other. A red Morris mail van halted beside them in a flurry of dust. A burly, bespectacled postman in a peaked cap shouted through the wound-down window, 'Want a lift?'

'You're an angel!' called Eadie. She had the door open and was clambering inside while Joy was still collecting her thoughts. Joy sighed. There was nothing for it but to follow her friend, so she squeezed inside.

'It's a long walk, this one,' said the man, accelerating.

Eadie winked at Joy. 'Not now, it isn't,' she said. 'My poor feet appreciate your kindness.'

'No problem,' he said. 'Who you visiting?'

'I forget his name . . .' Eadie began.

The man let out a guffaw of laughter.

Joy interrupted, 'Jim Tremaine.'

'Oh, I know Jimbo! The bomb aimer.'

'What's he really like?' Joy asked him. She was glad she and Eadie had come to the right place.

'Bit shy. Not a womanizer like a lot of the Brylcreem boys.' He slipped his hand into an inside pocket and brought out a packet of ten Player's Weights. One-handed, he flicked open the top and shook the cardboard packet so the cigarettes presented themselves. He offered them first to Joy, who shook her head, then to Eadie, who took one.

'Thanks,' she said, treating him to a grin.

'Light one for me,' he said. 'Matches on the dashboard.'

Eadie took another cigarette, lit both, then passed him one. Taking it, he said, 'Thanks.' After a drag, he asked, 'You relatives?'

Joy opened her mouth to speak but before a sound came out, Eadie said quickly, 'Not exactly.'

'You're not from the papers, are you? I can tell you now, he won't see you if you are.'

Joy peered at Eadie, then frowned.

'No! He wants to see my friend here,' Eadie said.

The driver nodded. 'I'll drop you off at the side entrance nearest his room. Any nurse'll point you in the right direction.'

'Is there somewhere I can get a cuppa?' Eadie asked.

'Walk on by the side and there's a small café that caters for guests and visitors who like to sit outside,' he answered. 'You won't find Jimbo there, though.'

'Oh, doesn't he like visitors, then?' Eadie wondered.

'Would you, if all they wanted to ask you is how you managed to set them bombs bouncing towards them German dams?'

There was a moment of silence. Only the vibration of the van's engine could be heard and heavy breathing from the vehicle's occupants.

'Oh, my God!' Eadie said eventually. 'Is he . . . ?'

'You didn't know?' The postman put out his cigarette on the front panel and threw the stub out of the window. 'There's several Dam Busters recuperating here, poor devils.'

'I can't go and act naturally when I see him. He's like a film star! He's famous!'

Eadie grabbed Joy's shoulders and shook her. A man hobbling along the hospital corridor with crutches either side of him stared at them, shocked.

'I'm not hurting her, just trying to shake some sense into her,' Eadie explained, as he tried to hurry past. 'Listen, Joy. He's the same man who had to pluck up the courage to ask you to dance. He set your heart beating fast then and none of that's changed. What's different is he's been injured doing his job and wants to see you. Are you going to deny him that?'

Eadie stepped away from the door to room ten, having banged loudly and waited for 'Come in.'

The door closed after Joy. Gathering her wits, she looked around. She took a deep breath and smiled as she stared at the man in the bed. Plaster-of-paris-covered arms lay either side of an upper body covered with what Joy supposed was a sterile sheet dressing to avoid contamination. Some sort of cage concealed his right leg. Her eyes travelled to the raised pillows.

The curly-haired man gave her a broad smile. When she saw the tiny chip in the front of his white tooth, the tiny imperfection that had tugged at her heartstrings months ago, she knew, despite everything that had happened since that night on the dance-floor, this was the man who had sent her senses reeling then and was doing the same now.

'A nurse told me you were on your way,' he said. 'Oh, Joy, I'm so happy to see you.'

She spied a chair in the corner of the highly sanitized room. His eyes had followed hers. 'Pull that up and sit next to me where I can see you properly,' he said.

When she was sitting opposite him, she wanted to lean forward and brush his dark curls back from his forehead. Apprehensively, she just sat and watched, and listened to him speak.

The nurse had already told her and Eadie that Jim discouraged visitors. Luckily, the same nurse had written the letter he'd sent to her, so when Joy showed her the envelope, a look of achievement passed across her face. 'I'm so glad you've come,' she'd said. 'And he'll be thrilled. He's told me all about you, you know.'

Now, he stared at her and said, 'You look wonderful. Tell me everything you've been doing. How's work in the armaments factory? Did you have a good journey up from Gosport?'

Joy laughed. 'Stop!' she said, breathing in the antiseptic smell. 'One question at a time, please.' She explained about the accident at Priddy's without dwelling on the severity, and told him she'd moved on to hop-picking for the season. She made him laugh telling him about Eadie's 'sister', Maureen, who was sharing their hut but was an actual godsend because they knew so little about hops. She tried to hide her hands, so he wouldn't see the discoloration the hops had caused.

He drew her attention to it, saying it was honest toil and she should be proud of it. 'I've never been hop-picking,' he confessed. 'Tell me more.'

Within minutes she had him spellbound, telling him about all the different characters she'd met, how efficient the Romany children were at riding and managing their horses and how quick at stripping the hop bines. She flitted from one subject to another, but she made him laugh and that seemed to her to be a good thing.

To Joy, it was as if the afternoon was a continuation of the short time they'd spent together on the dance-floor. Conversation batted so easily backwards and forwards between them. Only once did he interrupt and that was to say, 'It is true, isn't it, this earth-shattering feeling we have for each other?'

She nodded. 'Are you going to tell me what happened?' she asked.

It was as if a dark shadow had stolen all the brightness from his face, his demeanour. 'I'm not dwelling on what happened to me because I'm so relieved to be among the survivors. Our part in the operation was a success. But men died that night of the sixteenth–seventeenth of May. And one day I'll be as good as new with the excellent care I'm receiving. Opioids help.' He gave a small grin. 'You deserve to know about this.' He looked down at himself, at the dressings, the cage. 'I'll tell you a little,' he said.

'I'm not sure if you know what my job entails but the bomb aimer lies flat, looking through the front turret, the gun aimer directly above him. After we'd been hit, my controls failed. I managed to open the escape hatch and was confronted by roaring flames. Fuel tanks had been hit and were on fire. I had a seat-type parachute so didn't need to look for a stored one. I was lucky.' Again he looked down at himself. 'The burns will heal,' he said. 'So, too, will the bones. I'm a lucky bloke and I know it.' He gazed at her. 'I'm even luckier now my prayers have been answered and you're here.'

Joy was aware he'd told her all he was going to about that night. She wanted to kiss his forehead, his cheek, show him she was glad to be with him, glad he'd been able at least to speak a little of his trauma. Unsure of the correct hospital procedure for compassionate touching she refrained. 'Can I ask why you were in Gosport the night we met?'

'A funeral,' he said. 'My beloved grandmother, Nana, was buried that morning in Alverstoke. She wouldn't have wanted me to sit alone moping in her house. She'd have said, "Remember the good times and go out and make some more," so when I spotted the advertisement in the paper about the dance I decided to pop in for a while . . . and you happened along.'

'We've got fifteen minutes before the bus comes, Joy, else we'll miss all our connections.' Eadie's loud voice seemed to bounce about the room.

'That's telling you!' Jim said. 'If that's your friend banging on the door she'll break it down in a few minutes.' He laughed. 'Please say you'll come again, please, please?'

Joy got up from the chair. 'I'll come again,' she said.

Joy smiled into the darkness at the crackle the straw made as Eadie mumbled, then turned over on the palliasse. At least she wasn't moaning about the pain her bunion was giving her. The two of them had walked miles today, visiting Jim at Cosford RAF hospital and it was, to her, worth every step. She held her breath as Billy snuffled, then went on breathing steadily in his sleep, close to his mum. Joy thought how lovely it was lying there thinking about the young airman.

As soon as she returned home to Gosport after the hop-picking was over, she planned on visiting him again. And of course she would write. Already in her head she'd begun planning a letter. There was a big drawback, though. Jim had explained how he'd earned the massive burns that covered practically the whole of the front of his body as he'd managed to open the escape hatch of his plane to parachute to safety. His bravery was about so much more than fighting for his country. His courage was in refusing to be daunted by the severity of those injuries and burns.

Seeing Jim lying in that hospital bed, practically helpless, she'd had to steel herself from showing even a little outward shock and pity. She could see why he'd needed the kindness of a nurse to write the letter she'd received. For some time to come, he would need help even with the simple tasks of opening and holding a letter. Yet as soon as Joy had heard his voice, caught a glimpse of that small imperfection in his front tooth, she knew her feelings for him had not diminished one iota. Outward imperfections meant nothing to her. The man lying in that bed was everything to her.

Of course, knowing a third person, probably that same caring nurse, or perhaps someone else, would be party to their letters, meant she wouldn't be able to write all she wanted to say to him. Her natural shyness meant she would have to hold back her deepest feelings until she could talk to him face to face.

Not to visit Jim as much as she wanted would be awful.

While it was true she'd be returning to Gosport with wages from the hop-picking, she had, at the moment, no prospect of other work, and household bills would need to be paid, now and in the future. She wondered if Priddy's was rehiring yet. It would be a slog finding another job but Eadie would be in the same situation. Her wages wouldn't last for ever, either. Stop it! Joy told herself. Be positive! Hadn't she been working outside in the fields at Selborne? She could do similar work when she returned home, couldn't she?

Potato picking would start soon. General farmwork? There were smallholdings and farms galore just beyond Gosport, in Fareham, Stubbington, Titchfield. She wouldn't be out of work. She'd make sure of that.

But she'd need extra money to visit Jim at Cosford. Joy deliberated for a moment. There was nothing to stop her finding evening work as well, was there? She could apply for an evening barmaid job! Yes! With so many public houses always needing part-time staff and a town full of pubs, it shouldn't be too difficult to earn enough money for train and bus fares, should it? Joy smiled to herself. Then they wouldn't need to depend on letters. Visiting Jim as often as possible meant the two of them would be able to talk freely about their hopes and dreams. Week by week Jim would heal until somehow, someday they could make more permanent plans . . .

Chapter Fourteen

'Come on, tell us what happens next, Maureen.' Eadie sniffed the misty September air as she pushed Billy's pram along the muddy path. 'Not going to be as warm today, girls, not at all,' she added. 'Picking will be wet until the bines dry off.'

The long noisy caterpillar of pickers was now travelling in the opposite direction to the fields where they had first started picking weeks ago. The bines growing furthest from the Southerns' farmhouse had been stripped and left to dry off, and the workers were now picking closer to their huts and the pond. Eadie was curious to know exactly what happened to the pokes of hops after they were collected from the fields. 'You've become an absolute mine of information since working up at the farm,' Eadie added.

'Well,' said Joy, 'I never knew people could buy pillows

with hops in to help them sleep or that hop tea is said to improve a person's appetite . . .'

'I found that out from Queenie,' said Maureen. 'The Romany people know all about natural remedies . . .'

'Are you going to tell me about those funny buildings Joy and I saw from the train? The ones with cone-shaped chimneys— Blast!'

'Mind my pram!' Maureen yelled as Eadie had to yank the front wheels from a puddle across the path that was certainly deeper than it looked.

Billy, wearing a warm, hand-knitted woolly, giggled and waved his arms as he sat in his harness, happy to be tossed about by the sudden erratic movements.

'The pokes full of picked hops go from here to oast houses, or hop kilns, as we in Hampshire call them. These are one- or two-storey buildings with drying floors that are perforated so that hot air from wood or charcoal fires below can circulate about the hops until the moisture in them is dried out. The air comes from that funny shaped cowl on the kiln's roof. The wind turns it.'

'Then what?'

'I'm getting there, Joy,' Maureen snapped. 'The dried hops are bagged up in large jute sacks called pockets. When they're full they weigh about a hundred and forty pounds.

The growers' details go on the pockets. Then they go to market to be bought by the brewers. As you know, hops are used in beer-making to add flavour and act as a preservative.'

A moment of silence followed while Eadie and Joy digested Maureen's words. Then Eadie asked, 'Do we have anything to do with that final stage, the drying process?'

'Bless you, no!' Maureen said. 'Our job ends when the last field has been picked clean. We're paid then by Farmer Southern, who knows exactly how much money we're due because we've witnessed the tally-man write down the number of bushels we've picked. The wages are less any subs we've had off the farmer.'

'We've never subbed money because you, Maureen, have helped us out. You've been an angel in disguise,' said Eadie. 'Then it's back to Gosport,' she added. 'And I can have a proper bath in front of the fire, after I've dragged the tub off the nail on the wall outside in the garden, cleaned off the snails, and heated the water in the copper. I can't wait!'

Eadie felt bad remembering when she'd first heard of Maureen's arrival at the hop-fields. She'd felt jealous. She'd been worried that Maureen's presence in the hut would alter the long-standing friendship between herself and Joy. It had.

The feelings between the three women had now strengthened so much that by now they had earned their nickname:

the Three Musketeers. All for one and one for all! Eadie wondered how she could have been so mean-spirited and childish.

'Italy's surrendered!' shouted a man, waving a newspaper. 'The British have landed from the sea at the port of Taranto and now Italy's surrendered!'

Cheering erupted from the pickers.

'That's a lovely piece of news for a damp morning,' said Joy, with a broad grin. 'Bloody Hitler's not getting everything his own way.'

They'd reached their new field to be stripped of hops. It wasn't long before Joy spotted their numbered picking bin and squealed with pleasure to discover Maureen's was next to it. 'I'm glad we're together,' she said. 'We've got a good routine going between the three of us, taking turns looking after Billy.' She put her hand to her eyes to shield them from the brightness of the sun breaking through the mist and peered along the bines. 'We can see the farmhouse and that stinky old pond from here.'

Maureen was removing from the pram flasks, bottles, the tin of bacon doorsteps for their dinner, and setting stuff she thought any of them might need in a pile on the grass. Billy was dozing and she was making sure he would have uninterrupted sleep while they worked.

Eadie said, 'Maureen, it looks like you have visitors.' She could think of no reason why either she or Joy warranted a visit.

Queenie was being helped along the path towards them by Eli, who had one arm supporting his grandmother and tucked beneath his other her lightweight peacock-backed chair. Over one shoulder he carried a weighty-looking bag. Queenie relied heavily upon a stick. As soon as she saw Maureen, she said something to Eli, who spoke to the young lad trotting along beside them and he waved.

'It's the great-grandson, Vano, who I pulled out of the pond,' said Maureen, moving away from the pram, tying her sacking apron about her as she did so. 'The hospital must have discharged him. Apparently he had his stomach pumped. Don't suppose he liked that much.'

'He'd have liked it a lot less if you hadn't saved his life,' Eadie said.

Soon the three visitors were level with Maureen. The chair was set on the grass and Queenie practically fell into it. She mumbled her thanks to Eli, gave up her stick to him, then said, 'I'm not as young as I think I am.'

Maureen laughed, 'I know exactly what you mean, Queenie. Good morning to you.'

'I've brought young Vano along to thank you for saving his life.' Queenie's eyes glittered in the early sun.

The boy was standing so close to his great-grandmother that he was practically swallowed in her voluminous skirts. His usually tanned skin was pale and he was looking at his bare feet as if he'd never seen them before. He lifted his head, his brown, long-lashed eyes hinting at the heart-breaker he might eventually become. 'I shouldn't have been in the water. Thank you for saving me.'

Eadie wanted to move forward and gather him into her arms, he was so small and vulnerable. She watched as Maureen stared gravely at him then put out her hand for him to shake. Which he did with all the seriousness of a grown-up. Then he stepped back, lifted his head, and said again, 'Thank you.'

'You may go back to the others now,' Eli said. The boy turned and within seconds he'd disappeared into the mass of humanity beginning a new day's work.

Eadie could see Maureen gulp back her emotion as she said to Queenie, 'Thank you.'

'No, it's right and proper,' the old woman said. 'Life is precious.' Then she added, 'A handshake is a seal between us. You are owed. What you've done won't be forgotten. Not by me or mine.' Queenie's eyes, shining diamond-like in the sun, went towards the heavy bag on the grass. Eli picked it up and set it at Maureen's feet.

'There's two freshly caught and skinned rabbits inside and a dish of the finest and juiciest blackberries Vano picked earlier this morning from the bushes around our camp,' Queenie said. She began struggling to stand and Eli helped.

She paused, looked again at Maureen and said, 'Remember, you are owed.'

Her stick now held tightly in one hand, her arm slipped into the crook of Eli's and, with him carrying her peacock chair, light as a feather, Queenie began her regal trail to the midst of the hop-field, back to her own line and her willing young helpers.

Maureen opened up the bag and peered inside. 'Oh!'

She allowed the bag to fall around the rush basket as she lifted it out by its rope handles. Inside, ripe glossy blackberries shone. Eadie marvelled that someone had sat and woven such a pretty, yet useful container.

Automatically Maureen popped a plump berry into her mouth and revelled in the sweetness. She closed her eyes.

'Don't we get one, then?' Eadie teased.

'Sorry! I was off in a world of my own there,' Maureen confessed. She stepped towards Eadie and Joy and handed

Eadie the basket. 'They make these, I believe, and sell them door to door.'

'What? Blackberries?' Joy laughed, her hand snaking towards the fruit.

'No, these beautiful baskets,' Maureen said.

'Very clever folk,' said Eadie, slapping Joy's fingers away as she reached towards the basket a second time. 'Stop it, Greedy Guts! There'll be none left for our meal tonight the way you're going.' Joy looked chastened.

'There's a tin of cream in the hut,' Maureen said. 'Go lovely with those.' Already she was examining the cut-up pieces of rabbit, wrapped in clean cloth, smiling as she did so. 'We're going to eat well, today. Very well indeed,' she added.

Maureen began putting the food back into the bag, then twisted the top, secured it tightly and buried it beneath the base of the still damp hop bines. 'Should be cool enough there until the bell clatters for dinner,' she said. 'One of us could run the food back to the hut in case the sun warms up this afternoon. It'd be a shame to let it spoil in the heat.'

The pickers were singing as they worked and 'You Are My Sunshine' rang out across the bines. A handful of hops, thrown by Joy, landed in the bin next to Eadie. Picking had started a while ago and as yet today there was little to show that the three women had made any decent contribution towards it. Eadie took a last look towards the Spotted Cow and the field opposite, where the bonfire was growing nicely, piled with not only farm rubbish but some from the hostelry. The hopping season had begun with the fire and would end in the same way.

Eadie wouldn't have missed a moment.

'Unless I ask, you never tell me what Joe writes about in those letters you receive,' Joy said.

Eadie stared at Joy, who was wiping the few pieces of cut-lery in readiness for their evening meal. The delicious aroma of thick rabbit stew and vegetables that had crept inside the hut from the outside fire was making her feel queasy. 'Only because he made me promise to forget about everything that was happening in Gosport while I was away. He writes me only the bare essentials, the need-to-know news.' Eadie smiled at her. 'I promise you your house is still standing, still tidy, and that Joe's been watering your garden religiously because he knows how much you love your sunflowers!'

She laughed at the perplexity on Joy's face. Joy opened her mouth but Eadie stemmed her words: 'He's even collected your copies of *Picturegoer* from the newsagent for you.'

'Oh!' was Joy's eventual reply.

'Now, tell me, has knowing all that changed your world for you out here in the back of beyond?'

Joy stared at her. 'You're too clever by half,' she said. Then, 'You do realize Joe loves you?'

Eadie took a deep breath. Outside, Maureen was making clattering noises with the ladle against the side of the enormous pan that held the bubbling, fragrant stew. 'He's my father-in-law and I couldn't do without his help.' Eadie stared at Joy, still idly polishing with the tea-towel. 'You're making those spoons and forks very, very shiny,' she said. 'What's all this in aid of? Why don't you come out with what you really want to ask me instead of going all around the houses to get there?'

'All right,' Joy said. Eadie saw her glance towards the pram where Billy was fast asleep: she doubted he'd wake before tomorrow morning.

'I'm scared about everything changing if or when you tell Joe about Vinnie. Scared for you.'

Eadie stared at the girl she'd known for ever. No sound came from her as she replayed in her mind the words Joy had just spoken. Then she began to laugh, at first timidly, as if she wasn't sure whether Joy was being serious or not. Then unable to help herself even if her life depended on her answer, her laugh became a hearty roar that echoed around the small space. Tears sprang to Eadie's eyes and still her laughter rang until she noticed that tears were running down Joy's cheeks too. She stopped laughing immediately and crushed the younger woman to her body, regardless of whether Joy could breathe or not, or if the cutlery she was still gripping would stab either of them.

'Joy! This storm'll be weathered. With you beside me, I hope. Of course I have to tell Joe. I owe him that. I experienced a fit of passion on a whim with a man I'd just met. I'll never see him again. My life is in Gosport with my husband, with Joe, with you!'

Eadie pushed Joy away from her to arm's length. Joy was still gripping the cutlery and the tea-towel, which Eadie took from her clenched hand and began using to dab Joy's face, to wipe away her pain. Her voice was barely audible as she held Joy's chin, and said, 'It isn't that long since you had a nightmare in that very bed,' she looked towards it, 'and I told you I'd always be around for you. I meant what I said.' She paused. 'As for Joe and Will, Joe cares for me and I know his feelings run deeper than perhaps they should. Of course he'll be hurt I've betrayed Will. But he'll understand it was a moment of utter madness on my part.'

'You can't be one hundred per cent sure of Joe's feelings.'

There was silence as Eadie assimilated what Joy had said.

'No, you're right, I can't.' She took a deep breath. 'None of us can predict we'll even be alive tomorrow, with German bombs falling like rain on Gosport. So we have to hold on to what happiness and security we can grab now.'

'Perhaps you're right.' Joy's lips turned into a fragile smile that petered out as she said thoughtfully, 'Joe won't leave you. There's precious little housing available and he'd worry how you'd manage Will without his help . . .' Her words halted.

'What the . . .?' Maureen stood in the centre of the small hut. Eadie shoved the spoons and forks at her. She took them. 'What's going on?'

'Nothing now,' said Eadie. 'Everything's fine.' She bent her head and stared into Joy's tear-stained face. 'It is fine, isn't it?' Joy nodded.

Eadie tried a small smile. Then she said, 'Joy's just been quoting me a line from the United States Air Force song about the "wild blue yonder", haven't you, ducky?' She didn't wait for an answer but added, 'Everything's all right now.'

'You two are for it, if you wake my Billy up. You know that, don't you?'

Joy looked at Eadie and they nodded.

'Come outside and get your dinners. Don't let a good meal go to waste.' Maureen turned and left them to it.

'All right?' Eadie asked.

Joy said, 'I am now.'

Eadie put out a hand, grasping Joy's fingers. 'C'mon, let's go. The Two Musketeers . . .'

'Don't you mean Three?' Joy moved to the doorway.

'Oh, yes! And she's dishing up dinner,' said Eadie, walking towards the long plank settled on three piles of used bricks. The construction of the bench had caused much laughter between the three of them as they'd hunted high and low for the materials so they could copy the seating arrangement they'd seen outside Pat's hut.

Soon it would be dusk, thought Eadie. She had no desire to go visiting anyone that evening. She was tired and her body ached. In a short while the stars would light up the sky. She could hear, faintly, the water from the stream behind the huts burbling along, but every so often a spark would spatter sharply from the logs on the fire, pronouncing its noisy superiority.

'Move up, then,' Joy said, sitting next to her. Earlier she'd brought out the stool for Maureen to sit on. Eadie could feel the chill in the air. It wouldn't be more than another few weeks and the summer would have passed for another year, she thought. These huts would all be vacant. She looked along the path. Not everyone was cooking outside in the fresh air that night. Soon she'd be back in Gosport and this summer would be as a remembered dream. The monotony of her real, everyday life would chip away at her memories of hop-picking days until they disappeared and she had nothing to remember.

Eadie watched Maureen stirring the pot. Steam rose and scattered tiny droplets of meaty flavouring into the air. On a large flat stone another saucepan sat. Traces of deep red juice discoloured the outside, where Maureen had warmed and blended the choice berries with sweetness. In a small white jug, the cream, thick and glossy, waited. A huge pile of fresh-cut bread towered skyward from an enamel plate.

'Do you want a little or a lot, Joy, love?' Maureen asked.

Eadie watched the ladle dripping its goodness onto the enamel dish. She saw the perfectly cooked meat fall among the fresh vegetables and thick gravy.

'A lot,' Joy said. 'I'm starving!'

'Pass it to her, then! Don't let her die of hunger!'

Maureen's voice was sharp as the bowl came closer, its smell eclipsing all other night perfumes. Nausea rose sharply from Eadie's stomach, saliva flooding the back of her throat.

'Oooh!' Eadie rose from the bench in such an untidy manner that Joy only just managed to grab the bowl of stew before it fell.

'What the . . .' began Maureen.

Eadie ran, stumbling, for the anonymity of her secret place between the huts. Out of sight, she collapsed against the rotted wood and allowed herself to heave, closing her eyes to everything around her.

After a while, her mind and eyes focused on the fact that she wasn't alone.

Joy was by her side. Eadie was aware of her friend's hand on her shoulder, holding back her hair. In the dull light she could make out the blue-and-white check of a tea-towel. She smiled weakly at Joy and uttered, 'Not the dreaded tea-towel!' She realized, with amazement, that the sickness had passed and breathed in deeply.

Joy's worried eyes locked onto hers. 'How d'you feel?'

'Bloody marvellous!'

'Well, sip this and you'll feel even better.' Joy pushed the metal bottle top until it popped back and she could put it to Eadie's lips. Eadie drank some water, and passed back the bottle.

'Well!' Eadie said. 'I could do with a fag now. I'm really sorry for spoiling dinner. What an awful thing to happen.'

'Not at all.' Maureen took up residence in the small space. 'It's what happens in the early stages of pregnancy.'

Chapter Fifteen

'So, you'll be going back to Gosport with more than just your wages, then?' Joy let *Picturegoer* fall onto the blanket. She glanced in the candlelight at Anne Baxter's beautiful face on the cover and made a mental note that when she got home she'd find the time to finish the article about the actress she so admired.

'Looks like it.' The muffled reply came from the depths of the bed next to her.

'Do you want anything?' Joy tried.

'Actually, I'd kill for a cup of strong tea.'

'I can do that.' Joy slid down from the iron bedstead and padded towards the hut door, opening it just enough for fresh air to circulate inside when she lit the paraffin stove. Maureen wasn't expected back from the farmhouse yet:

Betty Southern had enlisted her help in secretarial duties now the final days of hop-picking were looming.

'Health-conscious?' muttered Eadie.

Joy faced her. 'Gotta look after you now, haven't I?'

'I'm not ill.' Eadie's voice was soft. 'I'm having a baby . . . Oh, Joy, you don't know how many times I've longed to say that.'

Joy struck a match beneath the kettle. Then she stepped towards Billy's pram and glanced at his dimpled, chubby cheeks. Gently, Joy disentangled his knitted blanket from its creased position and re-covered him. She turned to Eadie.

'Oh yes I do,' she said. 'You're aware of the problems this is going to cause?'

Eadie sat up. 'Don't spoil my happiness!'

Joy cut in. 'When are you going to tell Vinnie?'

Eadie lowered her eyes. 'I'm not. He doesn't need to know.'

Joy opened her mouth to protest but the steam shooting angrily from the spout of the kettle reminded her that tea needed to be made. After she'd pressed the lid onto the teapot, she said, 'If he's the father, he should know.'

'Of course Vinnie's the dad! What d'you take me for?'

'But you're not going to tell him?' Joy let out a deep sigh as Eadie shook her head.

'He's got enough on his plate with Ivy and Tim,' she said. 'Besides, I've told him I don't want to see him again, ever . . .' Joy said nothing, so Eadie carried on: 'I can cope with this.' A smile lit her face. To Joy she was like a red-haired warrior queen, Maureen O'Hara in a scene where she was about to conquer the world.

'How long have you suspected?' Joy began.

'Just a short while,' Eadie said. 'I missed my period. I began to hope, then. My breasts grew tender. Now I'm sure.'

'Eadie! You have to tell—'

'No!' Eadie's voice was shrill. Joy saw her glance towards the pram, fearful she'd woken Billy. Seeing him breathing peacefully, Eadie said, 'I can give my baby all the love it needs without disrupting Vinnie's life.'

Joy placed two enamel mugs on top of the box that served as the kitchen area.

She picked up the teapot and stared at Eadie. 'You've thought this through, haven't you?'

Eadie nodded. 'I don't think my news will raise an eyebrow among the neighbours at home. I'm a married woman with a decent home, as long as Hitler allows me to keep it . . .'

She paused and Joy jumped in: 'But you and Will haven't—'

'Neighbours know nothing of my love-life!'

'Joe does!' The silence in the hut was almost earth-shattering.

Then Eadie said, very quietly, 'I'm telling Joe everything. I have to.'

For a moment the only sound was the rattle of a teaspoon against metal mugs.

'He'll be hurt, angry too!' Joy's voice was cold as she handed Eadie her tea. 'A single moment of passion is one thing but that passion resulting in a child is an enormous event for Joe to accept.'

Eadie nodded. 'At first.' She took a deep breath. 'I'm praying we'll become a proper family. We've all got a lot of love to give. Especially me. Having a child around might even be the making of Will's rehabilitation.'

'Joe has feelings for you.'

'Love takes many different forms, Joy.'

Joy watched as Eadie drank some tea, then gave her a smile that reminded Joy of the sun coming out after a long bout of rain.

'You're incredible,' said Joy.

'First time I've ever been welcomed back to the hut with an open door and a teapot on the go,' said Maureen. She closed the door behind her and her eyes immediately went to the pram. 'Any problems?'

'You're early,' said Joy, taking another mug from the wooden box.

Maureen looked at Eadie who, having finished her tea, was setting her empty mug on the floor. 'How are you feeling now?'

Her answer was a big grin. Eadie was lighting a Woodbine, then echoed Joy's words, 'You're early tonight?'

'Fruit and veg are nearly picked clean. Kitchen garden and orchard under control. Maincrop potato-picking starts as soon as the hoppers leave. It gets dark earlier now so I've been helping with the bookkeeping. I shouldn't have opened my mouth and told Betty Southern I can type.'

'Can you?' Joy's eyes were as round as marbles. 'I never knew that!'

Maureen sipped at the tea Joy had given her. 'Not much call for it, being married to Mick, but amazing how quickly skills return when they're needed . . .'

'Is typing needed on this farm, then?' Eadie asked. She pinched the end of her cigarette, dousing it.

'Apparently, especially as I've been asked if I'd like to stay on permanently, move into the farm . . .'

Eadie slid from the bed and threw her arms around Maureen's neck. 'I'm so proud of you!'

271

'Steady on, you'll make me spill my tea. Get off!' Eadie was smothering Maureen's cheek with kisses.

'When are you leaving us?' Joy was so pleased for her. She suddenly realized how much she would miss Billy.

'I'll stay with you two until you leave at the end of hop-picking. It's only a matter of days, now.' Maureen put her empty mug on top of the wooden box. 'Billy and I will move into a pretty bedroom under the eaves of the farmhouse.' She gave a shy smile. 'I'll have a workroom below, which means I'll hear him if he cries.' She sighed. 'It also means I'll be able to spend more time with him. I've always felt so guilty, leaving him here with you.'

'Please don't say that,' Eadie broke in. 'He's a little love and you're a terrific mum.'

'Well, that's debatable,' said Maureen. 'But you've no idea how happy I am now I've escaped from Mick and his fists. I've negotiated a roof over my child's head,' Maureen raised her eyes to the corrugated-iron ceiling, 'a *proper* roof,' she emphasized. 'And just to have my own money makes such a difference.' Joy almost couldn't believe this was the browbeaten woman she and Eadie had worked with at the munitions factory. Maureen paused and retied the ribbon in her long, glossy hair. Joy pushed away the mental picture of Maureen's bald patches covered by the eternal turban. 'And,'

Maureen added, 'there's a village school within walking distance of the farm. Betty said the sooner I put Billy's name down for it, the better.'

'This is where I climb back into bed,' said Eadie, 'and try to get some sleep. We all have an early start tomorrow.'

Joy noticed Maureen staring around the hut. 'Everything's done! Everything's ready for work.'

Maureen frowned, then looked at Eadie. 'Have you eaten?'

Eadie grinned sheepishly. 'Blackberries and cream, just a little,' she confessed. 'I couldn't face the stew. There's plenty left for tomorrow.'

'Got to keep your strength up,' Maureen advised. 'Now I'm back I thought we might have a chat about your baby.'

'Too late,' answered Eadie. 'We've already done that. Don't worry, you won't get left out. Tomorrow is another day. We're the Three Musketeers, Maureen, all for one and one for all!'

Joy threw a handful of golden-green hops into the bin. 'We'll finish early today,' she said to Eadie. With a hand shielding her eyes against the sun, she stood watching the bonfire in the field next to the Spotted Cow. 'Just as well. It'll give us more time to get dressed up for the celebrations. Will you look at the size of that pile of rubbish?'

'I can't believe we'll be on the train going home tomorrow,' Eadie said. She stretched, and yawned. 'A lot of that bonfire stuff is junk the pickers don't want to take home.'

'We'll have some to add to it later,' Joy said. 'We've only got to finish this row and that's it till we come back next year.'

'If we come back . . .'

'If?' questioned Joy. She glanced around. Queenie and her retinue of children were still picking, tidying the line as they moved along it. Vano saw Joy and waved at her. She waved back with a smile. Eli looked up from the work-sheet he was writing on and acknowledged her. The Romany folk were hard and thorough workers, many staying on for the main potato harvest. Some of the men were picking hops from bine lines abandoned by workers eager to start clearing their huts and preparing for the journey home after they'd been paid.

'If we'd stayed later last night there would have been no need for anyone to come in today. The few of us in this field aren't gathering juicy hops, just collecting stragglers.'

'What's left here is still money for the farmer,' said Maureen. 'And the more hops, the better for the war effort.' In each hand she was holding a mug of tea from the flask. She passed them the steaming drinks. 'Actually, I've come to ask a favour,' she said.

'Oh, yes?' Joy responded. The tea was welcome. She sipped, then took in a deep breath of the sweet-smelling air. Not long and she'd be back in Gosport gulping the almond and metallic stench of the previous night's bombs. She pushed away the awful thought away and smiled at Maureen.

'Betty Southern would prefer me to move into the farm today. She says it would make things less chaotic tomorrow with pickers leaving.' Maureen looked so apologetic Joy wanted to cuddle her.

'So, you need a hand, today?' Eadie asked. 'You can leave Billy with me.'

'That's what I was hoping, except there's a problem.'

Eadie looked confused. 'Problem?'

'I was hoping you could manage without his pram.'

'Why?' Eadie's forehead creased.

'Remember I told you how I managed to bring all the stuff we needed from Gosport in the pram?'

Joy nodded.

Eadie jumped in: 'Well, you don't have to strap Billy around you, papoose-like, this time, do you? Why don't you take all we need from the pram, our dinners and drinks, nappies, blankets? It's a lovely day so I can look after him on the grass here. He'll be safe with me.'

'You'd do that?'

Eadie shrugged. 'Queenie's over there if I need anything.'

Joy saw relief cross Maureen's face. She knew how desperately Maureen wanted to go on making a good impression on Mrs Southern.

It wasn't long before Joy, her hand on the pram handle with Maureen's, was walking along the path back towards the huts. Despite the warmth of the late-summer sun on her face she felt saddened to think their glorious, but extremely tiring hop-picking adventure was practically at an end. It was strange, she thought, to see the place so deserted. It was usually alive with people lounging outside their huts or cooking over their fires. It reminded her of the first day she and Eadie had arrived when everything was peaceful and they'd had no idea what the future would hold for either of them. Once or twice she or Maureen shouted a greeting or waved to a picker sweeping out a hut.

'Funny to see the place so quiet,' Joy said.

'I'm betting everyone's sitting in the sunshine at the Spotted Cow. Especially those who've been paid.'

'For the price of a pint of beer, they'll be getting a free meal later, won't they?' Maureen said.

'We can join them tonight,' Joy said. 'It'll give us a chance to say goodbye to the friends we've made.'

Joy looked at Maureen and instantly knew what the other was thinking.

'Eadie'll maybe tell Vinnie about the baby, as it's the last time she'll set eyes on him,' Maureen said.

They'd reached their hut. Joy pulled up the brake on the pram. 'No. Once she's made up her mind, that's it.'

'You were the last to leave this morning. Did you know you'd left the door ajar?'

'I did not!' Joy was affronted. She was always so careful. Years of living alone had taught her to be aware of her safety.

'Well, it's open now.' Maureen's voice was curt. She pushed herself against the door and stepped inside. Joy heard his voice before she set eyes on him.

'Where's my fuckin' money?' She heard the slap, then a crash that sounded like the wooden box being knocked over. It contained their crockery, and the paraffin stove stood on it. Maureen screamed.

Joy turned and ran.

Mick's loud drunken voice seemed to echo among the trees, and oaths strung together, like paper chains, floated on the air. Joy sped back to the field she and Maureen had just walked from, thanking God that it was close by.

'Eli! Eli! He's killing her!' Joy shrieked, as she spotted him at the end of a line with another man, untying the wires and strings that had been a mainstay of the bines.

At the sound of his name, Eli looked up. The other man pointed towards her.

'It's Maureen's husband! He's found her! He'll kill her!' A flock of birds rose from a hedge, their wings fanning the air. Joy's voice was shrill.

And then Eli was beside her.

'Calm! Calm!' His voice was hypnotic.

Joy took a deep breath. 'She came here to escape him but he's found her! He beats her and Billy! You've got to come!'

Eli had a hand on each of her shoulders. He was staring at her but it was almost as if Joy could feel cogs and wheels turning in his head as her words sank in.

Then he put his fingers to his mouth and a long, sharp whistle filled the air. A brief silence followed, then Eli said, 'Come!' He swung away. Joy knew he meant for her to show him where she had just run from. He moved quickly, the other man at his side.

At the field's open gate Joy was panting heavily but maintaining pace with the young men, for now a third had joined them.

Then they were at the hut.

Through the open doorway Joy could see Maureen

huddled on the floor against the far wall, her head on her knees, her left arm hanging loose. She didn't look up despite the noise they made. Joy rushed at the door but Eli put out an arm, barring her entry.

'That floor's slippery. Careful. He could be hiding anywhere.'

He pushed Joy behind him so he could enter the hut first. She obeyed his unspoken order to wait because he was making sure the place was safe to go inside. Eli stepped from the dirt path to the wooden flooring in the small room, followed by his two mates. It was then she noticed for the first time the empty saucepan that had contained last night's stew of vegetables and rabbit meat congealing on the wooden boards. Joy's heart was heavy: her friend was so still and quiet on the floor. She looked like a broken doll.

Joy watched Eli take in the mess before he motioned for her to follow. If ever Joy had thought the hut was overcrowded with herself, Eadie, Maureen and Billy, she felt dwarfed and hemmed in now by the presence of the Romany men.

'He's scarpered,' one said.

'Stay here, Joy!' commanded Eli. Then, to one of his friends, 'Park yourself outside, Riley.'

Joy dropped to her knees beside Maureen and almost

cried when her friend opened her eyes. She leaned close to her. 'I'm sorry I left you to get hurt by Mick. Where is he now?'

On Maureen's cheek, a red mark was blossoming. 'Dunno. He's had a skinful. Could hardly stand . . .' she whispered. A huge shiver took hold of her and Joy put her arms around her to still her tremors. 'Said he saw my picture in the paper . . . Billy! Where's Billy?' Agitated now, Maureen twisted in Joy's arms, wincing with pain.

'He's safe. Don't worry.' Joy had no doubts at all about Billy's safety. After witnessing Eli's hurried departure from the hop-field Eadie would have scooped up Billy and lost no time in settling herself with Queenie and the other Romany folk. 'When Eli and his mates get hold of Mick, and they will,' said Joy, 'he'll wish he'd never laid a finger on you today.'

Maureen frowned. She looked down at her arm. 'Mick didn't do this.' She tried to shake her head but obviously it hurt to do so. 'No.' She tried again. 'He'd been eating our leftover stew but he must have dropped the pot on the floor. When I rushed in, I slipped in it. Ended up here.' She looked first at the corrugated wall then at her arm again. 'I don't think it's broken but my shoulder's swollen now and it hurts so much.'

Joy stared at her. 'I suppose the rest of the mess is because he turned the place over looking for his money?' This time

Maureen nodded. 'And that mark on your face came from nowhere?' She sighed. 'And now he could be anywhere?'

'Probably,' Maureen murmured.

'Oh, love,' Joy said. 'And I can't even make you a cup of tea until I find out if the paraffin stove's still working.'

Just then they heard a shout.

'It's Mick!' Maureen began to panic. The shouting went on for a short while. Then Riley, who'd been told by Eli to stay outside, poked his head around the door.

'They've got the *dinlo*,' he said, with a white-toothed grin. 'Tucked in a cubby-hole, asleep, between the huts.' As quickly as he'd appeared he vanished.

Joy grinned at Maureen. 'You realize he just called Mick an idiot?'

'Oh, yes,' Maureen answered. 'I've called him worse.' She winced again as pain caught her but managed to add, 'They've obviously found him in Eadie's secret place.'

The door opened once more. This time Eli came right inside. Careful of the mess on the floor he bent in front of Maureen. Joy, next to him, was suddenly aware of his absolute masculinity. She couldn't help but notice the muscles in his tanned arms below the rolled-up sleeves of the blue shirt he wore. He'd brought into the hut the scented air of the fields tinged with a hint of fresh male sweat.

'Manfri and Riley have taken your husband off to teach him a lesson.' He must have noticed Maureen's panic because he added, with a twinkle in his golden-brown eyes, 'Oh, don't you worry. This is Romany stuff. There's no real malice. He'll even enjoy most of it, until the fear sets in. Then I guarantee you'll have no trouble from him, ever again.'

Maureen opened her mouth. 'He didn't hurt my arm—'

Eli cut her off. 'Riley overheard you say that but we don't believe in slapping women and *chaves* about—'

'But—'

'Trust me.' His eyes twinkled. 'Would I jeopardize my family's good standing here, with the farmer who pays my wages and who will undoubtedly buy your Mick a drink, by doing something unforgivable?'

Joy could see Maureen wavering.

'Good,' he said. 'Now, let me look at your shoulder. Take off that cardigan.'

It took a little while for Joy to help Maureen remove the thin woollen top she'd put on earlier that day over a sleeveless blouse. Each movement caused her friend pain.

'Are you a doctor as well?'

Joy was being flippant and was surprised when Eli answered, 'Non-Romany folk don't often trust us despite the many talents we've taught ourselves, though we don't refuse modern medicine.' He stared hard at the swelling of Maureen's shoulder. 'I take it you can't move the joint?'

Maureen shook her head.

'Your shoulder is dislocated.'

'What does that mean?' Joy asked.

'It means her arm bone has popped out of its socket.'

'Can you do anything?' Joy asked.

'If Maureen is willing to trust me, I'll say yes.' He smiled at Maureen. 'Or is she willing to trust Farmer Southern to cough up for the hospital doctor's bill because you're a casual worker here at the farm? If it's the latter you'll have to wait a long while for an ambulance or doctor to arrive.'

'Can you do anything now?' Maureen asked. 'Please? It hurts so much.'

Eli grinned. 'I do things like this all the time.'

Joy saw relief wash over Maureen's face.

'First, I need you to swivel around so your back is against the wall. Can you help her, Joy?'

Joy nodded. After Maureen had managed to shuffle painfully about on her bottom, she was eventually sitting against the corrugated wall of the hut, her legs stretched in front of her, her right arm in her lap, holding her left wrist. Joy sat next to her.

283

'I'm going to hold on to your left wrist now, Maureen, so you let go of it.'

No sooner had she removed her fingers than Eli grasped her wrist, pulling it forwards and straight, very sharply and unexpectedly.

'Ouch!'

'Did that hurt?'

'You know bloody well it did!'

Joy saw the brightness of tears in Maureen's eyes but she knew her friend wouldn't let them fall.

'If I told you I was going to do that you wouldn't have let me, would you?' Eli gave Maureen another disarming smile, then said to Joy, 'Can you tear up a sheet or some other piece of cloth to make a sling?'

Maureen was experimenting with flexing her fingers. 'I'm cold. Can I have my cardigan back and will you help me on with it, Joy?'

Joy answered, 'I can do that. In fact, I can do both things.'

Almost in a state of shock at what had just happened so quickly, Joy rose, went over to the dishevelled bed, picking up Maureen's cardigan on the way, then ripped a large square of cotton from the worn sheet. She folded it into a triangle and passed it to Eli, but not before she'd managed to wrap Maureen's cardigan around her.

Without speaking, she watched him carefully bend Maureen's elbow at a right angle, making sure her wrist was higher than her elbow, enclose her arm, then tie the sling at the back of her neck.

'It'll go on hurting for about six weeks,' he said, 'not as severely as before because you're a healthy specimen.' He rose from the floor of the hut.

'Thank you,' said Maureen.

Joy said nothing. In awe, she watched Eli walk the few steps towards the empty upturned box and lift the paraffin stove from the floor. He shook it. Joy heard the paraffin swoosh inside. He looked the stove over carefully and stood it upright, then felt in his trouser pocket, pulled out a box of Swan Vestas and lit it. He smiled at the even flame the wick presented. Then he tested the temperature gauge. He set the stove on the floor and said, 'A cup of tea, and you'll both be right as rain.'

As he reached the door, he turned. 'Mrs Southern knows what happened earlier with your husband, Maureen. She'll be at the Spotted Cow tonight. Keep an eye open for Queenie. She'll give you some home-made stuff to keep the pain away. And come earlier – there's still the blackout to consider.'

And then he was gone. Maureen looked at Joy.

'Well!' was all Joy said.

Chapter Sixteen

'I don't really want to go to the Spotted Cow.'

Eadie looked at Maureen perched on the side of the bed and sighed. 'Bit late for that now. Anyway, you can't stop here because you haven't got a bed. There's nothing of yours here now except Billy and his pram, and you won't be coming back with us later because you're going to live in the farmhouse. How's your shoulder?' She continued brushing her red hair.

'It's all right.'

Joy, peering into a compact mirror while coating her eyelashes with mascara, said, 'She had that dishy six-foot, curly-haired Eli round her this afternoon, ministering to her every need, putting her arm in a sling, and all she can say is "All right"! So why doesn't madam want to go to the bonfire at the pub on our last night?'

'Because I don't know what's happened to my husband, who frightened the life out of me earlier, slapped me and ran off. I'm scared he'll do it again.' Her hand went to the side of her face where the bruise, coming along nicely, had been cleverly concealed by Joy with her Max Factor Pan Stik.

Eadie scooted over to Maureen, sat down beside her and slipped an arm across her good shoulder. She looked into her face. 'Eli and his mates won't let him within an inch of you.' She glanced at the pram where Billy was asleep. 'Or the little one. You've got to learn to trust people. Queenie said you were owed because you saved Vano's life. A promise that won't be broken.'

'I wouldn't mind Eli looking out for me!' Joy put in. She was now outlining her lips with a bright red lipstick.

'How many fellas do you want?' Eadie snapped. 'You've already got an airman falling over his feet for you.'

'Shut up talking about men!' Eadie saw Maureen was cross. And no wonder, she thought, after the day she'd had.

An uneasy silence filled the hut until Maureen said, 'I'm ever so glad you kept Billy with you earlier, and I'm thrilled to bits you had a go at starting him on solids with bread and milk. I've been meaning to but I've been scared to try.'

'I can't take the credit. It was Queenie's idea. Billy was

having a few tears and I couldn't pacify him. Queenie asked me if he wanted feeding. I thought then he must be hungry. She was so proud that you were still feeding him yourself. She said a lot of mothers put their babies straight on the bottle nowadays—'

'Oh, Eadie,' interrupted Maureen, 'I wanted him to have the best start in life. But I must tell you this. I had an awful embarrassing moment when Eli was trying to sort out my shoulder. I'd missed Billy's feed. My breasts were heavy and, horror of horrors, I only had that thin white blouse on and I'd started leaking.'

'So that's why you wanted your cardigan?' Joy laughed. 'I wondered why it was so important for you to have it round you at that moment. You said you were cold!'

Beneath the Pan Stik Maureen's cheeks were red. 'I was embarrassed! Anyway, thank you for feeding Billy. Did he seem to like being fed with a spoon?'

'Queenie said she'd never have guessed it was his first time. He ate every drop.' She looked towards the pram. 'That's probably why he's spark out now.'

'Well, thank you,' Maureen said. 'And thanks for sorting out this hut. Thanks, too, for helping me sign for my wages when the two land girls brought them round earlier. I'm a bit hampered with this sling. And thanks for helping me get dressed.' She looked down at the grey frock she'd borrowed from Eadie.

'Will you shut up thanking us?' Eadie said. 'You sound like a worn-out record! Anyway, as everyone's ready, shall we take a walk down to the pub? I've got the torch cos it'll be dark when we come back, won't it, Joy?' She didn't say a word about the lighter in her dress pocket. She intended to give it back to Vinnie tonight. After all, it would be the last time she ever saw him.

Joy pushed Billy's pram along the path, while Maureen, her good arm tucked inside Eadie's to steady herself, walked alongside.

'It's such a lovely clear night,' Eadie said. She was trying to lighten the sadness that hung like a cloud over the three of them. After tonight she and Joy would return to their lives in Gosport while Maureen and Billy would be living an entirely different one here in the country.

'Something smells different tonight,' Maureen said.

Eadie took a deep breath of the eau de Cologne with which the three women had drenched themselves. Something was missing.

'It's me,' she said. 'You can't smell Woodbine smoke anywhere on me, can you?'

'Have you forgotten your fags?' asked Joy. 'I suppose you want me to run back and fetch them.'

Eadie shook her head. 'No. I've given up smoking.'

There was a sudden absence of sound as the pram wheels stopped turning.

Joy said, 'I don't believe it!'

Eadie stopped walking because Joy had stood still on the path and Maureen said, 'Ouch!' as Eadie bumped her arm.

Joy said, 'You'll get withdrawal symptoms. You'll fancy sweet stuff and get cross because there isn't anything sugary in the shops. What's brought this on?'

The walk began again as Eadie said, 'Earlier today, when I was with Queenie and Billy in the hop-field and we were sharing our sandwiches, she grabbed my hand and said, "It's a girl! You're having a girl."'

'Did you say anything to her about the baby?' Maureen's voice was thoughtful.

'I haven't spoken much to you about it so why would I say anything to her?' Eadie's voice had a sharp edge to it.

Maureen took a deep breath. 'How did she know?'

Joy broke in, 'She can tell the future!'

'She said she could see it in my eyes,' Eadie said.

Maureen nodded. 'Well, I've come to the conclusion

that I'd sooner have Romany folk as my friends than my enemies.'

'She can tell the future,' Joy insisted. 'What's that got to do with you giving up smoking?'

'After feeding Billy, ducky, I lit up a cigarette and she said, "If you want a healthy baby, give that up. If you want to risk a miscarriage, carry on the way you are." That was all she said, but it struck the fear of God into me. You know how much I want this child.'

'What did you do with the rest of your fags?' Joy asked.

'On my way back to the hut with Billy, when Eli said it was safe, I threw my Woodbines into a ditch and watched the packet go all soggy.'

'It can't do you any harm to believe Queenie, can it?' Maureen said.

Eadie smiled at her. 'I'm not going to say I didn't feel sad at watching the green packet and tobacco fall to bits.' She paused, stared at Maureen and said, 'I'm going to miss you.'

'This is Selborne,' Maureen said, 'not Timbuktu!'

Eadie tutted. 'You know what I mean.'

'We can visit.'

'Yes,' said Eadie, though in her heart she knew the visits would fade away, replaced by letters, the odd phone call, then perhaps simply Christmas cards.

'You've a new life ahead of you. Me and Billy have different lives, too. It's all part of life's rich plan.'

'What about me? I'll miss you too!' Joy's voice was shrill.

'You won't miss anybody when your airman gets out of hospital,' chided Eadie.

'I'm getting a bit panicky now,' said Maureen. She didn't have to explain why because Eadie could hear the steady hum of voices interspersed with laughter and music coming from the field in front of the Spotted Cow. People might have heard about Maureen's husband discovering her whereabouts, causing a scene and hurting her. Natural nosiness and gossip would be rife. Eadie thought Maureen was extremely brave to come down to the pub to celebrate the end of hop-picking for another year. She squeezed her good arm.

'You're not on your own. We're with you. We'll look out for Queenie. Eli said she'd bring some stuff to help with your pain.'

The grounds of the Spotted Cow were as they had been at the introduction to the picking season, packed with people lounging, sitting on benches, on the grass, drinking, chatting, singing to the music coming from inside the pub. 'You Are My Sunshine' was blaring out. Eadie decided it must be the most popular song of the moment. Children played, laughed, chased each other in endless games.

Eadie could smell the heady sulphuric, earthy smell of hops, stronger here than it had ever been in the fields. She wondered if that was because the air was still. Usually a daily breeze would blow the bitter stench away.

'Oh, look what they've done!' Joy exclaimed.

No wonder the scent of the hops was almost overpowering, thought Eadie. The hedges surrounding the field were hung about with cut-down bines.

'They look like Christmas decorations,' said Maureen. Then she pointed her good arm to the corner of the field. 'Wow! Look at that brazier!'

'It's not the only one!' Joy cried. 'They're all around the field!'

Tall metal poles supported iron baskets that were filled to the brim with materials to burn.

'What's in them?' Joy asked.

'Not sure,' Maureen answered. 'Usually wood or charcoal so they stay lit for quite a long time, but in honour of the evening, aren't hop bines and trimmings hanging down?'

Eadie nodded. 'So, when they're lit and more scents fill the air there'll be no mistaking we're celebrating hops.'

'Exactly,' answered Maureen. Then, 'Oh, there's Queenie and her family. I need to see her, don't I?'

Eadie put her hand on the pram to help Joy manoeuvre

it on the grass, in the right direction, towards the throng of excitedly waving children spread about Queenie, who seemed very queenly: she was sitting in her peacock chair in her high-necked black dress. Her walking stick was propped by her side. Queenie waved and Maureen, using her good arm, waved back. Queenie made a sign that they were expected to join her.

'Cooee!'

The voice was familiar, thought Eadie. Pat was bearing down on them with her children. 'Come and sit with us! We've got some seats and a table saved!'

'I'm not su—' Joy didn't get a chance to finish making excuses to Pat, who was flanked by Mikey, the boys and Marlene, arm in arm with her friend Alma. Alma made a beeline for the pram and Billy.

Before she reached him, Eadie managed to let go of Maureen and grab Alma. 'Don't you dare wake him, missy!' Eadie said, laughing. 'You look very pretty, Alma. Actually, you both do!'

The girls wore flowered dresses, not new but clean and bright. Marlene's hair had been freshly washed and hung in reddish-gold waves over her shoulders.

Eadie looked around at the family group.

'He's not here,' said Pat. 'He left this morning after he'd been paid.'

Something of her disappointment must have shown on Eadie's face even though she managed to say, 'Who – who's left?' Her heart was beating fast and suddenly her hands and the back of her neck felt icy cold.

'Vinnie and his kiddies. And the bloody cat . . .'

Eadie thought she heard just a smidgeon of triumph in Pat's words. It unnerved her. Was Pat making two and two equal five? No. That wasn't possible, she thought. Vinnie and she had been careful not to let on to anyone there had been something between them. 'Said he needed to get back to his regular job,' Pat continued. 'Anyway, season's over.'

'I . . . I . . .' Eadie was searching for words.

'We need to go to Queenie. She's waiting for us.' Joy's voice was very clear. Eadie was grateful she'd interrupted before she made an even bigger fool of herself.

Pat, however, hadn't finished. 'I heard about your old man turning up.' She was addressing Maureen. 'Such a shame. I also heard he'd been carted off somewhere. How's your shoulder?'

'You've found out quite a lot, Pat, haven't you?' Maureen's voice was icy. 'I suppose you've also heard I'm staying on with the Southerns. I'll be working in their office, probably sending out the work-acceptance sheets and train vouchers for next year's hop-pickers. If you don't hear from us and you think picking's started, don't hesitate to get in touch.' Eadie saw Maureen stifle a giggle as she turned to go but not before she'd watched Pat close her mouth where it had fallen open.

Joy, pushing the pram and following Maureen and Eadie, heard Pat mutter to the kids, 'What did I say?' Joy stole a look and saw that Pat was most indignant. 'If you can't have a decent conversation among friends . . .'

Eadie said, 'You were a bit off with her, Maureen. After all she's been good to us.'

'She's a kind woman but a nosy one,' Maureen answered.

'You wouldn't really leave her off the hop-picking list, would you?' Joy looked worried.

Maureen laughed, 'Don't be daft! She's one of the best pickers!'

When they reached where Queenie was sitting, the children shifted round to make space for everyone. Eadie was touched to discover three tankards of beer had already been bought for them and were sitting on the table. Her mouth watered.

'Thought it'd go flat by the time you got here,' Queenie said. Vano was beside her, cuddled in, looking none the worse now for his adventure in the farmer's pond. Queenie proceeded to introduce Eadie, Maureen and Joy to the many family members they had previously seen picking hops in the fields.

Eadie saw Queenie pass Maureen a small bottle. 'A spoonful night and morning. I make it from willow bark. There's nothing in there to harm you.'

Maureen thanked her, then asked, 'I've yet to discover where the bonfire is. We've seen it towering to the skies from the field where we last picked hops—'

Queenie didn't let her finish. 'That's because it's been reshaped. It's where the braziers are.'

'Well, I never,' said Eadie. 'Fancy missing that!' She took a mouthful of beer, swallowed it, then licked her lips. 'I can see Eli with Manfri and Riley. Is that Jean, the land girl, and her friend?'

Queenie nodded. 'See Farmer Southern and his wife?' She gave a laugh that was more like a cackle. 'When Eli told him what he had in mind for a man who knocks his wife and baby about, he laughed fit to drop!'

'But the bonfire's smaller and flatter now,' Joy said. 'There's steps been fashioned up the centre, and isn't that an old chair perched in the middle, on the top of it?'

'Nothing wrong with your eyesight, missy,' Queenie said. 'And can you make out what's hanging on the chair?'

Eadie, who'd been listening, said, 'It looks like a cardboard crown of some kind.'

'You're right! It's for the hop king!' Queenie began to laugh. 'First hop king ever!'

'I didn't know there was a competition to find a hop king.' Joy was indignant. 'There weren't any posters up about that. If there's a king, shouldn't there be two chairs, the other for a hop queen?'

'Bless you, no! Don't matter about that. Eli only thought it out today, you see.' Queenie put a hand over her mouth. 'Oh dear! I'll be in trouble for telling you all about it before it happens, won't I?' She thought for a moment, then said, 'I will, though, because I had the last say in the matter of teaching Maureen's husband that it's not wise to bring his trouble to places of work – any more than it's right to hurt women and *chavies*.' Eadie saw her look towards the pram where, despite the noise around him, Billy slept soundly. 'Children are our future,' Queenie said.

Just then Riley's voice rang out loud and clear, causing the hubbub from the crowd to die down, and the music to fade enough for him to be heard. 'Good people! Any moment now, I give you the hop king!' He moved back towards the doorway of the pub.

There was a moment of anticipation, then out from the Spotted Cow, supported by two men, came Mick.

'You're not going to do Mick harm, are you?' Maureen frowned as the crowd began yelling again. Eadie could see she was not only surprised but worried.

'Of course not! Why on earth would you think that?' Queenie began to laugh. 'Mind you, he'll not realize that until his hangover clears tomorrow and by then he'll have fathomed out how he was fooled by his own greed. I promise you this, Maureen, my pet, you'll have no bother from him ever again.'

Eadie, concerned now too, was amazed when another cheer rang out.

'I don't think I've ever seen him as drunk as that,' said Maureen. Her face was a mask of anxiety.

'They're holding him up more for effect,' Queenie said. 'He's had plenty of beer. He only had to ask for a refill and it was put in front of him. But Eli promised me the publican wouldn't allow him enough to make him ill, or to take away his ability to think rationally in an emergency.'

Eadie was aware the onlookers were laughing as Mick appeared to revel in the attention. He began bowing to the crowd and swaying about.

'I see what you mean. He's always been a show-off,'

Maureen admitted. 'But I'll say one thing for him, he can drink anyone under the table . . .'

'Especially if he doesn't have to pay for his beer!' Queenie said.

'Whatever do you mean?' Maureen asked. Before anyone had a chance to answer her, Riley waved his hands, then lowered them, showing the crowd he wanted their silence. The noise lessened.

'Ladies, gentlemen, friends, we're about to crown the hop king.'

Loud cheers filled the air, with cat-calls and clapping that faded as Mick, led by Eli and Manfri, walked up the short incline towards the chair and the crown.

Queenie said, 'He's allowed his greed to get the better of him. I think you've had enough worry for one day so I'll tell you everything, Maureen. After what happened at your hut, the men brought your husband down here. They were intimating there was no hop king this year. There's never been a hop king, not that we know about, anyway. That was simply a fabrication. Then the men were saying what a shame it was because the hop king gets to sup as much beer as he can for free and is crowned during the evening when the bonfire is lit.'

Queenie giggled. 'Eli's not stupid. He guessed Mick's

greed fuels his need to dominate. He reasoned that's what makes him lash out at weaker people, namely, you, the baby.' She paused. 'I'm not going to lie and say we don't fight. We do. Some of the best bare-knuckle fighters are our people.' She smiled. 'And there's many a bout of fisticuffs in a pub yard after a spot of horse-dealing. But married couples are partners, not punching bags. And specially not children.'

'So, Mick seizes his chance for free beer and to be the centre of attention and volunteers to be the king,' said Joy, and looked pleased with herself for guessing right when Queenie nodded. Then she said, 'But if he's been drinking all that time how is he even standing up?'

'Because it doesn't dawn on him they'd water down the beer! Sure, he's drinking but he thinks he's clever enough to tolerate the alcohol! He's the hop king, or thinks he is!' Queenie smiled.

'Mick is actually acting more drunk than he really is, isn't he?' Eadie said thoughtfully.

'Showing off!' Maureen said. 'But I can tell he's over his normal limit.'

'But not so far that he can't think logically,' Queenie replied. 'Now just you keep watching because this is where Mick's attempt at self-preservation should kick in. That's if my Eli has thought this through properly and I see no reason why he hasn't.'

Eadie watched as Mick was led to the chair. He half sat, half fell onto the seat.

Everyone was staring as Eli unhooked the crown from the back of the chair and placed it on Mick's head.

Maureen stifled a giggle. 'He looks stupid with those bits of hop bines dangling over his ears,' she said. Mick had already searched the crowd and, finding Maureen, had treated her to a look of superiority that bordered on smugness.

Eli encouraged the crowd to cheer and stamp their feet. At the base of the bonfire Manfri had made his way to one of the tall braziers. He carried a long pole with what looked like material wound around one end.

'What's happening now?' Eadie asked.

'Manfri is about to light all the braziers in the field with his torch before the bonfire is lit,' said Queenie. 'Watch carefully. It should be over soon and Mick will hopefully be out of your life for ever.'

Eadie, listening to Queenie but not fully comprehending her meaning, watched as Manfri, using matches from his pocket, set alight the cloth wound on the long pole. It lit with a whoosh.

'I expect it's soaked in paraffin,' said Joy.

The light was just beginning to fade from the sky now and a huge cheer rose as the first brazier began to burn, sending orange sparks, like tiny stars, flying high into the sky. More cheers began, and continued as each successive brazier was lit. Manfri walked across the grass, reminiscent of a lamplighter from the days when gas was king, igniting each brazier until the field shone out as bright as a sunny afternoon.

All that remained was the central unlit bonfire with the so-called 'king' sitting on his throne, atop the rubbish.

All the while the burning braziers had been flaring up one after another and the crowd had grown ever wilder. Eadie had been watching the body language and the changing expressions on Mick's face.

At first, he seemed to relish the crowd chanting for him, the king, but now he was on his own, wearing the silly headpiece, sitting on a pile of rubbish: Eli and Riley had joined ranks at the base of the pyre gazing up at him. Mick was still waving at the people, but without the vigour he'd shown at the start of the escapade.

Manfri stood quite still, holding the fiercely burning torch. He was staring up at Mick, unsmiling.

Mick's expression had changed. It now held fear. Eadie

saw his body was tense. His eyes, unable at first to move from the swinging action of the flaming torch as Manfri waved it, back and forth, closer and closer to the rubbish, turned to Maureen.

Eadie watched spellbound as his wife, sensing his panic, smiled treating him to a wink that seemed to convey he was getting everything he'd asked for.

And then Mick was up from the chair and scrambling down to the base of the piled plywood, cardboard boxes, oily rags, dried garden and field rubbish, and broken furniture.

There was a sudden silence from the crowd, who watched as their hop king fled. As it dawned among the hop-pickers that he had foolishly thought he was about to be set on fire, people began to laugh.

Eadie, from her vantage point, watched as Mick broke through the hedge surrounding the braziers and the bonfire, and ran, stumbling once or twice, otherwise showing a perfect ability to put distance between himself and the farm. Eadie saw he'd lost his crown but definitely not his need to escape from the hysterical laughter.

'He won't show his face here again.' Queenie was using the hem of her dress to wipe tears of mirth from her eyes. 'Good riddance,' she added. She leaned across and patted

Maureen's knee. 'You see, it's all in his mind, dearie, all in his mind!'

Eadie watched Manfri walk to a galvanized bucket full of water and plunge in the burning torch, which sizzled, spat and died.

'Oh! Isn't he going to light the bonfire?'Joy exclaimed.

'Bless you, no!' Queenie said. 'Blackout restrictions mean there'd be no time now for cooking potatoes in the ashes. Food's been taken care of by an army of volunteers. There'd be another war on the Spotted Cow's doorstep if food wasn't produced on the last night of hopping. I can tell you what's being served. Salad sandwiches, corned beef and pickle, and Spam. To follow there's apple cake or chocolate cake.'

'Sounds pretty good to me,' Eadie said. She smiled to herself. It seemed to her that all eventualities for the evening had been covered. 'Do we go and get it?'

'No, they'll bring it round,' Queenie said. Just then a cry came from Billy's pram. 'So, the young master's woken up at last, has he?'

Maureen half rose to see to him.

'You sit still, Maureen,' Queenie said. 'Eadie pass me that bundle of joy. And a clean nappy. I expect changing's what he wants.'

'Oh, look, there's people dancing!' Eadie let go of Billy into Queenie's lap. Already the little boy had stopped grizzling and was staring at Queenie in wonder.

Eadie hadn't been aware of the music starting up again from inside the pub but couples were now dancing on the grass to the Andrews Sisters singing 'Says My Heart'. Queenie must have seen her watching the dancers. 'There's nothing to stop you joining them,' Queenie said. 'Why don't you? And you, Joy. We'll save you some food when it comes.'

Maureen said, 'Go on! Go and enjoy yourselves!'

Chapter Seventeen

'I suppose it's back to normal now for the pair of us?' Joy said, as the train pulled into Fareham station.

Eadie smiled a thank-you to a sailor who moved his kitbag along the floor with his foot so she could drag out her suitcase from where it had become entombed among other luggage on the fag-littered carriage floor. 'Whatever normal is,' she answered, feeling a little better when they were out in the relative fresh air on the platform and away from the stench of cigarettes. Since she'd given up her Woodbines the smell of tobacco turned her stomach. 'Even fresh air don't smell very fresh now we're nearly home again.' Eadie looked at her hands. Despite scrubbing and countless washes, they were still heavily stained with hop juice. She decided she'd do what Pat had suggested and scrub them with soda.

'Give us your voucher,' said Joy.

Eadie felt in the pocket of her slacks and produced the paper slip from the hop farm that entitled her to free travel home and passed it to Joy. Enclosed in the crowd of passengers making for the exit and the guard collecting tickets, she felt as if the past weeks weren't real but had somehow turned into a fabulous dream, and now she was waking up.

Joy handed in the vouchers and they began the walk down the slope from the station to the bus stop.

'Are you looking forward to being home again?' Joy asked, as they joined the queue.

Eadie grabbed Joy's arm making her halt. 'I was.' Eadie's forehead had furrowed into creases. 'All along I've been telling myself I can return home to Joe and Will, and after confessing I'm pregnant with another man's child, everything's going to come up roses. I've made myself believe this because it's what I want. But suppose Joe does up and leave, with Will?'

'Whoa! Stop right there.' Joy was staring at her. For what seemed ages she didn't speak. Then she said, 'So what?'

'What do you mean, "So what?"' Eadie's voice was cold.

'If Maureen can make a life for herself, I'm pretty sure you can. You're the strongest woman I know. All that matters is the child you've been blessed with. You've been given what you've always wanted.' She stared at Eadie. 'Besides, you're the one who's been earning the bulk of the money to keep a roof over everyone's head. If things get bad, move in with me.' Joy took a deep breath. 'I'll always be there for you. You should know that.'

'I don't know what I'd do without you.' Edie felt tears rise but swallowed them back. 'It's last-minute nerves I've got, isn't it, ducky?'

'Of course it is.' Joy grinned. 'Now, keep moving along with the other people or we'll lose our places in this queue. Why don't you finish telling me some of the things you've missed during the time we've been away? Not counting people,' she added.

'I'm looking forward to a few home comforts,' Edie said.

'Like what?' Joy persisted.

'A proper lavvy!' Eadie smiled at her friend. 'I'll have to stop myself searching for a secluded spot in the garden!' She felt better already. She was so lucky to have Joy as a friend.

Joy laughed. 'What else?'

'Electricity!'

'What else?' Joy asked doggedly.

'Water pouring out of the tap so I haven't had to carry a bucketful back to the hut!' Eadie began to laugh. 'Makes you wonder why we went hop-picking, don't it?'

Joy dug in her pocket and pulled out a small brown

envelope. 'Not really. This wage packet is why I went gathering hops.'

Eadie said, 'And we did have fun, didn't we?'

'You did!' Joy laughed, and a cross-looking woman in front of them turned, glared at them and tutted.

'You met up again with Jim, so you can't grumble,' Eadie said. It made Eadie so pleased that Joy was happier now than she'd ever been, with the airman, Jim, in her life. Then she thought about the precious baby growing inside her. A child she'd wanted all her married life. She knew that, no matter what happened from now onwards, she regretted nothing. But she was excited at seeing Joe again. She'd missed him and Will. The future, despite the war, was exciting, and whatever life threw at her, she'd manage, of course she would.

'Having money means bills will get paid,' Joy said. 'And that will enable me to look for more work. I can't wait to see Jim again.'

'When Joe sees my wage packet, I hope that puts a smile on his face before I tell him about the baby,' Eadie said.

'You don't have to say anything at all yet,' Joy said. 'You're not showing.'

'I do. You know I wouldn't feel right otherwise.'

'About bloody time!' a voice shouted from the queue, as

the green Provincial bus came lumbering along the road. 'These buses are never on time!'

'Don't go upstairs,' begged Eadie. 'The fag smoke'll make me be sick.'

'Two to the Criterion Picture House, please.' Joy held out the money to the conductress. From there it was just a short walk home.

As the bus trundled through Fareham on its way to Gosport, Eadie could see where the Luftwaffe had done its best to destroy everything in its path to try to obliterate Portsmouth's dockyard.

In the weeks they'd been living in the countryside gaps had appeared where houses and shops had once stood. Then it dawned on her that only last night, or possibly early this morning, there must have been an air raid.

The bus halted. A rescue truck was taking up space in the main road. Men were moving wooden rafters and joists, pulling bricks away from a building that was still smoking.

'That doesn't look too good, does it? I hope no one's underneath that lot,' said the conductress. She pushed standing passengers aside as she made her way up the aisle to the front of the bus and banged on the glass partition behind which sat the driver. 'Back up, Eddie, and go down Blake Avenue. It comes out on the main road further down.'

The driver shrugged and did as she asked.

Sitting next to the window, Eadie gave her reflection a ghost of a smile. 'Joy, we met some extraordinary people, didn't we?' She thought about Queenie and her relatives, Pat and her children. 'And I just know Maureen'll be happy now with Billy. Oh! I could have eaten Billy all up, he's such a gorgeous little boy . . .'

'What about next year? Are you up for it again?' Joy asked.

Eadie turned on the seat and stared at her. 'What? Sleeping on straw? Getting up at the crack of dawn? Cooking over a fire or a paraffin stove? Living in a space no bigger than a cupboard, with a baby as well?' She thought for a long moment, remembering.

'You bet I am,' Eadie said.

Acknowledgements

I'm grateful to the whole, fantastic team at Quercus for their expertise and encouragement. Especially the design crew for my brilliant covers. I love the hops! Thank you to Florence Hare. A warm welcome to Hannah Rossiter. Finally, a special thank you to my loyal readers.

RAISING READERS
Books Build Bright Futures

Dear Reader,

We'd love your attention for one more page to tell you about the crisis in children's reading, and what we can all do.

Studies have shown that reading for fun is the **single biggest predictor of a child's future life chances** – more than family circumstance, parents' educational background or income. It improves academic results, mental health, wealth, communication skills, ambition and happiness.[1]

The number of children reading for fun is in rapid decline. Young people have a lot of competition for their time. In 2024, 1 in 10 children and young people in the UK aged 5 to 18 did not own a single book at home.[2]

Hachette works extensively with schools, libraries and literacy charities, but here are some ways we can all raise more readers:

- Reading to children for just 10 minutes a day makes a difference
- Don't give up if children aren't regular readers – there will be books for them!
- Visit bookshops and libraries to get recommendations
- Encourage them to listen to audiobooks
- Support school libraries
- Give books as gifts

There's a lot more information about how to encourage children to read on our website: **www.RaisingReaders.co.uk**

Thank you for reading.

---

[1] National Literacy Trust, Book Ownership in 2024, November 2024
https://nlt.cdn.ngo/media/documents/Book_ownership_in_2024

[2] OECD. 2021. 21st-century readers: developing literacy skills in a digital world. Paris, France: OECD Publishing.
https://www.oecd.org/en/publications/21st-century-readers_a83d84cb-en.html